Why Not

Why Not

Lesta Bertoia

Copyright © 2017 by Lesta Bertoia.

ISBN: Softcover   978-1-5434-5607-3
             eBook   978-1-5434-5608-0

All rights reserved. No part of this book may be reproduced or transmitted in any form or by any means, electronic or mechanical, including photocopying, recording, or by any information storage and retrieval system, without permission in writing from the copyright owner.

This is a work of fiction. Names, characters, places and incidents either are the product of the author's imagination or are used fictitiously, and any resemblance to any actual persons, living or dead, events, or locales is entirely coincidental.

Any people depicted in stock imagery provided by Thinkstock are models, and such images are being used for illustrative purposes only. Certain stock imagery © Thinkstock.

Print information available on the last page.

Rev. date: 10/02/2017

To order additional copies of this book, contact:
Xlibris
1-888-795-4274
www.Xlibris.com
Orders@Xlibris.com
768364

In the beginning was the question, and the question was

WHY NOT

?

a metaphysical love story by

Lesta Bertoia

To my WOW friends
and to FFR, FW, and EZ:
your luminous awareness,
your openness to the divine masculine
matching your divine feminine,
and your beautiful dreams
inspire my own.

By the time you read this, my dear Louisa, you will probably have figured out that it wasn't what you received from me that gave you your abilities. But I'll get into that a little later, because the first thing you will be wanting to know is why we left. And the second is, did we find the person we were looking for? And perhaps the third would be, what ever happened to that dog?

PART ONE

Addie

When I handed my grandmother the small cloth-bound box, her hand flew silently to her mouth, whether to hide a smile of recognition or a gasp of surprise I couldn't tell, but her eyebrows said it was both. She smoothed her tentative fingers over the pale golden silk as if the delicately embroidered flowers were familiar treasures, and then she glanced at me, with such an expression of nostalgia and wonder that I felt like a mirage through which she was viewing some invisible, magical scene. She leaned forward from the green corduroy couch on which we were sitting, set the box down on her walnut slab coffee table, slid the peg from the latch, and raised the lid. Carefully and slowly she pulled out a thick envelope, made of textured rice paper and bound with a narrow gold ribbon. Beneath the envelope were a few loose photographs.

"Maudie! Mary Etta!" she exclaimed as she picked up a couple of the photographs. "Omigod. Wow. I can't believe this!" For a moment she was so immersed in her memories that I began to wonder if she would disappear into the mist of angel wings that seemed suddenly to surround her. But like a mirage that comes into focus and proves to be solid after all, she turned to me. "Where did you say you found this box, Addie?"

I hadn't told her my news until after we'd hugged. I love my grandmother's hugs. They make me feel like I've come home. When I was little I could just sink into them. Her arms would surround me, and we would sway, gently and slowly, as if we were in a treetop together, or rocking in a boat, with sunshine and fragrant breezes caressing us. Even now when it's my arms that surround her, my cheek that rests on her temple, time holds still while we close our eyes in one another's embrace and recapture the most wonderful reasons to be alive. When we pull apart, we've both found again that sweet refreshing contentment.

"You get more beautiful every year!" she'd said, pushing my short straight hair back behind one ear affectionately. She always says that. "My hair used to be this same light brown when I was, what, twenty-one, is that how old you are already? You have such grace, Addie. So much light in those beautiful brown eyes of yours." Her eyes and mine are the same color, and since hers are so full of light when we exchange glances, I have to take her word for it that mine are, too. "Come have a cup of tea with me! And tell me what you've been up to since last time."

When I'd let her know I was coming to visit, I hadn't told her that I'd found my house. Well, I'd found more than my house, but I was going to wait on that other part of what had come into my life until I was sure about it. I could surprise her, though, about the house, a deed already done. I'd been drawn to it just when the older couple living there had decided to move away to live with their son. They'd known, as I had, that the house and I were meant for one another.

"Gran, I have a house of my own! All to myself! It's just twenty minutes from here. I'll get to spend time with you every few days instead of every few months!"

"Addie! That's wonderful!" For a moment she'd looked like a sparkly-eyed child, despite the lines around her mouth and eyes, her almost shoulder-length graying hair. Her hands had come to rest on her heart. "I didn't expect this much happiness!"

"Wait till you see my house, Gran! It's such a gem. It's old, but it's been loved, you can tell. I haven't actually moved anything in yet. I've been too busy wandering through the rooms, exploring. I get the most wonderful feelings from this house, as if it already knows me. As if it wants me to know it. I think it must be harboring some delicious secrets. Gran, I'm telling you, this house is special."

I'd followed her into her kitchen, which looks more like a greenhouse than a place to cook, it has so many potted plants on the windowsill and on the moss-colored counter and even on top of the tall avocado-colored cupboard. It makes you feel like you're in a secret garden in the woods. You can't see the neighbors' houses through the window because of all the greenery in her back yard, palmettos and pink-lanterned fuchsia bushes, an apricot tree, a lemon tree.

"I found something in the house," I'd told her as we'd carried the mugs and teapot back out into her cozy little living room. She likes woven fabrics. They're draped over the couch, the armchair, even across the top of the bookshelf, all in shades of rust and dark greens and browns. "I sensed that I shouldn't open it, though. I felt I should give it to you."

When she'd accepted the little silk-covered box from me, something had shifted in the atmosphere; something had shimmered between us.

She looked up from the photos now spread out on the coffee table, her eyes alive with what seemed to be insights perched on the verge of cascading into the empty spaces in her being, subtle gaps which I hadn't recognized until now had been there for as long as I'd known her.

"I found it in the attic," I answered her question, electrified myself by her anticipation of being quenched with answers to long-hidden mysteries. "The house had been emptied, so I wasn't expecting to discover anything of interest. I just wanted to know every nook and cranny of my new home. I love the attic. It's been finished into one large room, with a wide-plank pine floor and mahogany storage cabinets built in under the slope of the roof and a casement window on either end. When I propped them open to air out the room, a starling flew in. I never would have thought to look on top of the rafters if the bird hadn't landed on one. It wasn't until after it had flown out again that it occurred to me that the starling was perched too high to be on the rafter itself. I woke up in the middle of the night thinking about it, so the next day I brought a stepladder with me. That's where the box was, on top of the rafter in the attic of my house."

"Your house." She said the words as if they had just fallen into place in a puzzle, with the mixture of satisfaction and stupidity one feels when saying, of course, how obvious, what took me so long? "Is the big old oak tree still in the front yard?"

Now my curiosity, already prompted by her recognition of the box, sent a ripple of goosebumps up my arms.

"Oh, Addie. Wow." She'd seen the look on my face, and the answer had told her something, but what, I wasn't prepared to fathom.

"Gran, what is it?"

"I didn't even know that I've been waiting all these years to have this story come full circle," she said, holding up a photograph. "Thank you!" She looked up at the ceiling. "Thank you." She opened the envelope, and as she read the small handwriting on the first piece of paper, her hand went to her heart. "This is going to explain it all," she said, scanning the first few lines of what looked like a minor manuscript. She put the folded wad back into the envelope. "I don't want to know any more, though," she said. "Not yet."

I frowned a silent question.

"Not until I've told you about what happened one summer a long time ago." She returned the photos to the embroidered silk box. "What are your plans for tonight, Addie? Will you stay here? I'll clear the stuff off the bed in my office. Yes?"

"Of course! I was hoping you wouldn't mind . . ."

"Mind? You know better than that!"

"Oh, good! I'll go get my bags."

I closed the front door behind me and stood in the recessed alcove, its arch made of the same mossy bricks as the path to the sidewalk, and took a deep breath. The front yard of Gran's little European-style chalet is shaded by two red maples and covered with a low spreading ivy. Across the street other houses of different styles, each with their own solar-tiled roof or sunflower arrangement of photovoltaic cells, hide the view, but I knew the ocean was out there. I'm glad I can see it from my house. My house. Gran was going to tell me something about my house. I was going to find out why I'd been drawn to it. Was I surprised?

I opened the door of the hover-car I'd borrowed, made a mental note to check the hydro-fuel cell, and pulled my bags out from the back seat. Yes, despite how many times my life, whenever it was intertwined with Gran's, had seemed to be woven into the mysterious and wondrous fabric of the universe itself, I *was* surprised.

And eager to know more. When I joined Gran again on the couch, she unfolded her memories for me, like some well-preserved tapestry whose every strand is still as vivid as the day it was threaded into the design, and I found myself falling in love with life all over again.

Louisa

The summer I met them was, oh, let's see, must be over fifty years ago, back around the turn of the century, when people were still using those big bulky computers, the ones that once you set them up on your desk, that's where they stayed, and they had a flat screen, two-dimensional, not holographic. A computer was what Maudie was unloading from their minivan — one of those old air-polluting gasoline-powered vehicles — when I think about how primitive the technology was back then, it seems so much longer ago — but I can remember them both so clearly, right from that very first day, as if it all happened this afternoon instead of that one. Maudie's fluffy hair was so white it glowed. Actually, she glowed. That's why I pulled my bike over on the sidewalk a couple of car-lengths from their driveway. When she straightened up from under the rear door of the van, she was in a patch of sunlight. Her pale yellow jumper was contrasted against the dark shadows under the old oak tree in the front yard, and her white hair was catching the sunlight. That was part of it. I leaned my bike against the sycamore tree in front of the Jamesons' house, the blue and gray one with the wrap-around porch and the high bushes all around it and a big old tent of an avocado tree in the front yard. I pretended to study the bark — sycamores have so many colors in their bark — and picked at a flake. There was a smooth patch of pale apricot green under it. When the piece of bark fell, I stooped to where the roots were pushing the sidewalk up, and sneaked another look at Maudie and Mary Etta moving into that cream-colored house next door to the Jamesons'. It's odd to think we called that color cream. Most people hardly know what cream is these days. Thank goodness we don't mass abuse animals like that any more.

Anyway, Maudie was glowing. She had that big bulky monitor in both arms, but she was looking up into the branches of the oak as if she were seeing angels, as if god herself was beaming down through the leaves. She turned, so slowly you'd think she'd never seen such a beautiful sky. I squinted up at it. It was just blue. But Maudie. Maudie glowed. And then she chuckled at something Mary Etta said and lugged the monitor up the walk toward the front porch. That's when I saw it, when she climbed the four wide painted wood steps, just before she angled the screen door open with her elbow and backed into the front door and shoved it open with her hip. She wasn't in the sunlight any more, but all around her was a dim white-gold haze, floating, like smoke. I rubbed my eyes as if to get the chlorine out — the chlorine in the pool at the Y — they used to put it into the water, awful, it messed up people's eyes, made the lights in the natatorium look like they had hazy rainbows around them — but of course I didn't have any chlorine in my eyes. Maudie was just the first person I'd ever seen who glowed that much. I wasn't even sure, that first time, that I'd really seen what I'd seen.

"You get used to it. She does that when she's happy. You live around here?"

I snapped out of my daze. Mary Etta had come around to this side of the van and was talking to me. I hadn't meant to be seen. She was probably just about as old as Maudie, but her hair was bright orange and short and perky, and she wore a chiffony kind of flowing red dress. She had a big carton in her arms.

I stood up and nodded, glancing part way over my shoulder up the street to indicate the direction from which I'd come.

"Oh, good, then you can clue us in to all the good places to eat and shop, and ice cream, I'm going to want some ice cream when we're done unloading, with chocolate syrup on it, I think, or maybe strawberry. You can help if you want. I'm Mary Etta. That's Maudie." Maudie hadn't reappeared from the house yet. "There's a couple of smaller boxes on the back seat . . . umph . . ." She grunted and hitched the carton up with her knee. "Just follow me. What are you, about ten, eleven? What's your name?" she asked over her shoulder, heading up the walk toward the porch steps.

I didn't want to tell her my name. Or my age. Not just because this was very personal information to be sharing with such an obviously loose-with-her-own-information kind of woman, and how could you know if you could trust someone who had brown pencil lines for eyebrows and that bright a red on her thin lips? but because, well, my age wasn't my age, I mean, I could say I had just turned eleven, but what would that tell anybody, nothing, and my name, I didn't like my name, it wasn't me at all. Louisa. My name should have been Estelle, was what I had decided secretly — I would never in a million years have told anyone — because it meant star, and Louisa didn't mean anything, it was some sour-smelling old aunt's name or something.

I found myself standing in the driveway beside the van, considering the boxes on the back seat. There was also a plastic laundry basket full of books under a slew of dresses on hangers, none of which looked like old ladies' dresses, they were all splashy colors and had to be Mary Etta's. Maudie would never wear anything splashy, I knew that about her right away, just like I knew she didn't ever wear any make-up.

"Don't be shy, I'm going to need a name," Mary Etta was calling from the porch, "so I can boss you around when you bring those boxes in here." She nudged the screen door open with her rear end and it slammed shut behind her.

Several jumpers, all of them plain solid colors, light mauve, pale olive, were hanging from a hook inside the sliding door. Now those were Maudie's. I looked down at my legs, smooth and tan except for the scabby bug bites and the scrape from when I'd crawled out the window, and at my lime green polo shirt and dorky purple plaid shorts that I never would have picked out for myself, but since they'd been a birthday present, well... and I pictured myself in a long pastel jumper and in sandals instead of white socks and sneakers, and I sighed. I picked up a couple of cartons, small ones, one on top of the other. They must have had glasses in them or something that didn't weigh much. The cement walk was cracked, weeds were growing up through it, and there was a cold moldy smell coming from under the front porch. A few dead oak leaves were scattered here and there, and the faded yellow paint on the steps was peeling. But the porch had a good feeling to it, like it would be nice to sit on a padded swing-chair, on one of these summer evenings, listening to the crickets and looking out across the street over the rooftops sloping down to the pier, and out over the ocean. You could see just enough of the ocean, under the high branches of the oak, because of the vacant lot across the street between the driftwood-colored house, the one on the left with the short steep driveway, and the palmetto-lined yellow stucco house on the right, enough of the ocean to feel the mystery when the sun would disappear behind the eastward roll of that vast curve of solid silver water.

The screen door popped open. "Right in there would be fine," Mary Etta pointed, "and I'll just call you Hey, unless you'd like to tell me your name, in which case I'd be able to invite you along for ice cream later." She cocked a brown pencil line at me. One of the things Mary Etta gave me right off the bat was that if a person has enough quirky things going on about them that induce an inclination to judge, you're so busy trying to figure out whether or not to judge them, or how, that you forget about whether or not it matters if they're judging you.

"Louisa," I finally told her, entering the empty living room and squatting to lower the cartons carefully onto the hardwood floor. The windowsills were deep, which made the house feel solid, and despite the faint musty odor, there was a cozy, safe warmth to the room, like a friendly cave with amber yellow walls and rich walnut trim.

"Oh, my." Maudie was coming in through an archway from what was probably the dining room, although I couldn't tell. My heart fluttered in confusion for a second. If I looked up at her, would I see it again? "Louisa," she said.

I looked at her. No, the glow wasn't there, but the way she was eyeing me, slightly tilting her head, a little question in her almost invisible eyebrows, the hint of a smile at the corner of her lips, even though that might have been a permanent feature, it all added up to making me feel like I could almost glow, if I weren't so plain and my short hair wasn't so no-color brown and I wasn't wearing lime green and purple plaid.

"I would have thought your name was . . . Estelle," she said, twinkling her eyes at me, while mine were probably showing white around the irises, they were so wide open, but only for half a second or so before I looked down again. I didn't know how she knew, or did she guess, but I guessed if I could have opened up my chest right then and taken out my heart and handed it to her, it wouldn't have been a grand enough gift in exchange. Even though it *was* beating almost like music. I stood up and glanced over at Mary Etta, but not before I'd seen the smile of pleasure on Maudie's face, at how she'd made me feel when she said Estelle. How *did* she know?

"You get used to it," Mary Etta said. "Maudie, don't try to bring the bottom part of that damn computer in here all by yourself, you'll crack a rib. Louisa will help you. And, personally . . . ?" she'd started up the stairway on the left, old bronze-colored wood steps with faded ivory risers and a well-worn walnut railing that curled at the bottom, ". . .I think the name Louisa is elegant. I like it a whole lot better than Mary Etta. Whoever would think to respect a Mary Etta like you could respect a Louisa? Did they leave any toilet paper in the house or do I have to figure out which box . . ." Her voice drifted, like the flowing chiffon dress, into the upper regions of the house. I stood there thinking I might see a trail of light on the stairs, but I didn't.

"Would you mind, Louisa? Mary Etta's right." Maudie's voice wasn't potato-chip crisp like Mary Etta's, it was silken, whispery, like stream water rippling over green waving plants. I didn't know what she meant at first, would I mind if they called me Louisa, even if Estelle did fit me better, because Mary Etta was right, Louisa was a respectable name, an elegant name? She nodded at me slightly, as if she knew what I was thinking, but then she said, "I *could* use some help with the bottom part of that damn computer." She was quoting Mary Etta, I could tell, laughing inside. It seemed like she meant two things at once, though. I knew people could do that, mean two things at once, but usually they were trying to hide something when they did that. Maudie was trying to let you know something extra. I almost couldn't breathe at how excited that made me feel to think about. Like there really was a different world, and I'd been missing it even though I hadn't been sure it existed. I followed her out onto the porch. I noticed that I was only about a head shorter than she was. Even though I wasn't all that tall for eleven, I guessed maybe she was short for sixty-five or so.

"I like this porch," she said, pausing and looking out over the rooftops sprawling down toward the ocean. They didn't have the sunflower solar cells on them back then. It took people scaring themselves almost to annihilation before they were willing to turn good old sunlight into electricity. "We need one of those double-seater swings with cushions. I think we'll be able to watch the sun disappear from here, all the way down behind the planet." She was gazing at the horizon, holding her arms and vaguely smiling, and I was just slightly behind her, to her right — thinking how nobody else I knew talked like that, like the way I thought but couldn't say out loud, seeing things that differently, seeing a planet instead of a horizon, but even more, like she was saying *we* on purpose, and *we* included me, like she just knew . . . something — when I saw it again, just a hint of it, for a second, coming off her shoulders and hair, misty light, pinkish this time. She was moving away and it was flowing after her, but then she was in the sunlight and I wasn't sure I'd seen it and by the time she was under the branches of the oak, all dappled and in motion, it wasn't there.

"Louisa!"

I looked up from the walkway toward Mary Etta's voice. She was leaning halfway out of an open window above the porch, her palms on the roof, her bright orange hair sticking up every which way, as if she'd just made it do that on purpose.

"Bring me some toilet paper so I don't have to do anything disgusting!"

I cringed a little, wondering if anybody in the neighborhood within hearing distance was home, but Maudie was smiling and rolling her eyes and handing me a grocery bag — they used to make them out of paper made from trees back then — *trees* instead of bamboo and hemp! "You get used to it," she said, grinning.

By the time I handed the paper bag into the upstairs bathroom, I thought I was about as used to Mary Etta and Maudie as if I'd known them all my life instead of just fifteen minutes.

* * *

"This is the creamiest ice cream I've had in a long time. You don't want the rest of yours, do you, Maudie? Mm-mhh!" Mary Etta, wiping the corner of her lip with a bright-red polished fingernail, pointed at her dish imperatively.

"It *is* good." Maudie spooned her second scoop of plain vanilla into the strawberry and fudge sauces swirled together in Mary Etta's dish. "It's so rich, a little goes a long way for me."

We were sitting by the lace-curtained bay window at a little wooden table in Cooper's, surrounded by paintings of flowers on the brick walls. The place was almost empty. It tended to get busier later in the afternoons. It wasn't far from the house Maudie and Mary Etta were moving into, just back along Sycamore and then instead of going straight and then up and around to Uncle Rim's, we walked down and around to Ardmore, under the eucalyptus trees and past the cedar two-story with tall narrow windows of stained glass. I knew a shortcut between the deck of the cedar house and the ugly turquoise San Francisco-style house next to it, but I didn't think Maudie and Mary Etta would do too well on the rickety wooden stairway.

"I'm so glad you knew about this place, Louisa." Maudie touched one of the leaves of the speckled begonia on the windowsill, gently, as if it were a new friend. "I like the homey atmosphere. Do you come here often?"

I scrunched my shoulders together. She had turned to me just as I was sucking the orange sherbet out of the bottom of my cone.

"Now that's the way to enjoy a cone," she said, smiling broadly at me. "Louisa, it seems to me you're a curious kind of girl. You must know quite a bit about the people in this neighborhood. Is there anything interesting you could tell us about anyone?"

I tried to catch the drip before it landed on my shirt, but I missed. I frowned at the splotch as I wiped it off with a red cloth napkin. I couldn't believe my ears. Was Maudie asking me for gossip? That didn't fit what I'd been thinking about her at all. I didn't want to look at her. I knew about the people in the area, of course I did, probably more than anyone else did.

A girl on a rusty bicycle isn't paid much attention to by neighbors talking on their phones beside open windows, or noticed by mothers yelling at their kids in back yards. You never hear that kind of yelling any more, thank goodness, but back in those days it was way too common. I never told anyone about what I heard. Sometimes what I knew weighed heavy on my heart, but who would be able to change anything? Not my Uncle Rim. He was too busy organizing his files, making phone calls and filling out forms on his computer, whenever he was home long enough for us to have a meal together, which was mostly every night, but our conversations, what conversations we had, were generally about school, till a few weeks ago when summer vacation had started, and about real estate, or what national park we'd go visit the next time he had a free weekend, and then dinner was over, and we'd watch a video together. Videos. Haven't thought about them in a long time. Looking at flat images on a screen. Stories made up to look like real life by setting up millions of dollars' worth of situations to film. That was before people could produce animated holographic imagery that was as real-looking as reality without going to all the trouble. Anyway, I didn't mind Uncle Rim not asking me about what I did when he wasn't around. But I did mind Maudie asking me. What did she think I was, anyway, a snoop?

"Maudie, I swear," Mary Etta said, "you have no tact. You can't start it that way."

I put down the napkin and looked at Mary Etta. She was rolling her eyes. "Louisa, what Maudie means is, do you know about anybody who might have a secret or seem to be, well, lost, or in trouble?" The look I gave her must have clued her in to the fact that I was about ready to excuse myself and get as far away from the two of them as I could. I would never have pegged them as busybodies. "Oh, nuts!" she exclaimed. "What I mean is we need somebody to do some sp . . . aye, aye, aye . . . I'm really botching this up."

"Oh, dear, Louisa, Mary Etta didn't mean that the way it sounded," Maudie tried to reassure me. I didn't want to hear any more. "Maybe this isn't the time or place to bring this up after all?" she appealed to Mary Etta, who was scraping the last of her sweet sauces out of the bottom of her dish with a fingertip and muttering to herself. I heard the words *stupid* and *fool*. I pushed my chair back.

"Oh, for crying out loud," Mary Etta groaned. "Louisa, don't go."

"I have to be getting home," I said. Having lost my appetite, I dumped the remains of my cone into Mary Etta's empty dish, got up, and turned toward the door.

"Estelle." Maudie's voice had stopped sounding like rippling water. It had taken on the tone my teacher used with students who were caught talking. Students had to stay indoors almost all day in those days, except in the summers, obeying what their teachers believed were good rules to live by. What a waste of the natural learning capacity of childhood. Well, Maudie had my attention, calling me by that name. I resented her using it that way, but I turned around and waited for what she had to say. She glanced around the ice cream parlor. There were a couple of teenaged girls on the wire-backed stools by the counter, talking to the guy behind the counter, but the other tables were empty. She motioned me to sit down again, and she looked so conspiratorial and inviting that I had to do it, however reluctantly. Then she leaned over toward me. "Did you ever wish you could help someone, but you didn't really want them to know that you'd helped them?"

"Now why couldn't you have said it that way to begin with?" Mary Etta wanted to know.

"Mary Etta, give Louisa a minute to think about what I just said," Maudie admonished her. "Oh, Louisa, it's true, isn't it? You *have* thought about doing something nice for someone without them knowing about it."

I had that same feeling again, like Maudie knew me from way long before that afternoon. In fact, I'd done just what she was talking about. When the Jamesons' big ugly mongrel got out and tangled with another dog and tore up old Ms. Pritchard's pansies that lined the walkway to her front door, that night after dark I went and pulled out the mangled ones and put the soil back around the live ones until it looked almost as good as before. I didn't let anyone see me do it, though. That's why I had that scrape on my leg, from climbing out my bedroom window. I'd done a couple of other things like that, too, but Maudie was right, I hadn't told anyone, not even Uncle Rim. Especially not Uncle Rim.

"Well, what we'd like to do, Louisa," Maudie nodded at my memories as if she'd heard me thinking about them, "is find out who needs help with something. And help them. Only they can't know about it, because, well, that would spoil the fun, wouldn't it?"

It would. I felt really good when I overheard Ms. Pritchard telling her grown daughter that somehow her pansies had just straightened themselves up during the night, so she wasn't going to press charges against the owner of the dog after all, not this time, anyway. Pressing charges, that was what people did in those days instead of working difficulties through to mutual satisfaction face to face. I was glad to know she wasn't going to do that, but I wouldn't have felt right if I'd gone up and told her what had really happened. Besides, then she'd think I was protecting the Jamesons or something, and I wasn't. Jeely Jameson had been in my class, but he wasn't one of my favorite people. Not that my favorite people even knew who they were, but he was definitely not one of them. I hadn't fully figured him out yet, why he was so surly and unsociable. I had my suspicions. I'd heard some yelling and screaming from his house, and anybody who owned a dog like that . . .

"So Mary Etta didn't mean spying, really. She meant . . ."

"I meant," Mary Etta leaned toward me and croaked in a hoarse whisper, "if you could tell us about some of the folks who live in this neighborhood, maybe we could figure out something the three of us could do, together, in secret. To help." She glanced at Maudie and shrugged, while I checked to see if anyone was wondering who was croaking to death at our table. "So we *would* be spying. But not for the same reasons that other people spy. See?" She leaned back. "So do you mind," she said in a normal tone of voice, "if I finish your cone?"

She'd already started peeling the waffle away and poking her finger into the sherbet, so I didn't see any point in telling her it was okay. I didn't want to smile, but I was relieved. I hadn't misjudged them after all, and besides, Mary Etta was letting orange sherbet drip into her upward-tilted open mouth from a finger raised as high as her arm could stretch. A sputtering giggle broke through my lips. I tried to grab for the remains of my cone, but Mary Etta, head still tilted back, slapped at my hand like it was vermin, while Maudie reached over and snatched a piece of soggy cone out from under the slapping hand and popped it into her mouth. I swiped a fingerful of what was left of Maudie's vanilla ice cream, and when she went after me with her spoon I started laughing, protecting my head with my arms and screeching like a donkey. Mary Etta and Maudie started laughing, too, flicking fingertips of ice cream at one another. I glanced over at the teenagers to see if they'd noticed that Maudie was glowing, but they were still hunched over toward the soda jerk. Soda jerk! He looked soda like a jerk! I hadn't felt like laughing that much in a long time.

Maudie chuckled, and gave Mary Etta a funny glance and a little head tilt in my direction.

"What?" I asked defensively.

Mary Etta was looking at my shoulder and raising a brown pencil line. Did I still have some sherbet on my shirt? Then I saw it, just barely, out of the corner of my eye, just for a fraction of a second. A rosy glow was rising off me, like a mist.

* * *

"Hey, Looze, you're wearing the outfit I gave you for your birthday. I thought you were just being nice when you thanked me. I guess I was wrong." Uncle Rim looked pleased. He was around thirty that summer, so you'd think he'd have known better, but his taste in clothing was deplorable. He was wearing a pink and green plaid short-sleeved shirt with a pink tie and teal slacks. I gave him as unfake a smile as I could manage and slurped up another strand of spaghetti. "Thanks for whipping up dinner," he said, "again." I nodded. He sighed and poked at the overcooked broccoli. "I appreciate that you didn't impose on Mrs. Pritchard for our evening meal. She's a bit on the cranky side, but at least I know you have someone to call on when I'm not here. Not that I seem to be getting much done when I'm not here."

I felt sorry for him, sitting there so downcast, pushing his broccoli around the plate. His dark lashes were so long I couldn't see the beautiful gray of his eyes. A shock of his short dark hair hung across his forehead. He was really good-looking, in a sorrowful kind of way, like a poet who'd cheated on his soul to sell real estate. What a waste, how people used to get all caught up in ownership of property and advertising of products and everything else the monetary system we used to use back then could twist into futility. I didn't know enough to feel sorry for him about that kind of wastefulness and enslavement, though. I was just thinking it wasn't his fault he'd gotten stuck with me until Dad got out of the situation he was in, which I didn't really understand and didn't like to think about at all. "I never had a lime green shirt before," I said as cheerfully as I could.

He managed a half-hearted smile. "I never had anybody cook dinner for me before on such a regular basis. Well, not in a long time, anyway."

Well, there you had it. He was lousy at picking out clothes, and I was lousy at cooking. I didn't realize that my mouth was twisting kind of funny until I heard him chuckle. "I have to say, though, this broccoli is about as dead as broccoli can get."

I couldn't believe my ears. He'd never, ever, said anything that might have hurt my feelings in the whole three months I'd been living with him. We'd always been family, Rim and my dad and me. I'd stayed with him almost every time my dad went out of the country for a few days. But he'd always been appreciative and upbeat, I guess because in a way he felt kind of sorry for me. So of course I'd had to be careful with him, too, because people who are careful with other people's feelings are fragile themselves, was what I'd figured out. I studied him, and it seemed to me, despite his droopy face, that he was playing with more than his dead broccoli. "Well, I have to say that this lime green shirt is about as ugly as they come," I retorted with a straight face. We looked at each other, and both of us glanced down before we could be hit by the full impact of the other's grin.

"Do you want to go out for Chinese?" he asked.

"Not until I go change into something less embarrassing."

"Loozie, is it that bad?"

I picked up a stalk of broccoli. It was so limp it bowed its head in dismay.

"That bad. Maybe after Chinese we could go check out the mall."

"Jeez, Rim, the mall? That's where you got **both** these lame outfits, isn't it?"

"Whoa, wait a minute. Are you saying you don't like my pink tie?"

I gave him my best imitation of an imp in dork's clothing mouthing the word duh, and he leaned his head back and moaned out loud. Then he leaned forward and peered at me with narrowed eyes.

"What?"

"There's something different about you today."

"Yeah, well, there's nothing different about you, so we gotta fix that. Come on." I emptied our plates into the trash and went to change into my jeans and a T-shirt.

The next morning I helped him straighten his new plum-colored tie over his dove-gray long-sleeved shirt in front of the mirror. Charcoal gray slacks, with a nice trim waist. Toned down elegance, I thought, just like his own hidden soul, and his eyes, you really noticed his eyes when he was wearing the right colors.

"Not bad, huh?" He tilted his angular chin at his reflection.

"You're going to sell a house today, Rim, I can feel it in my bones."

"Oh, you can feel it in your bones, can you? And what do you feel in your bones *you're* going to accomplish today?" There was certainly something different about Rim that morning. He'd almost lost that mopey look.

"Oh, so now that I've helped turn you into a halfway real person, you want to know what it is I do all day."

"I was just wondering who you're all dressed up for." He made me turn around and show off my new tan brushed-denim jumper. "Hey," he finally heard what I'd said, "what do you mean, halfway real?"

"I don't know yet, Rim. See ya." And before he could turn into a pseudo-parent on me, I scooted out the door, only to discover that trying to ride a bike with a dress on, especially a boy's bike, wasn't the smartest thing I'd ever done in my life. As soon as Rim left the house, I went back in and changed into some spying clothes.

Rim was right, of course. There was something different about me, too. Yesterday morning I had felt small and tired and just barely patient with the way people were. I'd hardly noticed that feeling unnoticed in a confusing world had been getting to me. Today I was surprised I hadn't grown too big for my jeans. Shouldn't my ankles be showing or something?

I probably knew enough already to give Maudie and Mary Etta an idea of where to start with their secret plans, but just in case, I thought maybe I'd see if I could round up some juicy details to add to the generalities. Besides, I was curious. What was it about Jeely Jameson that made him so unapproachable and sour? It couldn't be just his orange hair and millions of freckles, although that would have been enough to put me in a foul temper for more than a few years. Not that I liked my own hair, I noticed again as I frowned at the full-length mirror in the bathroom. My complexion was okay, except for the dozen or so freckles across my nose, but my hair, ugh. Why couldn't I have been born with hair like Rosalie Grant? Hair to die for, all soft auburn waves, and her eyes, such a gorgeous jade green, not just plain old mud brown like mine. And her nose, her nose was perfect, not a dumpy little wad of flesh stuck onto the middle of her face. I turned away from the mirror and went into my room and plopped myself down on my unmade bed. Why did I even care about trying to figure out what Jeely's problem was? Didn't I have enough of my own?

There was something about the way people lived in those days, being expected to compete in school, not knowing enough about their own families, not connecting to what was real inside themselves, that was eating away at me more than I knew.

I didn't even feel like going down to Sycamore to see if Maudie and Mary Etta needed any more help unpacking their stuff. They were just a couple of weird old ladies with weird ideas. I probably hadn't seen Maudie glow at all. Had I?

* * *

I leaned my bike against the rough trunk of the old oak, but the minivan wasn't in the driveway. I could tell even before I knocked on the screen door that no one was going to answer. Well, so much for having any kind of an interesting day. If I'd brought my swimsuit along I could have coasted my bike on down to the Y, but going all the way back up the hill just seemed like too much trouble, and I really wasn't up for pushing the rusty old thing all the way home again anyway. I guessed it wouldn't matter if I just left it there by the tree and went down to catch the bus to the pier. I turned from the door and did a double take and wondered why I hadn't already noticed it. There was a swing seat hanging on the porch. With cushions on it. Wow.

"Well, aren't you a pretty picture!" Maudie nearly scared me out of my skin. I'd been humming to myself, rocking back and forth with my eyes closed. She was standing under the oak. "Louisa, I'm so glad you're here. I could use some help putting the kitchen stuff away, if you wouldn't mind?" It sounded to me like she was trying extra hard to be cheerful. I wanted to ask her what was wrong, but I didn't feel like it was my place to pry. "Oh, honey, Mary Etta's gone off again, and I don't know when she'll be back," she said, answering my thoughts again. She opened the door, and I followed her inside. "I walked all the way down to the mini mart to use the phone. They'll hook us up tomorrow. Whew. That's quite a hill." She took off her white sweater and tossed it onto one of the cardboard boxes in the living room. "Our furniture was supposed to get here this morning. I don't know what the delay's about. Some days just don't want to straighten themselves out right, do they? They usually end up all right, though, sooner or later, so I guess there's no sense in fretting. If you weren't here, though, I probably would have gone upstairs and laid down on that pile of blankets and squirmed around about as much as I did last night trying to get comfortable. Well, I don't have to waste time feeling sorry for myself after all, do I? In fact, I just happen to have some great music to put dishes away by."

We hauled two cartons each through the dim little dining room, which was papered with a pale goldenrod design above the knotty pine wainscoting. A small crystal chandelier hung above the empty space of broad floorboards, which was a good thing, because the light from the single window was filtered through a tall bushy lilac into mottled shadows The kitchen was bigger and sunnier than I'd expected, and it sparkled as if it had recently been scoured. I handed the plates and mugs and things up to Maudie, and she arranged them in the oak cupboards, but halfway through the tape she'd put on, she stopped and turned up the volume on a song by somebody who'd heard it through the grapevine. She grabbed my hand and twirled me under her arm and boogied me into bopping along. "How much longer will you be mine?" In unison we switched our hands across our knocking knees, marched sideways with our upraised palms twisting, and spun around and clapped to the beat until we were both doubling over laughing.

"Some people just don't care *how* foolish they look." Mary Etta stood in the doorway with her hands on the hips of a splashy garden-scene dress. On her red hair was perched a jester's cap with jingle bells suspended from each of the three sagging points. "Oh, yes, I heard it through the grapevine," she sang at Maudie, pushing her chin from one side to the other. Then she turned on her heel and walked off.

Maudie and I looked at each other and cracked up, and then she turned the music down and we went to find Mary Etta.

"Don't ask me where I've been, Maudie," Mary Etta said from the bottom of the stairs. "It's obvious that I needed to get myself a thinking cap on my way back from the lawyer's office." With that, she swept grandly up the steps, tripped on one halfway up, swore about having to live in a body that didn't know clumsy from Camelot, and disappeared around the railing of the landing. Maudie looked at me. "You gotta love her."

"Yeah, I guess." I rolled my eyes, but Maudie knew I'd fallen hopelessly in love with both of them.

* * *

"No, I didn't sell a house today, Looze," Rim told me even before I asked. He plopped his overstuffed briefcase onto the sagging armchair by the door and loosened his plum-colored tie. I was kind of hoping that he'd notice the difference in our living room. I'd put the newspapers and magazines into a neat pile on the garage-sale coffee table, straightened the knobby old afghan on the back of the couch to hide the bursting seams, and swept the dustballs out from under the crates and plank that served as a bookshelf. He hadn't sold a house? My shoulders sank. He'd been getting more and more discouraged. If changing his style and attitude wasn't going to do it . . . "I sold two."

"What? How can you sell two houses in one day? I thought it took all that paper work and all those phones calls and everything!"

"Yeah, all that paperwork and all those phone calls finally paid off, and the deal was closed on one of the houses this morning. The second one, that was a gift from the angels."

Oh, wow, now he's believing in angels, I thought. I grinned. "Well, slap me five!" He grinned back at me. I noticed something behind the sparkle in his eye. Something secret, and downright luminous. "Rim, what else happened today?"

"What else? Well, I'll tell you, Loozie, something really strange is going on. Somebody hired a cleaning lady while I was out." He took a look around the room. "I don't know if I can handle all this neatness. You must have been bored out of your mind."

In fact, I'd had such a full day, I'd made it home just twenty minutes before Rim. I'd stayed at Maudie and Mary Etta's while their furniture was being unloaded, probably getting in the way more than helping, drooling over their walnut end tables and the luxuriously plush couch and the elegant lamps with dangling beaded trim. After the movers left, the ladies invited me to "join them in a cup of tea," with cucumber sandwiches, served in grand style in the dining room on a round oak table draped with a lacy tablecloth. It was really nice, the pretty cups, the matching saucers, the three of us quietly enjoying our first meal in the dining room with the sunlight filtering through the lilacs. It made *me* feel like a lady.

"And now for my favorite thing to do," Maudie had said as we finished washing the dishes. "Unwrap all my treasures and find special places for them in their new home."

"Maudie is a pack rat, Louisa," Mary Etta warned me, pulling a large ceramic bowl and a glass casserole dish from one of the cupboards. "Didn't we have a box of macaroni in here somewhere?"

"Oh, look at this, isn't it beautiful?" Maudie was lifting small items wrapped in tissue paper from a cardboard box. She held up a narrow glass box with a scene inside it, little Chinese pagodas perched on cliffs under trees intricately carved out of cork. "And this!" She unwrapped an ebony statuette of an Egyptian in a curved headdress holding a scroll. Soon the dining room table was littered with tissue paper and mementos from all over the world. I picked up a tiny silver bowl with a crackled blue ceramic lining, inside of which was a tiny silver spoon. "That's for salt," she explained. "I don't remember where I got that. Do you like it? Why don't you keep it? Maybe you can think of something useful to do with it."

"Really? Wow." I'd never had anything silver before, anything so elegant and petite. I almost wanted to hug Maudie, but I didn't know how she would feel about that.

"Any time now . . ." The embroidered gold silk box, latched with a peg, that she pulled out next, she placed on the table beside a jaunty little ceramic elephant. "I think there's something else here that will be even more meaningful for you, but I'm not quite sure what it is yet, so that'll do for now."

I slipped the miniature bowl and spoon into my jeans pocket. "I don't know how to thank you, Maudie."

"Well, now, just hearing you say my name like that is thanks enough, and besides, what would we do without all your help?"

Mary Etta came out of the kitchen. "Okay, dinner's taken care of, we can just pop it in the oven later, so now we can get to work on . . . more important things." She lifted a penciled eyebrow at Maudie.

"Louisa," Maudie said, "will you come back tomorrow? So we can discuss our . . . project." She tilted her head, and I knew what she meant.

It was time for me to do some snooping.

I pumped my bike up the hill and left it in our driveway. I wouldn't need it to carry out my plan. The back yards of the houses across the street sloped down toward the back yards of the houses on Sycamore. I'd never had any reason to look for a shortcut from here, but I figured that the Jameson place, hidden by tall bushes, was probably below the square two-story house, the one with forest-green shingle siding and brown trim. Kind of a dreary looking place, with all the curtains drawn, but that was fine with me. It made it easy to avoid being seen from the windows.

A steep, narrow, crumbling stone stairway led down the slope beside the house under a tangle of bushes and vines, through a rickety trellis, and into an overgrown jungle of tall dry grasses choking out a few straggly palmettos. Whoever lives in this house isn't much into gardening, I thought. From the lower corner of the building I could see, beyond a sagging chain link fence choked with brambles, the roof of the Jameson house. I figured if anybody happened to be looking out of a window, they wouldn't think much of a kid crossing their back yard, but just in case, I ran for what looked like a curl in the bottom of the fence with enough space for me to squeeze under.

Suddenly I realized I wasn't alone in the yard. I nearly tripped glancing back at the sound of a menacing growl. Out of the corner of my eye I caught sight of a huge ugly beast tearing after me through the tall grass, its bared fangs frothing and snapping. It had mangling on its mind. As it leapt into the air, aiming for my back, I dove for the bottom of the fence, scrambling to save my skin. Hot breath and slobber closed in on my ankle, with a clamp of teeth about to follow had the dog not suddenly been choked against its collar, so enraged I thought it would snap its chain. I belly-crawled under the fence, ripping my T-shirt from shoulder to waist, and tried to catch my breath. My heart was racing fit to burst.

It was no good hiding under the bushes that lined the Jamesons' back yard. The brute — that monster of a dog who'd torn up Mrs. Pritchard's pansies and didn't belong to the Jamesons after all — was raising a frantic alarm that would set the whole neighborhood on alert. What had I gotten myself into? Well, I most certainly couldn't go back the way I'd come. I took a deep breath and slid on my rump out from under the bushes and smack into the Jamesons' back yard.

Two women were sitting at a round white table under a big scallop-edged umbrella, staring at me with their eyebrows up and their red plastic cups poised halfway to their mouths. Jeely was sitting on a stool on the brick patio next to a skinny ginger-haired girl in a wheelchair, with his neck craned around, gawking at me. He was holding an open box with blue tissue paper in it.

"Good Lord, Louisa, what on earth are you doing?" one of the women asked. I assumed she was Jeely's mom, since she had red hair, too, but I couldn't figure out how she knew my name.

"Hi, Mrs. Jameson, sorry to barge in on you like this." I was about to brush off the back of my jeans, but thought better of it. "I guess I'll just be moseying along now." I headed for the sidewalk.

"Louisa, look at your shirt! Please don't go yet. Let me get you another shirt. Just listen to that awful dog. Did he rip your shirt? Are you okay? Would you like some pizza? We haven't had a chance to get to know one another. Jeely's told me so much about you."

While I was answering this outburst with nods and shakes, I glanced at Jeely. I didn't want him to know I was surprised by that last bit of news, and besides, I was more insulted than surprised that anyone would be talking about me without me knowing about it, so I shot him a quick piercing glare before smiling sweetly at Mrs. Jameson, who was a little on the plump side, but she had a nice smile, if you didn't pay too much attention to the way her eyes looked so sad. "Oh, I'm afraid I have to be getting home," I said as politely as I could.

"We've got cake, too. It's Julie's birthday. Jeely's sister turned twelve today."

The girl in the wheelchair gave me a tiny bland smile, as if it took all her energy to express that much acknowledgement, and the embarrassment I'd felt about my explosion into their little party doubled for having glared at Jeely. I noticed then that the girl had what looked like a new pale blue sweater in her lap. There didn't seem to be any other presents. "Oh . . . well, uh . . . happy birthday, Julie." Her smile broadened a little, and the sincerity of her pleasure made me feel about two inches tall. There was a long moment of awkward silence. "I, uh . . . I didn't know it was your birthday," I said. "But I have a present for you." I reached into my pocket. I cupped the tiny silver bowl and spoon into my hand, and placed them into Julie's palm and curled her fingers over them, and then I ran, out to the sidewalk, along Sycamore, and back around the curve and up the hill to my house. I didn't stop until I was inside the door, panting.

And then I ran to my room, tore off my T-shirt, threw it into the wastebasket, and pulled on another one on my way back down the hall. "Look at this mess!" I said to the living room. It just stood there and shrugged. I attacked it.

"Yeah, I guess I was just bored," I said to Uncle Rim. "Don't get any ideas about me cleaning up like this *every* month." I expected him to smile at my wit, but he shook his head.

"Louisa, you shouldn't have to clean up at all. I've been a real slob. And letting you cook as often as you do. What a rotten way to be an uncle."

"Yeah, well, you're the best uncle I have."

"I'm the only uncle you have."

"Having you is better than having no uncle at all."

"Having you is better than I deserve. Where's that book about national parks? We're taking the weekend off! Time to celebrate! Time to start fresh. Here it is. Where shall we go?" He sat down on the couch and patted the threadbare cushion for me to join him.

I'd given up on taking a camping trip with Rim, even though it was something I'd wanted to do as soon as he'd suggested it, months ago, and now it was going to happen, and I didn't want to go anywhere. Maudie and Mary Etta needed me. I had some news for them. We had plans. "Oh, I don't know." I sat down. "Are you sure you want to do this?"

"What's up, kiddo?"

"Oh, nothing."

"Boring day, nobody to play with, just a boring old uncle to go camping with?" He closed the book and studied me, his eyes roaming all over my face. "I've been so absorbed in my own problems I haven't even thought about what you do all day, all by yourself." I didn't say anything. He ran his fingers through the shock of dark hair on his forehead. "I wish I had some news for you about your dad. The embassy people don't know anything more than they did a week ago, as far as I can tell. I don't know what Clay was thinking. I always thought he was smarter than that, being older than me. I guess even if I knew anything, I couldn't tell you much, though, because I'm sure he'll want to explain it you himself, once they let him communica . . . once he gets home, which has to be sometime soon, it has to be, and until then, well, you're stuck with me, Looze. I know that going camping with a bimbo who can't even dress himself right isn't the greatest prospect in the world. Do you have any friends you'd like to invite along? Someone from school?"

I sighed and leaned my head against his shoulder. "I don't know."

"Well, we don't have to decide anything right this minute. Are you hungry?"

"I guess so." Actually, I was starving. "I could go for some pizza, and some cake."

"Some pizza, and some cake. Okay . . . Would you like some strawberry-olive icing on that cake, or would you prefer lemon creme with anchovies?"

I elbowed him in the ribs.

"Hey, hey, a little gratitude is in order. I'm making a big sacrifice here. I was going to stay home and write some poetry, but, no, I have to take milady out for cake."

"You were going to write some poetry?" I *knew* he was a poet in shark's clothing! "What made you decide to write some poetry?"

"Nuh-uh, a true poet never reveals his source of inspiration."

"You have a secret, don't you?"

"Well, aren't we the sharpsters today. I'll tell you mine if you tell me yours."

"What do you mean?"

"I mean, you've been up to something."

"How can you tell?"

He tilted his chin back in a silent laugh. "Out with it!"

I narrowed my eyes at him. "I don't think so."

"Well, okay, then." He got up and hefted his briefcase from the armchair. "I'll put this away, and we can go for pizza, as soon as you comb those leaves out of your hair and wash that blood off your neck."

Addie

"Oh, look at the time!" Gran exclaimed. "I'd almost forgotten. Addie, I'm meeting with some friends in half an hour. I expect to be back in about three hours. Why don't you just make yourself at home, and we'll talk some more later. Well, just listen to me. I'm the one who's been doing all the talking. I promise to let you get a word in edgewise this evening! I want to hear all about how you found your house. Oh, I'm so glad you're here!"

"Me, too! I think I'll meet you back here . . . around seven, then?"

She smiled. She understood why I couldn't wait to get back to my house, knowing what I knew about it now.

But when I pulled the hover-car into the driveway, it wasn't *my* house that beckoned to me.

The house across the driveway, which Gran had described as surrounded by bushes, was no longer blue and gray, it was silver, and there were neither bushes nor an avocado tree hiding its wrap-around porch. I knocked on the front door. It was opened by a slender woman in her late thirties, wearing a close-fitting khaki-colored aviation jumpsuit that matched the color of her short wavy hair. The smile lines around her eyes encouraged me to announce myself. "Hi, I'm your new neighbor." I pointed to my left, about to tell her I was moving in next door.

"Oh, come on in! I'm Karen Firth." She led me into what might have been a sunny living room, if the light from the large front windows hadn't been muted by iridescent silver curtains. A black couch and two single-pedestal black chairs surrounded an oval brushed stainless steel coffee table. The wall toward my house was shelved from floor to ceiling, neatly stacked with sets of mini-discs arranged under labels and divided by abstract glass figurines. "Welcome to the neighborhood!" She opened her arms and we hugged long enough to dispel the initial sense of strangeness.

Her energy was airy, as if she merely tolerated being on the ground, but her warmth was genuine. Gran has told me that when she was a child, strangers didn't hug as a matter of course upon meeting. If they touched at all, it was a shake of hands. It's hard for me to imagine not exchanging the information that only an embrace can communicate. "And this is my dad, Jeely Jameson."

A man with curly white hair still tinged with traces of pale orange turned from the holographic display on his curved stainless steel desk. His gently amused face and the muscular arms emerging from his black cotton tunic were sprinkled with freckles. His matching drawstring pants revealed bare feet. He rose to greet me, an inch or two taller than me. "Pardon me," he said as we pulled back from our hug, "if I seem a little distracted. I'm so fascinated by the recent inroads into time travel . . ." He paused to let me introduce myself.

I was quite distracted myself. I hadn't expected to find Jeely Jameson still living here. The contrast between Gran's description of her childhood schoolmate, a surly and unhappy boy, and this virile man whose energy was abuzz with eager curiosity foretold an interesting story, if he was willing to share it. "Jeely, I'm so pleased to meet you. I'm Addie Crest, Louisa's granddaughter."

"And you're moving in next door?" He checked with Karen.

"I'm so sorry I can't stay and talk, Addie," Karen said, "but I was just on my way out. Next time I visit Dad, I'll check and see if you're home . . . ?"

"Oh, please do, Karen, and Jeely, if you're busy," I'd noticed that the name Louisa hadn't seemed to register any reaction, "I don't want to interrupt . . ."

He waved away my concern, walked his daughter to the door, and asked if I'd like some iced tea.

Three hours later, after having grabbed a bite to eat, I joined Gran on her cozy couch, nestled myself into a rust-colored velour throw rug with a cup of steaming peppermint tea between my palms, and reminded her where she'd left off. "Uncle Rim told you to wash the blood off your neck." I had to smile, not at the picture of what kind of girl Gran had been, although that, too, made me smile, but because of what Jeely had revealed to me over the course of several hours.

Louisa

"I'm not sure there's a whole lot we can do for the Jamesons," was Mary Etta's response to my disclosure of their unfortunate circumstances the next morning, "other than to poison that beast that waits in ambush for innocent children."

"Mary Etta." Maudie frowned at her. "Of course there is. They are obviously not rolling in money, and with Jeely's sister being in a wheelchair, he is no doubt expected to help out, and if there is no father on the scene, which for some reason I suspect is the case, he probably feels he is expected to be a man and not express his feelings, no matter how weighted down or how lonely he might feel. Does he have any friends, Louisa?"

Maudie's words had a shadowing effect on me. They were rays of light trying to pierce a cloud of shame. "No."

"You're not his friend?"

"No." From my perch on the armchair, I studied the Persian rug on the living room floor, avoiding looking at the couch, where Maudie was working on a handmade quilt and Mary Etta was peering over her glasses at me, I could tell, looking up from the tablet on which she was making notes. "Well, I didn't know!" I said defensively, hugging my knees. "I thought he was just, I don't know . . . no, that's not true, I did know, I knew there was something. But . . . well, I thought that dog was theirs, and that threw me off. They're . . . they're really nice. And sad." I looked up. Mary Etta was looking down at her tablet again, and Maudie was looking at me with that little hint of a smile and a gentle light in her eyes. Then she looked back down at her quilt and smiled for real. "So, I guess . . . I could try to be his friend," my shoulders sagged, "only how would I do that without him, like, noticing? I mean, that's not . . . I mean, I don't see . . ."

"Think about it, dear. You could become his friend without him noticing it, if it seemed that he would have some resistance. But what if he's *looking* for a friend, what if he's *waiting* for *you* to say . . . something? He told his mother about you."

I squirmed. "Whoa!" My hands flew up, somewhat to my own surprise. "I don't mind doing things for people who won't ever find out it was me . . ." I had forgotten about offering a gift to Jeely's sister, had swept it right out of my mind along with the dustballs under the bookshelf in the living room, ". . .but, look, this is different." My stomach was in a knot. "This is hard!"

"See?" Mary Etta turned to Maudie. "I told you. There's not much we can do for the Jamesons. Now you let her be. And you tell her what we are really looking for."

I sat up in my chair. Wow. Mary Etta was taking my side. And there's more here than meets the eye, just as I suspected, I thought to myself, although it hadn't occurred to me that I'd suspected any such thing until that very moment.

"Go on. Tell her!"

Maudie knotted her thread and bit it off with her teeth. She zigzagged the needle into the most recent patch and folded the half-finished work. She took off her glasses and put them down on the folded fabric, and then she took a deep breath. "Louisa. We had another sister, who died, a long time ago, giving birth to her daughter. We raised our niece, Samantha, as if she were our own daughter. And then one day she . . . she just . . . disappeared. She was twenty-two. That was twelve years ago." Maudie looked at Mary Etta, who gave her an impatient nod to go on. "We think we've finally zeroed in on the area of where she ended up. We think it might have been in this area. So we are keeping our eyes and ears open, and that is what you are doing for us, and with us. Helping us find a relative of ours."

I was so struck by this information that it seemed an invisible thunderbolt had flashed through me. Why this was so, I couldn't imagine, because what they were telling me made sense. I could understand why they hadn't told me right away. I could understand why they were telling me now, these two sisters — of course they were sisters. Even though that hadn't even occurred to me, I could see it now. They were sisters, and they were looking for their thirty-four-year-old niece, which was the same age my mother would be, if she hadn't died giving birth to me. Another thunderbolt flashed through me. No way. There couldn't be a connection. I shook my head slowly. No, it didn't compute. I looked a question at Maudie.

"We don't know," Maudie said. "We don't know what we will be finding out. But we're pretty sure we will be finding *something* out."

"Oh, my gosh, this is too nuts!" I exclaimed. "You are blowing my mind, I swear. Wait. Let me get this straight. You want me to go ahead and make friends with Jeely, but you'll keep your noses out of it, because that's my business . . ." I stopped at the sparkle that flashed at me from Mary Etta's eyes, a glint that told me, for the briefest fraction of a second, that I had just been seen. Recognized. Acknowledged for who I was, really. And I had just lost all notion of who I was, really. I didn't have a clue, at that moment, who I was. "So let me get this straight," I repeated, concentrating on the pattern in the Persian rug. "You are looking for your niece, who disappeared twelve years ago, and so she's thirty-four, and you think she lives around here." I glanced up. They were both looking at me. "Why wouldn't she have contacted you? What happened to her? Do you know *anything* about where she's been or what she's been doing?"

"Yes. Yes, we do," said Maudie. She glanced at Mary Etta with a question on her face, and Mary Etta shrugged. And then she began to tell me what they had learned.

Meanwhile, just because I hadn't been able to wheedle Rim's secret out from between his sealed lips, that didn't mean I wasn't going to hone my expertise.

* * *

"I bet it's some mysterious woman. I bet she has some strange aura to her, as if her past is forgotten in a cloud. She's elusive. But she's soooo alluring . . ." I left my mouth in the shape of a foghorn as I leaned across my plateful of crisp broccoli, mashed potatoes, and a breaded filet of fish I'd found in Rim's freezer.

"You're getting mashed potatoes on your chin, secret agent number nine," Rim retorted.

I stared at him, secretly trying to flash a bolt of lightning from my intense eyes into his shaded ones.

"Stop looking at me like that!"

"Like what," I narrowed my eyes. Then I sat up, scooped a smear of mashed potatoes off my chin and popped it into my mouth, and ate my food, bite after bite, in silence, savoring every delicious flavor as I licked it off my fingers. (Silverware distinctly diminishes the pleasures of eating.) Biding my time. Waiting.

"What made you say that, anyway?"

Yes. Now I had him. "Say what?" Innocence would have been too unctuous, so I uttered these words as a challenge. He gets it, I thought. I can corner him now, or he can spill the beans on his own, or we will have a stalemate. He's considering what to do. God, he has a beautiful face. Especially when he smiles. This smile just doesn't want to quit. I was right!

"You were right."

"I was right?!"

"She's like that."

"Oh my god. This is too bizarre. This is too nuts."

"What?"

Oops. What am I doing? The less information shared, the better, for now. "Um, well, you know, that I guessed right! So who is this person and where and how did you meet her and what's she like and where's she from . . . ?"

"Whoa, girl, whoa now, hold your horses. Let's just trot through this, not gallop. In fact, let's just walk through it. How does that sound to you?"

"Uncle Rim, I think you are in serious danger of becoming real."

"Yeah, kiddo, I think you're right about that, too." He didn't look sad anywhere on his whole face. He looked like someone who has just found a glow inside him, and he's listening to its music, which is coming from somewhere in the near future and has already pervaded him, both at the same time.

"Uncle Rim, if you would rather go and write some poetry right now, we can always talk later, right?"

"Loozie . . . Do you mind me calling you that? No, let me rephrase that. What would you like me to call you?"

"I like Loozie okay, and Looze. Just as long as you don't put an R on the end of it. Or maybe Loose would be better!"

"No, I don't think so, my innocent cherub. Shall I call you Louisa?"

I expected myself to flinch, but the name didn't sound so bad after all. Maudie and Mary Etta had made it sound okay. "Yeah," I nodded, "Louisa's okay."

"Louisa. Either you are more perceptive than the average bear, or you are a mind reader. I really would like to go spend some time with my own thoughts and feelings right now, if that's okay with you."

I was dying of curiosity, but pulling information out of him when he was looking like that seemed like poking at a box turtle that had just opened its shell. "Can I have a hug first?" What a great hug that was. It was the first time we had really hugged since I was little.

"Don't go getting caught in any more bramble bushes, now, okay?" he said, heading toward the hall.

"Yes, Uncle Rim. No, Uncle Rim." I had left out most of the truth about how I'd gotten blood on my neck the day before. About ninety-nine percent of the truth. "I'm going to read." I smiled at him winsomely. He rolled his eyes.

Rim hadn't been in his room for more than half an hour, though, when there was a knock on the door. I'd washed the dishes and was sitting on the couch with a book I wasn't reading. I looked out the window to see who it might be, but all I could see was the back of a wheelchair. "Uh, oh." I jumped up and ran down the hall. "Rim," I said to the closed door of his room, "there's someone at the door." Then I dashed into my room and bolted out the window.

* * *

I knew, when I hitched myself over the windowsill into my bedroom later, that what was waiting for me wasn't going to be another hug. I'd spent the two hours until dusk sneaking through people's backyards until I reached the top of the hill where it was too steep to build on, and I'd sat and looked out over the ocean, trying to piece everything together as the sunset blazed above its own immense and dazzling reflection. Three mystery women, but one of them was dead, and there might be no connection at all between any of them, and even though Maudie and Mary Etta had told me the name of their niece — which wasn't the same as my mother's, of course, no matter how much I wished I was related to them, because she was the one who was dead — wasn't she? — they were pretty sure the woman they knew as Samantha wasn't using her original last name any more. Maybe not even her original first name. The last they'd heard from her, she'd left on a road trip with a friend right after graduating from college. She'd sent postcards from various places around the country, where she and her companion (whose name she never mentioned) would stop in to visit someone they knew, but then the postcards stopped arriving in the mail. At first they hadn't been too concerned, but after a few months, they'd started writing to the addresses on the cards. It wasn't until after Maudie got herself a computer that their search had led them here, to the Pacific coast. When I asked her why she and Mary Etta hadn't gone to the police, the two of them looked at each other. "Not yet," Mary Etta said, still looking at Maudie, and I had that sense again that they were saying more than they were saying. "Just you keep your eyes and ears open, Louisa," Mary Etta had instructed me with a tone of finality in her voice.

And meanwhile, I didn't know anything about the woman that Uncle Rim had just met . . . so my thoughts just twisted and looped around on themselves without me getting anywhere, but trying to unravel them was better than thinking about what I was going to have to tell Rim after the visit from Jeely's mom. I peeked out my bedroom door and looked down the hall. There was a light on in the living room. No voices, though. Just silence.

"Loozie, you're the strangest kid I ever met." Rim was sitting on the couch, alone, his elbows resting on his knees, gently jiggling something in the palms of his hands. My heart sank. I knew what it was. "I don't mean that in a bad way," he added, noticing the look on my face. "I'm sure you have an explanation for this." He put the little silver bowl with the blue ceramic lining and its little silver spoon on the coffee table. "I don't like having to pry into your affairs." He ran his fingers through the shock of dark hair falling over his forehead. "I wish I didn't have to ask you about this."

"I wish they woulda just let her keep it! Now I'll have to give it back to her again! It was hard enough the first time! What's the matter with people? Why did she bring it back?" I started groaning as I paced the floor, and then a roar just uttered itself right out of my throat.

"Loozie . . . I'm sorry, Louisa . . ."

"Oh, Uncle Rim, just call me Loser and be done with it! I mess up everything!"

"Well, I don't know about that. But I must say, it was a little odd, the, uh, the way in which you presented this as a gift to, Julie, is it? who, by the way, was very gracious about returning it, although I could tell she was sorry she had to give it up, and if you do want to give it back to her, I'm sure she'll be pleased. The reason Mrs. Jameson brought it back was because it seems like a pretty valuable object, and she just wanted to make sure it was okay with me. I was a bit at a loss for words, since I didn't know anything about it." He paused, waiting for me to say something.

I figured that if I didn't tell him where I got the little bowl, then *he* wouldn't feel like he'd have to share his secrets with me, either, and that would really put a kink in recent developments. I sighed.

Rim studied me. "Mrs. Jameson was also worried about what that dog did to you. I had no idea you were getting yourself into such dangerous situations! I've been really irresponsible, Loozie . . . I mean, Louisa . . ."

"Uncle Rim, please, don't try to call me Louisa if it doesn't sound right, that only makes everything worse."

"And everything is pretty bad right now, isn't it?"

"Well . . . actually, not that bad."

"No?"

"No, actually, everything is pretty good. I don't think we have to worry about that dog any more, because if Mary Etta doesn't poison it, I will, and I can just leave the bowl on the table in their back yard, and what if you just found their niece, I mean, that would be so incredible, Maudie would just glow like a freaking light bulb!"

"Whoa, girl, slow down a minute. What's this about poisoning that dog, and who is Maudie, and no, I don't think so, just leave the bowl . . . ? Why don't we just back up here and take this one step at a time?"

"Not gallop through it."

"Right."

"Okay."

"So, come here and sit down. How about we start with where you got this? What is it, anyway?"

"And then will you tell me about your mystery woman?"

"I think I have two of them in my life right now."

"What?! There's another one?"

"I'm looking at her."

"Oh." I liked that. Being called a mystery woman. "Well, okay, Maudie and Mary Etta are these two ladies who moved in next door to the Jamesons . . ." And I told Rim everything. I sat on the couch cross-legged and stumbled through my story, back-tracking and inserting my omissions, admitting that I'd straightened out Mrs. Pritchard's pansies, reveling in Maudie's glow and Mary Etta's jester's cap, describing every one of Maudie's treasures, using my hands to impart the details of their charm. I hadn't talked this much to anyone, ever, and once I got started, I couldn't stop.

Rim listened with an attentive face, interrupting only with exclamations of "Really?" and "Huh!"

"And she knows what I'm thinking before I even say it, Rim! She makes me so happy . . . Look! Do you see it? Just thinking about her does this to me!" I was glowing. I could see a faint wispy pale peach light over my shoulder, out of the corner of my eye.

"You really like her." He smiled, but I knew by the way he wasn't surprised that he couldn't see it.

"So, anyway, that's it, I guess. They're looking for their niece, and *what if you have already found her*? What if . . . ?"

"Louisa." The way he said my name as he put his hand on my shoulder, I knew it was time for me to put a stopper on it. "I don't really know this 'mystery woman' very well yet. I mean, she just bought a house from me yesterday, almost right out of the blue, and so we went for coffee together . . ."

"Ooh, your first date in how long?"

"It wasn't a date. We were discussing business."

"Yeah, right."

"We were discussing business."

"And that made you go all fuzzy and poetic."

"Okay, we talked about some other things, too."

"I knew it!"

"Louisa, what I'm trying to tell you is that you're galloping again."

"Oh, Rim, I'm sorry." It suddenly hit me. "I'm all excited about finding Maudie and Mary Etta's niece, and you just met somebody, and whoever she is, it's just great that you just met somebody!"

"Yeah." His eyes went dreamy again. "Yeah, it is."

I had to bite my tongue not to tease him. Meanwhile, I could hardly stand the suspense, but he was right, there was nothing to do about finding out anything more, not tonight, anyway. "I'm really happy for you, Rim."

He smiled at me, a little crookedly, I thought, for a poet in love. "It seems to me," he said, "that you have a not too secret admirer yourself."

"What? Who?"

"Somebody with red hair."

I groaned.

Addie

"You said you're Louisa's granddaughter," Jeely Jameson had opened our conversation as he placed two tall glasses of iced tea onto cork coasters on the brushed steel coffee table, "and you said it as if I'm supposed to know a Louisa." He frowned and shook his head. "Which I don't. Excuse me for just a minute . . .?" He went to his desk and switched off the hologram. "Louisa," he said, settling into the other single-pedestal chair, tugging at the knees of his black cotton trousers and lifting his legs into a lotus position. The dense sprinkling of freckles beneath his haphazardly curly, peachy-white hair and sparse eyebrows were an odd contrast to the look of black-belt mastery conveyed by the rest of him. He looked like a sprightly leprechaun poured into a twenty-first-century spiritual athlete. His obvious interest in matters scientific bespoke a wide range of intellectual pursuits, yet he was not in any way intimidating. He had felt, in fact, despite his apology for being distracted when we had hugged, exceedingly accessible and warm. I was about to explain further, when he spoke again. "I did once, though. I knew a Louisa once. When I was, oh, about ten years old." He shook his head slightly, staring through the highly polished tile floor and smiling vaguely. "That summer . . . I never expected... Louisa." He looked up at me. "Could it be the same . . .?"

"Yes!" I encouraged him. "That Louisa! Louisa Bylander."

I thought for a moment that an electric spark had passed through the room, but which one of us had generated it?

He stared into space for a moment, looking as if he were listening to some whispered indication of significance, and then he returned his focus to me. "Yes, I can see it," he said, his green eyes scanning me, "the family resemblance. You have the same beautiful color of hair. I love that color. It has no proper name, does it? It's like the color of a dappled path through the forest, or of a deer in the shadows in the fall. And you have her eyes, that sparkling amber brown, like the deepest, rarest shade of topaz." I must have looked somewhat surprised, for he commented, "I seem to have a very vivid memory of Louisa after all, don't I?" and he raised his hand to his lips. "I don't know whether to laugh or to cry!" he announced, more to himself than to me. "But I'm being rude! You are my new neighbor, and I haven't asked you anything about yourself, and here I was about to plunge into a memory..." He let his sentence drift off into the distance he was gazing at.

"Oh, plunge, Mr. Jameson, please, plunge! I would like nothing better than to hear about my grandmother when she was a girl . . ." I almost grimaced at what was decidedly a deception on my part, "and about you when you knew her. Really!"

"But, Addie, is it? Addie, you are her granddaughter? So you know where she is now?"

He must have had a tingling chill course through his body at the realization, one that was contagious, for I felt suddenly electrified. "I do." His eagerness to hear more was evident. "And I will be happy to tell you more," I assured him, "if you don't mind me striking a bargain with you."

He smiled. "My story first?" he asked.

I nodded.

"A fair bargain." He leaned forward and took a sip of iced tea. "I have the oddest sensation," he confessed. "I want to cry." I looked at him with a compassionate question in my eyes. "With joy," he said. "And with..." He set the glass back down on the low table. "That summer... that brief summer... was so wonderful. And then so . . . Oh, where do I start?" He uncrossed his legs and planted his bare feet on the tile floor. "I can't sit here." He rose abruptly, paced to the window and clapped his hands three times. The silvery curtains drew themselves apart. He seemed to be elsewhere for a moment, collecting something. "There was an avocado tree in the front yard back then." I could see his shoulders heave in a silent sigh. "I used to climb up into its branches to get away from everything."

Suddenly I wondered if it was such a good idea after all to let him pry open what must be very painful memories. What was I doing? "Mr. Jameson . . . ?"

"One branch had a particularly accommodating coziness to it," he went on, oblivious to my interruption, "and from that hideaway I could see the sidewalk and the houses across the street and even the house next door . . . Your house, now, isn't it?" He turned around.

"Mr. Jameson . . ."

"Life is miraculously strange," he observed, and I thought to myself, oh, you have no idea . . . but then, maybe he did . . . or maybe he didn't. Maybe I didn't. He glanced out the window again. "I was secretly thrilled every time I saw Louisa go by on her bicycle." He stood there for a moment, and then nestled himself into the cushiony black couch, suddenly looking so small, I could clearly imagine that ten-year-old boy huddled into himself against too much to handle in his young life. Before I could try to offer again that he didn't have to do this, not for my sake, he spoke again. "I had a mad crush on her," he admitted, as if that fact weren't written all over his suddenly very youthful and sweetly sheepish face. "She was the one bright light during a very difficult . . ." He paused. "Addie, are you sure you want me to go into this? I'm afraid that once I get started, it might turn into a bit of a long story. You just stopped in to introduce yourself, and I . . ."

"Oh, I would love to hear your ver . . . your story, Mr. Jameson, really! But I don't want to impose . . ."

"No, no, this is no imposition at all. And please, call me Jeely. This is a rare opportunity, Addie. This is a . . . a very special moment."

"Oh, I agree! Please, do go on, then."

He nodded. "That was the summer that my father left us, finally, for good — us being me and my mother and my sister Julie. He'd done it before, but this time, as it turned out, was the final time. There'd been a lot of screaming and yelling between my parents, and then he took off — a few months before school was out for the summer. We had no money, no insurance, we were living on government support . . . and Julie's disease was draining the life right out of her. She was in a wheelchair and her strength was deteriorating. My mother was . . . she'd always managed to be a source of stability, and hopefulness . . . but that year she could just barely hold things together. Our world seemed to be falling apart." He tapped his chin with a knuckle. "But then . . . along came . . . Louisa!" He smiled, flashing an opened fist at me.

"I probably fell in love with her the minute she walked into our classroom, but if I didn't then, I most certainly did when our teacher introduced her. I can't believe I'm remembering this in such specific detail. It must sound odd – to think of a ten? yes, I was still ten, I didn't turn eleven until the end of August and that must have been, oh, maybe in March or April — a ten-year-old boy . . . falling in love? Our teacher told the class that Louisa — who was standing at the front of the room in a baggy, wrinkled T-shirt and jeans that were, well, rather well-worn — she told the class that Louisa was something of an orphan. Those were her exact words, something of an orphan. So it would **behoove** us to treat her with kindness.

Mrs . . . what was her name? Mrs. Ford? Forge? Anyway, she went on, while Louisa was still standing there looking extremely uncomfortable, to explain to us fifth-graders what the word *behoove* meant, but since my eyes were fastened on Louisa, I saw, with some astonishment, that this exceedingly lovely young girl was eyeing the teacher with . . . disdain! Her lip was unconsciously curling into a sneer! It wasn't the kind of sneer that was full of malice. It was an irrepressible expression of, oh, how can I describe this . . . it was as if I could hear her thinking, 'Oh, my *god*, this woman is *brain-fried*!'" Jeely laughed. I had to join him. I could just picture Gran's eleven-year-old self rolling her eyes at the situation she'd just been thrust into. "'Excuse me?' Louisa said, and, Addie, I sat there in total shock, and eager anticipation — Louisa was interrupting the teacher, this fifty-something-year-old woman who had, in my mind, just been exposed as a fraud. Louisa's sneer had materialized my own take on the woman so precisely that I was jolted out of some, what was it, some *resignation* that had been engulfing me for months, if not years. Mrs. Ford or Forge or whatever turned toward Louisa with a mildly supercilious expression, which she was obviously trying to twist into an expression of *kindness*," he grinned, "and said 'Pardon me?' Louisa somehow managed to replicate the teacher's expression exactly, at which I wanted to cheer — seriously — she was so *bold* it was bowling me over! 'Are both of your parents alive?' Louisa asked. Mrs. Whatever was visibly taken aback. 'Why, no, dear.' She strained the words through her self-image and added, 'How kind of you to ask. My father is no longer with us.' Addie, I could have died with delight right there on the spot. I could hardly wait for whatever Louisa had to say next. I even planned her answer for her, phrases flashing through my mind like, so you're somewhat of an orphan, yourself, then, or, what exactly *is* somewhat of an orphan? 'I'm sorry to hear that, ma'am,' Louisa said. 'May I sit down now?' 'Of course, dear,' Mrs. Whatever said, composing herself, 'your seat is that one,' pointing to the empty one right next to me. Oh joy of joys! She was going to be sitting next to me!" Jeely clasped his heart and grinned up at the ceiling, and although I knew he hadn't done that in the classroom, I also knew that was exactly what he had felt like doing. "I was mildly disappointed, though," he went on, "the opportunity for a verbal jab to the solar plexus having been what I'd hoped she would follow up on, but then, I realized, that was *me, I* was angry, I was angrier than I knew, about *everything* — all of this was tumbling through my mind in an un-thought-out kind of way as Louisa walked toward her seat. 'Mrs. Forger?' Louisa said then — that's it, that was the teacher's name, how could I have forgotten that? It's too appropriate! 'Yes, dear?' Louisa sat down and placed her books on her desk. 'I just wanted you to know that my father is not dead. He's a prisoner. I'm not an orphan. So you don't have to be kind to me.'"

I looked at Jeely, startled. Gran's father had been in prison? I'd suspected something along those lines, but I hadn't gleaned that she'd been aware of the fact at the time. I was going to have to ask her about that.

"Suddenly this terrible silence fell onto the whole room," Jeely said. "Everybody waited with bated breath for whatever Mrs. Forger would do next. Mrs. Forger herself looked like she'd just left her body and been transported to somewhere else in the universe, or wished she had. She placed her fingertips on her desk, as if to steady herself, because there she was, after all, in front of her class. I almost felt sorry for her, for a moment, this fifty-something-year-old woman who didn't have a clue. 'It isn't really necessary for any of us to disclose the details of our background in this classroom, is it?' she finally offered, not even hearing her own words — their reversal of what she herself had just done. 'We're here to learn, and it's time for us to enter the exciting world of geography!' and with that, she told us to open our geography books. I looked over at Louisa, hoping to catch her eye, to let her know that what she had just done was the most amazing thing I had ever witnessed in my life! And, Addie, when she looked back at me, what she did just threw me into the worst — and best — turmoil I'd ever known in all of my ten years. She *scowled* at me." He showed me the expression he remembered, and I grimaced. "No, it was wonderful! She was angry, too! Just like me! But then I realized that she was just as angry at *me* as she was at the rest of the world. I was just another thorn on her rose bush, and it seemed doubtful that there were very many roses on it, if any, more thorns than roses, anyway. Oh, how I wanted to let her know that I understood! She wouldn't have anything to do with me, though, not for the whole rest of the school year." Jeely shook his head. "I was miserable. My mother didn't need me to be miserable, though, you know? She had so much weighing her down already. So when she asked me how school was going and who my friends were, I started making up things about Louisa. Well, not making them up, really, there was plenty to tell about Louisa, and I got some kind of sublimated satisfaction out of talking about her, but I made it sound like Louisa and I were friends. So my mother wouldn't feel bad about me, too. Because the truth was, I didn't have any friends. I didn't want to tell anybody about what was going on in my life, nobody was real enough, except Louisa, and Louisa pretty much gave me the impression that I was . . . scum!" Jeely laughed.

"Oh, Mr. Jameson . . . Jeely . . ." I reached my hand toward him. His hand was dry and warm, and he squeezed my fingers. When he withdrew it, he seemed lost, in some other time, in the time he had been revealing to me with such poignant honesty. "Are you sure you want to go on with this story?" I asked him.

"Oh, I do!" He reached for his iced tea. "Are you sure you want to hear the rest of it?"

"I can't tell you how much! This tea is delicious, by the way."

"My own special brew. I grow the herbs in my back yard. Addie! Come with me." He popped off the couch and led me through the house, through a mostly stainless steel kitchen and a small laundry room and out the back door onto a beautifully tended garden. Neatly curved rows of herbs and vegetables created an artistic design bordered on three sides by a low stone wall. "We were sitting in this back yard," he said. "There was just a sparse lawn here off the patio in those days, and a table and chairs. That was the day my mother told Louisa that I'd been talking about her, and by the look on her face . . . but I'm getting ahead of myself." He plucked a leaf of peppermint and handed it to me. It smelled wonderful. "I'd been pining over Louisa since summer vacation had started, that's the only way I can describe it, pining for her, torturing myself by sitting up in the avocado tree watching her go into the new neighbor's house — your house, now, Addie — and wishing I had the courage to, I don't know, steal her bike or something so she'd have to talk to me! It was my sister Julie's twelfth birthday, and Louisa had sneaked down to the edge of our yard through the uphill neighbor's yard, there," he pointed at whatever lay beyond the immensely tall bushes that hid even the roof of what I knew to be a dark green house, if it was still there, still the same. "I had no idea why. Was she spying on me? The thought crossed my mind. I hoped she was spying on me! But didn't she know about the dog? She was attacked by this vicious mongrel that used to get out and terrorize the whole neighborhood. That dog disappeared a few days later, come to think of it. I never found out what happened to it, but I was relieved beyond measure, one less thing to weigh on my poor mother. Anyway, Louisa came tumbling out of the bushes and caught us all totally by surprise. That was when my mother told her I'd been talking about her, and when I saw the look on Louisa's face, I was . . . I was positive that mine was a lost cause! I had obviously become not merely one of the general enemy, but a specific traitor. And then Louisa did something that completely melted my already totally mushy heart!"

I didn't give Jeely any indication whatsoever that I already knew this story from someone else's perspective, but I think a trace of the same reaction of meltdown must have crossed my features. I had been more moved by Gran's account of her presentation of the silver bowl, and her speedy exit, than I had let her know. That confused and temperamental child who had tried to be so tough on the outside and was so soft on the inside . . . was that child still inside my grandmother somewhere? Was she still putting on a front of independence belying an unmet need? Her husband, my grandfather, died when I was little. I have very few memories of him. Gran is always so happy to see me, it occurred to me as I stood there with Jeely in his garden, that I have never thought about what she's like when I'm not around. Listening to this beautifully unselfconscious man describe his feelings for her . . .

"She gave my sister Julie a precious gift, a little silver salt bowl," Jeely interrupted my thoughts. "Come," he said, and led me back through the house. He went to his desk and buzzed open a drawer. "She gave Julie this."

Unbidden tears sprang to my eyes as I accepted the small object. *Jeely* had the silver bowl? I fingered the tiny silver spoon. So Julie was . . .? I looked up at Jeely.

"Julie gave me the bowl just before she died," he said, his own eyes moist. "You know, Addie, until this moment, this . . . you being here . . . you knowing where Louisa is! Oh, what am I saying?" He wiped his eyes.

"Oh, Jeely, I'm so sorry. I'm so sorry about Julie."

"Oh, no, no, you don't understand! I haven't told you the whole story! There's so much more! But, oh, my, look at what time it is! You've been here almost an hour." I was about to tell him that it didn't matter what time it was, when he said, "Are you getting hungry?"

Hungry? Food was the last thing on my mind. "I don't know . . . now that you mention it . . ."

"I just noticed that I'm ravenous! And I have just the thing. Karen brought over a spinach quiche. Let me just pop it in, and we can . . . do you have to be anywhere? I'm so glad you're here. I can't tell you how amazing this is. And you live next door! What a most marvelous turn of events we are right smack in the middle of!" And with that, he disappeared into the kitchen without even waiting for a response to his questions. I smiled at his boyish eagerness and was glad that Gran wasn't expecting me for at least another two hours. He was back in two minutes with a steaming dish and two plates. "Mmh! Doesn't that smell wonderful!" he exclaimed, breathing in the aroma with a delight that was infectious. "Would you care for a glass of wine, my dear neighbor? I think we should celebrate your arrival!" At my expectantly lifted eyebrows he brought out two stemmed glasses and a dark green bottle. "To your new home!" he toasted.

"To your feeling welcome in it any time, my new friend," I answered, clicking his glass and sipping the clear pale gold liquid.

"So, where was I?" Jeely asked around a mouthful of quiche. I had to hide a smile. I could tell that the next part of his story was going to be accompanied by grunts of pleasure and minced words and bits of spinach being wiped from his lips. What a mass of odd dichotomies this white-haired, freckled man was, sitting in his polished black and silver living room in an outfit whose similarly stark color contradicted the roguish affection he obviously felt for the more colorful things in life. "Louisa had come tumbling out of the bushes, and she had leaves in her hair and blood on her neck and mud all up her backside and a shirt ripped from here to there, and yet, she moved toward Julie with the loving grace of an angel, and she put that silver bowl into Julie's fragile hands, and looked at my poor sister with so much light in her beautiful brown eyes — I was sure that for a moment I saw her actually glow! I was frozen in awe. And then suddenly she had dashed around the corner of the house. She was gone as quickly as she had appeared, leaving all of us at a total loss for words."

I caught my breath. Listening to Jeely's version of this story was moving me even more deeply into a realm in which my grandmother was a shining star, a catalyst for magic, a harbinger of purity in spite of herself.

"That seemed to be her style," he said, and for a moment I wondered if he'd heard what I was thinking. "Appearing out of nowhere, and disappearing into nowhere." He wiped a bit of cheese from the corner of his lip with a cloth napkin. "She disappeared into nowhere at the end of that summer," he said. He stopped chewing. "After everything that happened, she just . . . disappeared. I never had the chance to thank her."

I was about to say, well, maybe you will, but, really, that wasn't for me to decide. I wasn't even sure how I was going to approach Gran about the fact that Jeely Jameson was my next door neighbor, let alone that he had turned his heart inside out in front of me, and some part of her had tumbled out in all her ragged, torn, and shining glory.

"My mother and I wheeled Julie up to Louisa's uncle's house the next day. Of course I knew where she lived. I was sorely disappointed that Louisa wasn't home. My mother had told Julie that she had to give the present back, but I don't think Louisa's uncle felt very good about accepting it. He didn't seem to know much about it, as I recall, although I was hardly able to pay any attention to him. I was in a mild state of shock. I had thought *we* were poor. But at least we had decent furniture, and enough of it to make our house feel cozy and lived in. This house Louisa was living in was more like a pit stop, a few articles of absolute necessity strewn around to make do in between relocations, is what it felt like. Louisa's uncle didn't seem to know very much about her, either, and that bothered me no end. Wasn't it bad enough she didn't have a mother, from what I'd deduced from her first day at school, and her father was in prison — I really wanted to know what that was all about — but here is her uncle in some fancy clothes, I mean, way fancier than anything Louisa herself ever wore, and he's too dazed to make any sense of what my mother is saying to him? Like, niece? What niece? Once I got over the appalling condition of the living room, I wanted to *shake* that man and turn him upside down! That would have been a bit much for my mother, though, don't you think, Addie? This red-headed kid of hers ramming into a perfect stranger with fists flying?"

While Jeely smiled at this memory of himself, I wanted to embrace him for feeling so protective toward the girl who was now, I was more than convinced, a lonely old woman with no one to . . . *Stop that!* I reprimanded myself. Gran is right now out with friends! She's involved in so many things, she's so creative, she has her family, her children, she has me. What am I doing? Gran is fine just the way she is! Maybe it's Jeely who never . . . *Addie Crest!* Stop jumping to conclusions! He has a daughter. What makes you think he isn't married? Besides, Gran didn't like him much as a youngster. Oh, but look at him now! She would . . . Married? He must be married. Before I could embarrass myself further by actually verbalizing any of these thoughts, Jeely continued.

"And then, suddenly and wonderfully, everything changed! It happened the day Louisa brought the silver bowl back for Julie."

Now he was getting ahead of what Gran had told me, and I was all ears.

Louisa

Well, there it was, coming at me from all sides, Maudie and Mary Etta telling me to be Jeely's friend, Jeely himself talking to his mother about me, and now Rim was poking at me.

"Why the groan? Don't you like him, what's his name, Genie?"

"Genie?! What, like something in a bottle? No, Rim, his name is Jeely, and, well, I guess he's okay, if you like people who never, ever smile. He's kind of in a bad situation, I guess, so I've been thinking maybe I should try to . . . well, Mary Etta and Maudie think I should try to be his friend."

"You feel sorry for him."

"Well, yeah. It doesn't seem like his dad's around much . . ."

"And yours is."

"Yeah, but, I mean, no, but . . . but, look at his sister, and his mom . . ."

"What about his mom?"

"Well, jeez, what kind of a mom names her kids Julie and Jeely, seriously? And besides, she's not nearly as much fun to be around as you are."

His eyebrows went up. And his face softened. "I think that family could use all the friends they can get, Louisa. Why don't you take that silver bowl and give it back to Genie's . . . uh, Jeely's? sister . . . ?"

"Julie."

"Julie, I knew that, why don't you just, you know, spend some time with them, work some of your magic on them."

Work some of my magic on them? What magic? I frowned at Rim.

"Who made me get new clothes so I would look like a million bucks when some special lady was about to walk into my life?"

I arched my own eyebrows at that.

"Who's been helping two old ladies move into their new house without anybody telling her that was a really great thing to do?"

"Oh, Rim, you have to meet Maudie and Mary Etta! You wouldn't call them old ladies if you knew them. They're not, like, old, not the way I always used to think of old, anyway. Can we invite them over for dinner some time?"

Rim scanned the living room, and I knew what he was thinking.

"Rim, instead of going on that camping trip, why don't we use the money to get some new furniture?"

"See what I mean? Light bulb lady. Brilliant. Yes. Let's do that. *Okay.* And then we can invite people over, without being afraid they'll go off and send the Goodwill people to us with donations."

"You could invite your new lady friend over!"

"And you could invite *your* new friend Jeely over."

I twisted my mouth. "I guess so." But first I was going to have to return the little silver bowl. I picked it up from the coffee table. It looked even more beautiful than I remembered. And Maudie had given it to me. What had I been thinking? Giving it away to . . . to somebody who needed something special in her life a whole lot more than I did. I bit my lip. How did I always manage to get myself into so many awkward situations? I suddenly felt so sorry for myself that tears came to my eyes. "Uncle Rim?"

"Yeah?"

"I love you so much."

He tilted my chin up, shook his head at me with a frowning wet-eyed smile, and pulled me into his arms. "I'm the luckiest uncle in the whole world," he said.

Snuggled into his arms like that felt so good that I suddenly missed my dad terribly. But since I didn't have him, I felt like the luckiest niece in the whole world. I sighed. Then I pulled away and wiped my eyes and narrowed them at Rim, trying to turn what wanted to be a smile into a pout. "Yeah, but do you *love* me?"

"Yeah!" he said, narrowing his eyes back at me and scrunching up his nose. "I *love* ya, kiddo."

I backed off the couch and got ready to make a dash for it. ***"Then why aren't we at the furniture store already?"*** I yelled.

He grabbed for me, but I was outta there, fleeing down the hall with my Uncle Rim on my heels, both of us roaring and laughing.

* * *

Sunlight poured down through the leaves of the oak tree and dappled the front yard of Maudie and Mary Etta's house. The yard was raked and trimmed and looking well-loved.

"Maudie, can I ask you something?"

She was on her knees, wearing work gloves, scraping old paint off the wooden steps leading up to the porch, and I was squatting beside her, brushing the flakes into a dustpan and dumping them into a bucket. "Of course, Louisa. Anything."

"Okay, well, actually, first, I have a confession to make."

She glanced up, one of her pale eyebrows arched into a question. She had a soft sky blue bandana wrapped around her white hair to hold it back, but a few wisps were trailing along the velvety pallor of her cheekbones. "Okay," she said softly, inviting my confession into her confidence as if it were a treasure she would protect from harm.

"Well, you know that little salt bowl you gave me? Well, I gave it away." I told her about Jeely's sister. "I hope you don't mind that I did that," my shoulders hunched as I spoke, but Maudie's expression relieved me.

"Louisa, that's the loveliest use for that little bowl that anyone could have thought of!" She pushed the scraper under a loosened layer of paint. "I couldn't have thought of anything better myself."

"If you have another scraper, I could do some of that."

"Maybe we can round something up, but let's worry about that later. What was your question?"

"Well, her mom made her give it back, but I still want her to have it, only I don't know exactly how to manage that. How do you give something to someone without feeling all weird about it? I mean, it was hard enough the first time." I sat back on my haunches and rested my chin on my knee.

"Oh, my, that's a good question." She picked up the hammer lying on the top step and tapped the scraper along, peeling back a long curl of dried, dirty paint. "Maybe the answer is a little like this," she said, considering her work. "Most people seem to have some layers of stuff on them, just like this old paint, which was a great way to protect the wood once, but, really, the wood is so beautiful, once you get to see it without all the layers of protection, it seems a shame not to let it show itself off." She paused and studied the steps. "I'm thinking that once we expose this lovely oak and sand it smooth, we could cover it with something clear. That way it would still be protected, but we would never forget how beautiful it is in its own right."

I thought I understood what she was getting at, but I knew I wasn't quite making the connection.

"If you clear away the outer layers, you know, the way somebody dresses, or the way their body says something about them, and you look deeper, at what's real inside them, well . . . what would you see if you looked at Julie that way?"

The light clicked on. "I would see somebody who deserves a gift as beautiful as she is, and I wouldn't even be thinking about how dumb I felt. I wouldn't be thinking about me at all."

"I think that's what you were just about doing when you gave your gift to her the first time, Louisa," Maudie gazed at me with an appreciative smile, "but this time you'll really be noticing what you see in her, and that will make it hard for you to notice anything else."

I sighed. I was most certainly one of the luckiest kids in the world. What Maudie said was making perfect sense. I had looked through the layers of Uncle Rim, and I'd painted over what was inside with something that clearly revealed his true beauty. I could do that with Julie, too. Maybe I could even do it with Jeely, although the thought of gazing at him long enough to see what was under that perpetually somber expression made me wince.

"What?" Maudie asked.

"Oh, you're right, Maudie. You're so right. I was just thinking . . ."

"It's harder to see into some people than into others?"

How did Maudie always know what I was thinking like that? "Why is that, Maudie?"

"Well, I don't know. Why is that?"

"It's because some people," Mary Etta said, appearing behind the screen door, "are more afraid than others of showing their true colors." She pushed the door open and went and perched herself on the swing seat, drawing her high-top sneakers in under her skirt, which was splattered with large blue and green flowers. Her yellow top, with its scooped neckline, was uncharacteristically plain-looking, but she'd taken care of that with three or four strands of different-sized beads, most of them sparkly, and a pair of multi-hoop dangling gold earrings. "Those are the ones who need somebody to do a little scraping, if you know what I mean."

"Sounds kind of painful," I ventured.

"Do you hear those steps complaining?" she asked. She batted her mascara-thickened eyelashes at me, giving the distinct impression of cowering before my dreaded answer, and I had to snicker.

"I think I have a possible, uh," what was the word, oh yeah, "*candidate* for your missing niece," I said, changing the subject. I was going to have to think about scraping away at Jeely later. It was going to take some serious thought, and Mary Etta wasn't going to help get me into a serious frame of mind, I could tell.

"Well, spill the beans, kid, I don't have all day," she said, languishing back against the cushions after setting the swing into motion, closing her eyes as if she had all the time in the world. Maudie returned to her task, looking like she couldn't be bothered with our silly banter, but I noticed a few sparkles bouncing off her shoulders as if they couldn't help but be curious.

"Well, I don't have any beans to spill, yet. I'm still busy collecting them. Maudie, this bucket is just about full. What do you want me to do with it?"

"More like me than you," Mary Etta snorted, her eyes still closed, and her words sounded like the end of a long conversation that had started when they were teenagers.

"How much older were you than the sister who died?" it suddenly occurred to me to ask. It was as if I could almost trust the image that had just flashed into my mind, of the two of them having a competitively protective affection for their much younger sister.

"We were thirteen when she was born," Mary Etta said, opening her eyes and glancing at Maudie, who glanced back at her as if she'd just let some cat out of the bag, and then she looked down, with a little secret smile playing at the corner of her mouth.

"You were both thirteen?" Something about the way they had just communicated something between them felt so familiar I wanted to smack them and laugh at them both. "You're twins?"

"Sororal twins," Mary Etta said, getting up and heading for the door. "Well, you could hardly call us fraternal." She opened the screen door. "I think we should have beans for dinner tomorrow," she mused. "I'll be waiting for someone to show up with some."

"You won't have to, Mary Etta," I told her. She turned around and looked back and forth right through me, as if she couldn't figure out how any words could have come out of that blank space on the porch. "Wait for someone to show up, I mean. Because you and Maudie are coming over to my Uncle Rim's house for dinner tomorrow."

"Oh, well, in that case," she said without skipping a beat, "I'd better go air out my champagne chiffon gown." She scratched a bit of bright red hair into an erect tuft, lifted her chin into the air, and marched into the house with a regal sweep.

"Louisa," Maudie said. I turned around. Her face was all soft with sweet silent laughter. "You can empty that bucket into the trash can by the driveway, and I think I might be able to find another scraper in the garage. I'll go check."

As I lifted the lid on the trash can, a flash of blue where a flash of blue shouldn't have been caught my eye. I peered into the avocado tree in the front yard of the Jamesons' house across the driveway, but I must have been mistaken. I couldn't see anything but branches.

* * *

"Uncle Rim, what does sororal mean?" I asked him as he handed me the other dish he'd just washed so I could wipe it dry and put it into the cupboard.

"So rural? Well, I guess it means way, way out there, way out away from everything else, way out in the country." He swished the two glasses under the faucet and set them on the counter for me.

"Okay, that makes sense. What does fraternal mean?"

"Fraternal? Where are you getting all these words?"

"Rim, just tell me what it means!"

"Okay, okay. Fraternal means brotherly. Fraternities are brotherhoods. It comes from the Latin *fra* . . ."

"Brotherly? I wonder why they didn't think they were brotherly. Oh, brother! No, sister! I get it!"

"Get what?" He turned off the faucet and wiped the counter down.

"I invited Maudie and Mary Etta over for dinner tomorrow tonight." I stepped down off the little square stool and shoved it into the corner.

"You did what?" He looked mildly horrified. "You invited your two old lady friends . . . ? Okay, okay, they're not as old as they look," he said at my open mouth about to protest, "they're young, and they're coming over here *tomorrow*, Looze? Why didn't you check with me first? How do you know I didn't already make plans? How could you ask . . . ?"

"Uncle Rim, slow down, you're galloping! I am checking wi . . . Make plans? You never make pla . . . oh, no. You didn't! What plans did you make? I can't tell them not to come! You have to change your plans! And you have to tell me about . . ."

"Hey, whoa, okay, we're both galloping. Hold it. Just hold it."

I folded my arms over my chest.

"I invited Mona over for dinner tomorrow night." He looked at me with a wry smile on his face. I would have wanted to throw my arms around him, for being so bold about his own life, finally, if he hadn't just spoiled my . . . wait a minute.

"Wait a minute! You invited Moh-nah over, ooh, what a puretty naame . . ." I shrank back at the suggestion of a threat in the tilt of his chin. "Sorry! Rim, that's so perfect! Mona — I really like her name, really, Rim, I do, it's a really pretty name — Mona's coming over and so are Maudie and Mary Etta and this is so perfect! Can we serve beans for dinner?"

"What are you talking about, Looze?"

"Oh, please, we need to have some beans, it's, like, a private joke, but we can serve whatever else you want to serve, and Maudie and Mary Etta can meet Mona in person right off the bat, so I don't have to . . ."

"Somebody is certainly off the bat, or off the wall, or something . . ."

"You don't like it."

"Well, actually, what I was hoping," Rim said, putting his arm around me, "was that you and Mona and I, just the three of us, could get to know each other a little better . . ."

My shoulders slumped.

"But . . ." he turned me toward him with both his hands on my shoulders, "I don't see why we can't all get to know one another better all at once."

"You mean it, Rim? Really? That would be okay with you?" His smile had a little strain in it, but hey, if he was going to let this happen . . .

"I'd really like to meet Maudie and Mary Etta . . ."

"You will love them!"

"And, well, what can I say . . . ?" He scratched his head and bit his lip.

"I really want to meet Mona! She must be pretty cool if she said okay to dinner this soon. I mean, it's only been a week . . . not even . . . ?"

"She is. She is pretty cool." He slipped his hands into his pockets and gazed past me, taking a deep breath.

"So, we'll have to go shopping, right?"

He opened the cupboard where our meager supplies were stored. "I'll take half a day off tomorrow, unless you want to go down to the market right now?"

"Oh. Well. No." I walked into the living room and surveyed our new furniture. We could serve buffet style, and everyone could sit around on our new couch and our new easy chair and we could bring Rim's office chair out from his room. "Rim, this is going to be so great! I'll go shopping with you tomorrow, but there's something else I have to do first. Like, now. So it's not on my mind tomorrow."

He followed me into the living room and sank into the plush cushions of the chocolate-colored couch and hoisted his feet onto the elegant walnut slab coffee table. "Let me guess," he said, picking up a magazine and looking like the picture of satisfaction. I didn't think he was going to read it, though. He looked more like he was going to gaze dreamily into space as soon as I walked out the door, and might be doing the same thing by the time I got back. "Does it have anything to do with a little silver bowl?" he ventured.

"Uncle Rim," I whispered into his ear, hugging him, "who would have thought there was such a beautiful grain under all that old paint?"

As I shut the door behind me, it occurred to me that he might not have had the foggiest idea of what I was talking about. Then again, considering the grain itself, maybe he did.

I fingered the little silver bowl in my jeans pocket as I walked down to Sycamore. Look for the grain, look for the grain, I kept repeating to myself as I stepped up to the porch of the blue and gray house. The front yard was mostly dirt, strewn with scattered leaves from the avocado, curling into brown around their edges. What would it be like to live in this house? To walk out the door and not be able to see the ocean because the bushes were so high? To not be able to see the sky because the avocado tree was so . . . what was that? A blue rag stuck behind the trunk? No, it was a sleeve . . . Hey! "Hey! You in that tree, I see you! What do you think you're doing? Nobody around here needs anybody spying on them! Hey!" I put my hands on my hips as self-righteously as if I'd never been guilty of spying myself, mainly because I hadn't intentionally spied on anybody, well, not until Maudie and Mary Etta . . . but this was different, somebody was right in the Jameson's front yard where he could look right into their windows, and probably look right into Maudie and Mary Etta's . . .

"Hi, Louisa."

"Jeely Jameson, you . . .! You just about scared me to death!" I guessed that must have been the case, because my heart was pounding fit to burst. Only I was more irritated than scared, I quickly decided. Then I remembered the little silver bowl clutched in my fist. I felt to make sure the tiny spoon was with it. Okay. Calm down. Look for the grain, look for the grain . . . Oh, man, who could care what kind of grain . . . and then I realized that the expression on Jeely's reddened face was so full of embarrassment and shame and . . . something else . . . hope? It better not be hope! As soon as I thought that, his expression changed.

"It seems to me you're the one who's spying, Louisa Bylander." His mouth clamped up so tight on his words, it practically turned upside down.

I was just about ready to give up on this whole ordeal, but, wow, Jeely Jameson . . . challenging me?

"It seems to me you do a *lot* of spying," he said, and suddenly something flamed up inside me and burned away whatever foolishness had been about to rise. Okay, so I'd come sliding into their back yard, but hey, I'd ended up giving Julie something, it's not like I was . . .

"So why don't you just leave us alone and go spy on someone else!" he blurted out. He was so mad there was a glint in his eye. I knew that kind of mad. So mad you could cry. So mad you didn't care what anybody thought or did.

I opened my fist and looked down at the little silver bowl. As I did, I could feel Jeely's silence, like a dead weight turning into a feather that floated down and landed on what he saw in my hand. I looked up at him, almost ready to cry myself, but not because I was mad. I was tired. I was tired of having to do everything for everybody. I was tired of being the one who was better off, because I wasn't better off. "Could you give this to Julie?" I said, taking a deep breath to keep everything in and putting the bowl down on the ground and turning around.

I'd taken two steps when there was a thud behind me and my arm was grabbed and then let go of as if it was too hot to touch. I turned around. Jeely was holding the bowl toward me.

"You could give it to her yourself, if you want to," he said in a gentle voice.

I shook my head. "I already did. I don't think I could do it again." I didn't take the bowl.

"Well, then, I'll give it to her." He slipped it carefully into one of several zippered pockets in his khaki pants, making sure the little spoon was inside it. "I know she'll be really happy you came back. *I'm* . . ." he stopped. "I was wondering if you felt like, uh, maybe going down to Cooper's for some ice cream?"

I took a long hard look at him. There wasn't any sign of that mushy hope on his face anywhere. His face was a blank. A controlled blank full of a million freckles and two red eyebrows that wanted to squirm but didn't. "I don't have any money," I told him.

Jeely reached into another pocket and pulled out a few coins. "Hold on a minute," he said, and after stuffing the coins back in and pulling the zipper across the top of the pocket, he swung up into the avocado tree. He was as lithe as a monkey. He disappeared around the other side of the trunk for a minute, and then clambered down, limber and sure-footed, and landed squarely on his feet near the roots. "Okay, let's go," he said, his eyebrows keeping the same low steady line as his voice. I just stood there, speechless, which was something I hadn't been in two weeks — speechless.

"Come on," he said, and he took my hand and led me out of the yard. He let go of it when we reached the sidewalk. "I know a shortcut down by that ugly old turquoise house. After we get our cones, we can go down to the pier. I have enough money for the bus."

* * *

The waves splashed and curled around the rows of thick posts, echoing within the shaded underbelly of the pier, and rolled up in a thinning foam sheet to within a few inches of our bare feet. Both of us had rolled up our pants, which were splotched with wet stains anyway, before we'd made ourselves comfortable on the sand.

"Won't your mom wonder where you are?" I asked Jeely. We hadn't spoken at all, except to tell the soda jerk that we both wanted orange sherbet cones, and to say hi and bye to the bus driver.

"It's okay with her if I'm not there every single minute," he said. "What about your uncle? Does he even care about you at all?"

"What do you mean? Uncle Rim? He's busy a lot, but, yeah, he cares about me, a whole lot! Why are you even asking me that dumb question?" I heard what I was saying. "I'm sorry, I guess it wasn't a dumb question. But, I mean, what do you even know about my Uncle Rim?"

"Well, his house isn't exactly . . . I mean, when we went over to . . ."

"Oh, Jeely! That dumb furniture! Is that what you mean? We fixed that! I made him go and buy all new stuff! He was going to take me camping, but then we figured we better do something about . . . well, what if we wanted to have company or something . . ." Uh, oh. I didn't want to take this into the wrong direction. I didn't want Jeely to think that just because he'd bought me an ice cream cone, I was going to invite him over to my house or anything. "Thanks for the ice cream cone," I said.

"You're welcome." He dug his heels into the sand, scooping two ruts out in front of him. Even his legs were covered with millions of freckles. He pulled his feet back and leaned his chin on his knee. Not liking that position either, apparently, he picked up a piece of driftwood at his side and started flicking grains of sand from its tip toward the incoming rush of salty foam.

Grains of sand. Look for the grain, look for the grain. "You help your mom out with Julie a lot, don't you?" I asked him. The sun was nearing the horizon, but the sky was so clear that only a pale gold wash was being reflected on the shimmering silver surface of the sea.

He shrugged. "I guess."

"What's wrong with her? With Julie, I mean."

"There's something wrong with her muscles or her nerves or something. She's been in that wheelchair for about a year now. My mom has to help her in the bathroom and everything. That lady that was here, that day? She's a nurse. She stops in once a week. But Julie is a full-time job for my mom, so, yeah, I try to help out some."

"Is Julie going to get better?"

He shrugged again.

"Don't they know what to do?"

"I don't think they know **anything**. Nobody knows anything! Nobody knows when my dad's coming back! Not that I even want him to. Nobody knows where the money is coming from . . ." Suddenly he was tossing the stick into the waves and darting out from under the pier and splashing through the water along the dark gray sand toward the setting sun.

I threw my own stick away and ran after him. "Hey!"

He stopped and turned around and waited until I'd walked up to him. I didn't know what to say. It seemed like we were in the same boat, but his end was sinking faster than mine.

"You don't know when your dad's coming back, either, do you?" he asked. I shrugged, and then let my shoulders sag. Maybe this boat was just plain going down on both ends. "What's he doing in prison?" He said it the way you'd hold out a bit of food to a feral cat. He wasn't trying to trap me, he was just aware of why I was the way I was.

"He's not in prison."

"Oh." He looked out at the colors deepening on the water. He wasn't looking at me when he went on. "But you said, in class that first day...?"

I flashed back on that day, not *that* first day, *my* first day, when that brain-fried Mrs. F needed to be reminded that kids are actually people. "I said he's a prisoner." I had sat down at the desk next to Jeely's, and he'd looked like he couldn't contain himself, like he'd never seen anyone be real before, and I knew right then I'd be in big trouble, I'd have to deal with the worst kind of anti-hero-worshipper, if I didn't set him straight right away, so I looked at him as if he smelled really bad. Which he didn't, of course. And I'd thought I was right to do that at the time, because who needs an Eeyore following you around. Out here by the ocean, though, away from that cage called school, I was starting to see a lot more grain under the peeling paint. "At least that's what the embassy people told my uncle they think — about his not reporting back from, what was it, the 'area of political turmoil' he went into. That he's been taken prisoner."

"He's a soldier?"

"No, he's a photojournalist."

"What's that?"

"He takes pictures for the news people to show the rest of the world what's really going on. And nobody has heard from him for over three months now." I almost felt like doing what Jeely had done, just start running, but then I remembered why I was here — trying to be a friend to someone who really needed one. "But it's not all that bad, I mean, the not knowing is bad, but I have my Uncle Rim, and something else, too. Something else really great."

"What else?" He had this encouraging look on his face, like it was a relief to change the subject.

What else? How could I tell him what else? There was so much to tell. "Jeely, do you think you could come over to my house for dinner tomorrow night?"

His eyes widened for a second. "Uh, yeah."

And then I decided I could tell him. So I told him. Everything. We walked back to where we'd left our shoes — we had to rescue one of my sneakers from the sneaky waves — and we walked back up the hill, instead of taking the bus, even though it would be dark long before we arrived. I told him about Maudie and Mary Etta and their niece and Uncle Rim's Mona. "So, you can't say anything about any of this to anyone, Jeely, at least not until we know more."

"But won't they know right away as soon as they walk in the door and see your uncle's girlfriend if she's their niece?"

"Oh." I hadn't even thought about that. We were standing on the sidewalk in front of his house. "Jeely?"

"Yeah?"

"Can you see Maudie and Mary Etta's house from your tree?"

He gave me a look bordering on sheepish, but it had kind of a satisfied grin hiding underneath it. "You're not the only one who's a good spy, Louisa," he said.

This time it was my eyes that widened a little. "Jeely Jameson, there's a lot about you that I never noticed before."

He shrugged. "That's okay."

And it was. It was okay. "See you tomorrow, then. At five-thirty. Don't forget!"

He looked at me as if I'd told him not to forget his own head, and I turned around and dashed up Sycamore so he couldn't see how much my mouth wanted to smile and how high my eyebrows had shot up.

Addie

I still had half an hour or so before Gran would be expecting me. I'd hugged Jeely warmly when we parted, promising to stop by again later in the week, and as I walked across the driveway to my house, I felt inundated with history, with changes and personalities and possibilities. I stopped at the edge of the walkway and turned around and pictured the old avocado tree that once shaded my neighbor's yard. I could almost see a ten-year-old boy among its branches. I turned around and imagined Maudie and Mary Etta's minivan, one of those old-fashioned cars that ran on high-pollution fuel, parked where my borrowed hover-car was sitting. It was odd to think that people owned the vehicles they drove in those days. It just makes so much more sense that the solar- and water-powered vehicles we have now are simply available to whoever needs them, for however much time, in whatever capacity. But people didn't operate then under the assumption that whatever was needed would become available. Under the rule of government and the institution of finance, Gran once told me, an imposed sense of scarcity had created all manner of problems between what she called the haves and the have-nots. I can hardly fathom the imbalance created by the wealth being so unevenly distributed. I can't imagine people not trusting that they will somehow be provided with what they need, that what will solve a temporary problem can be traded for one's own talents, that in one's own community there is always plenty to go around.

Gran also told me it was an almost unheard-of rarity, back then, for someone to do something like what I'd just done, followed my inner senses and the outward signs to the house that was calling me from the deep fabric of existence, to find exactly where I belonged so that my sense of belonging was inextricably woven into that fabric. It would have been considered a miracle that just when I arrived where I was supposed to be, the people who had been there were ready to move on, and I could never, in the old days, have simply moved right in. There would have been all kinds of intricately involved money exchange and paper work concerning ownership, the kind of work that her Uncle Rim had done, what she called not only time-wasting but soul-wasting.

I thought about Maudie and Mary Etta as I walked toward the steps to the front porch. I pictured a swing seat suspended from the rafters, and I could almost see an eleven-year-old girl sitting there with her eyes closed, dreaming of belonging, not yet knowing what a sense of belonging those two women would infuse into her world. To what extent, I had yet to find out, for I hadn't heard the whole story yet, and apparently Gran didn't know it yet, either, since she'd tucked that thick letter back into the gold silk box after reading the first page. Even what I did know from the rest of Jeely's account, I would need to have embellished with the details Gran would provide.

I walked into the living room and listened to the echo of Maudie and Mary Etta suggesting to my grandmother, when she was a soft-hearted, tough, bright young girl, that she could befriend the boy next door.

I paused in the dining room under the old chandelier, glad that the former occupants had never replaced it, and pictured a table spread with treasures from around the world. If Maudie hadn't given Gran that miniature silver bowl, the one that Jeely right now had in his possession, some of the things he'd told me about would never have happened. Some of the things that were still possible wouldn't even be in the realm of consideration.

Maybe I was being an impetuous romantic to hope that a meeting between them would rekindle the innocent spark they'd shared during a summer of their childhood, but it was becoming an impossibility, in my mind, to allow for no meeting at all. Jeely's former partner lives in Australia.

I turned back into the living room and climbed the stairs, running my hand along the smooth curl of polished walnut, and I could almost hear the jingle of bells from a jester's cap bouncing on the head of a woman who muttered complaints to herself. It made me smile.

I leaned out of the upstairs bathroom window, my palms on the roof of the porch, and looked down at where Maudie had walked by, a soft glow wafting from her shoulders, followed by a shy girl in jeans, and an unexpected wave of nostalgic affection surged through me.

I peeked into the bedrooms, warmed by the activity and thoughtfulness that had once been generated into the atmosphere by two profoundly aware women, and knew that I would be inspired in my own work and in my own thinking when I arranged my office and sleeping quarters.

I stood in the attic and gazed at the rafter where either Maudie or Mary Etta — and I suspected it had been Maudie, she would have been the one to write the letter — had entrusted the solution of Gran's mystery not only to the protection of unnoticed years but to the inevitability of its discovery. That the starling had been part of the fabric of Gran's story, and now mine, was beyond doubt, and although I was starting to feel the deep comfort of the thread of my own life being embedded into such a finely and intricately woven tapestry, tears of overwhelming gratitude sprang to my eyes.

And then a sense of anticipation flooded over me. Something was happening that was even bigger than I could project from what I already knew. Something was billowing up inside me and around me that felt so full of unimaginable promise that I was buoyed into a sense of indescribable wonder and knowing.

A fluttering at the casement window startled me from my reverie. A starling, perched on the sill outside the windowpane, chirped at me. It hopped two steps, and chirped again.

Oh! I have to get going!

The bird ducked its head in a quick nod and flew off.

And I hurried down the steps, on my way to find out Gran's version of what Jeely had told me.

Louisa

There *was* something that could be called mysterious about Mona, I thought when I got up from the couch and answered the doorbell, although that description might have left a little to be desired in the nuances of shadows. She looked like a lizard. Or at least she was dressed like a lizard, in a scaly, skin-tight, long-sleeved, low-neckline emerald and gold top tucked smoothly into slender shiny emerald slacks that tapered smoothly toward black high heels. Something inside me began to glower in alarm as I stood holding the door open, taking in her frontward-angled short black hair and neatly manicured arched black eyebrows. Her eyes were such a dark brown they were almost black, and her lipstick bordered on bruised purple, which made her complexion appear to be haunted by hints of pale green. I had to admit that she was stunning, but my opinion of Rim's sensibilities were already smoldering beyond any conceivable recovery.

"Mona!" Rim exclaimed, emerging from the kitchen wiping his hands on a dish towel. "Come on in!" How could he be delighted to see her? "This is Louisa," he said, stepping forward and glancing at my tan brushed-denim jumper with a fleeting trace of regret, which ignited an already red-hot ember into a flame of indignation.

"Hi," I said, swallowing back dark smoke and allowing her to take my limp hand briefly in hers. We stood there, the three of us, in what suddenly looked like a very shabby living room, despite its walnut slab coffee table covered with neatly arranged plates, napkins, glasses, and silverware. Rim and I had prepared a feast of baked salmon and sweet potatoes and spinach salad and lima beans, all of which were awaiting final touches in the kitchen until everyone arrived.

"Oh, and this is her friend, Jeely," Rim added, turning toward the couch.

Jeely, sitting up straight as a pin, lifted the fingers of one hand from where it rested on his khaki-clad thigh. "Hi," he offered, with as controlled an expression as he could muster. A quick glance at me before he lowered his eyes to make an apparent appraisal of the coffee table reassured me that he was sharing my opinions of both Rim and Mona.

"Jeely, I need your help with something," I said, and turned on my heel and headed down the hall.

"Louisa . . . ?" Rim was making my name sound like that of an estranged orphan, and I wasn't about to turn around. "Jeely, why don't you go and help Louisa," I heard him change his tactic. "And Mona, maybe you can help me in the kitchen?"

"Jeely, oh my god," I whispered to him when he joined me in my room. He looked at my expression, and a smile flitted through his reflection of my curled lip. "You think it's funny?" I croaked at him. His eyebrows went up, and the corners of his mouth turned down, and then suddenly his shoulders hunched over as he tried to bar a giggle behind his freckled fingers. "Jeely, she's a reptile!" He grimaced in agreement. "If Maudie and Mary Etta weren't coming over, I'd climb outta my window this minute and never come back!" I grabbed my head and paced the room. "What was he thinking?" I slumped onto the edge of my bed. "The whole evening is already ruined."

He sat on the bed beside me and cocked his head at me. "It's not totally ruined," he said quietly.

"Oh, Jeely, the whole point of it was to introduce Maudie and Mary Etta to their long-lost niece! That . . . that *thing* out there isn't anybody's niece! She was hatched out of a leathery egg!"

"Well, I still get to meet Maudie and Mary Etta," he said.

"Yeah, I guess." The whole evening *was* already ruined, though, as far as I was concerned. "I hate this dress. Close your eyes. I'm changing." He obliged, and I flung my jumper into a corner and pulled on my jeans and a baggy T-shirt. "Come on, let's go watch the lizard dart out her tongue." Jeely rolled his eyes and grinned. He opened his mouth to say something, but I cut him off. "Don't even say it. Rim is a total idiot, and I'm not even going to *try* to be nice to **Moh**-nah."

"I was just going to say," Jeely scratched his thick curly red hair, "maybe we should catch some flies before we go back, you know, so she could have some dinner, too."

I wanted to throw my arms around him, but instead I got an idea. I went over to the windowsill, ran my finger along its dirty surface, and pulled him over to the mirror on my bureau. "I think you must not have noticed," I said, wiping a dark smudge across his forehead as he watched, "that you forgot to wash your face."

He spit on his finger, smeared the smudge into a dull gray cloud, and then pressed his fingertip onto the end of my nose. I liked it — not so noticeable an effect on either one of us that it would draw immediate attention, but just disturbing enough to elicit a comment from an intelligent and honest person, if there were any left in the world.

"Oh, before we go back in there," Jeely said, reaching into his pocket, "I think Julie would really like it if you gave this back to her yourself."

Just as we returned to the living room, the silver salt bowl having been tucked under my pillow, the doorbell rang again. "I'll get it," I yelled toward the kitchen, and there stood Maudie and Mary Etta, one in a tan jumper and the other in a champagne-colored gossamer gown. For a moment I regretted changing — I wouldn't have minded being Maudie's little twin — but I was too eager to communicate with a sullen shake of my head that there was nothing for them to anticipate niece-wise in this house.

"Well, Louisa, don't you look lovely," Mary Etta offered with a wry arch of one her brown pencil lines. She touched the tip of her nose with the knuckle of her index finger. "I see we've all dressed for the occasion." Oh, great, set me on edge, I thought, as if enough hasn't gone wrong already. But then I saw her smirking, and I knew she was already on my side, no matter what. "And this must be Jeely." She swept grandly into the living room and offered him a hand. "How do you do, young man?" Jeely looked slightly stunned as he took her hand briefly. "It's a pleasure to make your acquaintance," she told him. "Since we're neighbors, an introduction is long overdue, don't you think? And if we hit it off tonight, and I don't see any reason why we shouldn't, since we seem to have something in common, I'd be delighted to have you visit us upon occasion." Something in common? I glanced over at Jeely. He was turning red. What did they have in common? Red hair? Mary Etta glared an intent at me for a second, and I got it. Me. They had me in common. Duh.

"Hello, Jeely," Maudie said, closing the door behind her and offering him her hand as well. "It's very nice to meet you." She glanced around the living room. "Louisa, this is lovely. What a beautiful job you and your uncle have done, with all of this," she waved her hand over the coffee table, "and with the furnishings! That is a very inviting couch. And I bet you helped pick out those end tables, didn't you?" I couldn't remember telling her about our shopping spree. "Louisa, you know that one lamp we have, the one with all those fringes on the shade? Don't you think it would go well on that end table?" My eyebrows went up. "I've been thinking of replacing it, and I don't know what I'll do with it if you don't take it."

"Oh, Maudie, I'll take it!"

"Oh, good. It's out in the van. I'll bring it in . . ." She was about to open the door when Rim and Mona appeared from the kitchen.

I cringed. Did I have to make all the introductions? I didn't think I could say Mona's name without drawing it out into a moan. To my relief, everyone introduced themselves. I glanced over at Jeely. He shrugged, but then he grinned at me, and I knew he liked Maudie and Mary Etta.

In fact, he did quite a bit of grinning that evening. I never would have guessed how much fun it could be to have people praising our cooking and talking about all kinds of things. Everyone seemed so comfortable. Mary Etta was hilarious, especially when she refused to crack a smile at something she'd just said, even though everyone else was laughing. Maudie was warm and gentle, interested in what people had to say, asking questions to draw them out. Rim looked unusually handsome, the way his gray eyes sparkled when he offered more food or drink or spoke about his work. I even found myself retracting a little of my first impression of Mona. She was a bit stiff, and maybe a little too aware of how she looked, but it seemed that behind her facade, she was reserved more because of an uncertainty about herself than because she thought too much of herself. And she had a nice smile. Maybe if she had been dressed differently, I thought . . . and then I remembered what Maudie had said about looking for the grain. I couldn't see it, but I wanted to.

For about two minutes I wanted to, for Rim's sake, but it had been evident by the way Maudie and Mary Etta had reacted to Mona right from the start that she wasn't their niece, and by the time everyone left, after all the clean up was done and all the hugs and thanks and promises were exchanged, even though the living room looked even better in the glow of our new lamp, I was not only disappointed, I couldn't even stand to look at Rim, whose vague smile made me grit my teeth. I told him good night and ducked away before he could lavish any of whatever he was feeling all over me. I closed my bedroom door with extreme control, since I felt like slamming it so hard it would splinter into smithereens, and threw myself down on my bed.

"Louisa?" It was Uncle Rim at my door. "Is everything okay?"

Oh, sure, everything's just hunky-dory. "Everything's fine! Good night!"

"Can I come in?"

"No."

"Louisa."

"What?!"

"I'm coming in."

"No!"

He came in. "Hey, kiddo, what's up?"

I could feel his weight settle itself on the edge of my bed, but I didn't want to look at him. "Rim, just leave me alone!"

"I just . . . I don't understand, Louisa. What's bothering you? The evening went so well, a hundred times better than I expected. It was great! And it was all your idea. I don't think it would have been nearly as terrific if it had been just you and me and Mona . . . ." He paused. "Oh."

Oh, he thought he had it all figured out, but he didn't. He didn't have a clue. Nobody did. It was like Jeely said when he ran off at the beach. Nobody knows anything. Well, maybe some people knew something. When Mary Etta asked Jeely about his sister, Maudie wondered if they'd ever tried an energy healer with Julie. He didn't know what that was, and neither did I, and when Maudie explained it, Jeely just said he didn't think it would work, nothing had worked, and so Maudie dropped it. She looked like she knew something, though. Or maybe I'd just wanted her to look like she knew something. Lying on my stomach with my face in my pillow, waiting for Rim to make his inaccurate observations, it seemed like there were way too many questions and no answers at all. Questions with no answers are like walls around empty rooms. If the walls weren't there, it wouldn't seem like an empty space, it would just be part of the whole big outdoors looking to be explored, but the walls make you notice how there isn't anything inside the space, no cozy, comforting answers, just . . . nothingness.

"I'm guessing," Rim said, "that Mona isn't what you might have been expecting."

I lifted my face from my pillow and gave him my oh-aren't-you-ever-so-clever look.

"Actually, Looze, I was a little startled by her outfit myself. It was kind of, well…"

I sat up. "Like a chameleon?"

He sputtered a laugh. "I was going to say, kind of, like, really…" he scratched his arm, "…really *green*. But you know, you have a point, chameleons change colors, and Mona was not dressed anything like that when we were negotiating the purchase of the house. I guess I thought she'd turn up in a regular skirt and blouse. And what was the color of that lipstick she was wearing?"

"What was she thinking?"

"I've been trying to figure that out, actually. Maybe she runs with a different crowd in the evenings, you know, not like the business people she works with during the day."

"But why did she think you would be that kind of person?"

He shook his head, frowning, shrugging.

"Was she trying to impress you?"

He shrugged again.

"Did it work?"

"Um, well, she certainly did make an impression, didn't she?" He threw a hand over his mouth to hide his grin.

I was so relieved. He could see it, too. She just wasn't right for us. And then it occurred to me that Uncle Rim had had high hopes about this person. "So, what now?"

"You know what, Looze? I think I'm going to give her a second chance."

"What!?"

"Have you ever given anyone a second chance, Looze?"

I thought about Jeely. He had seemed so different from what he turned out to be. I was even thinking of him as a friend.

"I really like your friend Jeely," Rim said. "And Maudie and Mary Etta? Wow! I think you hit the jackpot in the friends department!"

I just had to lean over and give him a big hug.

* * *

It was drizzling when I left the house the next morning. I'd told Rim at breakfast that I was going to return the little bowl and spoon to Jeely's sister, but before I did that, I needed a dose of M-and-M-type courage, so I rode my bike past the Jamesons' place, leaned it against the van in the driveway, admired the beautiful wood of the four wide steps as I climbed them to Maudie and Mary Etta's front porch, and called through the screen.

"Louisa! Just the person I wanted to see! Come on in!" Maudie's voice made my slightly skittery insides settle into a deep calm by the time I'd walked through the warm coziness of the living room into the little dining room. Someone had trimmed the lilac bush outside the window, just enough so that a little more of the day's gray light illuminated the display of objects on the table. "I knew I had something that was meant just for you. These things weren't in one of the boxes. I'd forgotten that I'd wrapped them in washcloths and packed them into the corner of one of my suitcases. Oh, my, don't you look lovely this morning," she said, glancing up and smiling at me.

I peered down at my same old T-shirt and jeans outfit and shrugged my eyebrows. I knew by now that Maudie was a rainbow-in-the-sky-kind-of-guy, but come on, this old bunch of rags?

"Oh, I'm not talking about your outer layers! I'm talking about that soft light beaming out from inside you. It's funny how that happens — when you look for it in other people, it shows up even more in you. Now, Louisa, honey, I could let you pick out one of these items for yourself, or I could give you the one I think belongs to you. Or maybe that's not an either/or," she muttered to herself, sorting the various objects into equidistant spaces from one another. "Right." She tilted her head at me. "Why don't you take a look at each one of these, handle them if you want to, and see if anything seems to want to be with you."

See if *it* wants to be with *me*? I hadn't done much choosing of things — some clothes, some books, this or that pair of shoes — but when I had, it was about what I thought I would feel comfortable in or enjoy reading. It wasn't about did that shirt want to be mine! Did that book feel like it wanted to be read by me? I was about to say something, when my attention was drawn to one of the items. That's how they say it, isn't it, one's attention is drawn, but that implies an agent doing the drawing, and that's exactly what was happening, my eyes felt pulled over and locked onto, not by me, but by the object itself. Wow. Okay. But wait. Could I even look at these other things? I took a deep breath, found a neutral spot inside me to fit myself into, and scanned the table.

There was a solid rose quartz heart, next to a tiny cylindrical box with an inlaid abalone-shell lid, and next to that a colorful jointed Chinese-looking fish. There was a brown leather medicine bag on a leather cord, with a tiny feather and a bead attached to its front by a miniature dream-catcher. There was a ring with a carved image of some Greek goddess on it. There was a white ceramic duck and a hand-carved wooden zebra and a tiny blue crystal chalice and a bracelet of opals. There was a small paperweight with what looked like glass candy inside it. I could feel Maudie's eyes on me as my own wandered over her collection of mementos from around the world. Each item was beautiful, a little treasure, and I wouldn't have minded being given any one of them. None of them, though, was pulling at me the way the first one I'd noticed had done.

Attached to a necklace of colorful beads was a curly-cue white shape that looked like a fish hook. I couldn't tell if it was ivory or bone or even plastic without touching it, so I looked at Maudie to see if it was okay with her for me to pick it up. I was almost startled to see how much her eyes were glistening, how much love, how much joyfulness was beaming at me. For a moment I experienced a kind of zooming in, or out, the world disappearing, or being contained in the vastness, a light-filled sense of connection, an all's-right-with-the-cosmos sensation that tingled a shower of starlight through my cells. It lasted for only a second, or was it a minute, or an eternity? I felt I'd been charged with something, or given charge of something. When I looked down, the curly-cue carving was in my hand. I must have been about to pick it up and didn't notice when my fingers grasped it. Right away I knew it wasn't plastic.

"It's carved from whalebone," Maudie said. "It once belonged to a kahuna. Her son made it from a rib washed up on the shore of her island. So it carries more than one kind of energy, you see. The energy of the whale is free and grand, benevolent and powerful, fluid and far-reaching. The fish-hook is a symbol of the tool used by her people to supply themselves with nourishment from the sea. It promises plentifulness, ongoing success with the right use of the tool, intentions turning into the best outcomes for all concerned. And, well... does it look like anything else to you, Louisa?"

"Maudie, I can't believe you want me to have this!"

"Do you still think it is one of us who has made this choice?"

I had to sit down. Thankfully there was a straight-backed chair almost directly behind me. What had just happened? I looked at the necklace in my hands. I felt its smooth curves, the pointed curl, the way it fit into my palm. It was the size of a seahorse. "It looks like a seahorse," I told her.

"And what does a seahorse make you think of?"

"A seahorse is so little," I said. "It's so little it can hide in coral and seaweed and disguise itself to look like nothing but another waving leaf in the current. But it's different from other fish, as different as it could be, because all the others are built to swim straight ahead, but the seahorse is vertical. It's always upright." Even as I made these observations, I felt as if I were describing myself. Well, maybe not the upright part, so much, although as I said the words, I wanted that to be true about me, too, as true as the part about being small and invisible.

"And does it remind you of anything else?"

"Well, it's kind of like an upside-down question mark, too."

"Oh, yes, what a smart observation. So even though this looks like an insignificant little being and a common enough means of making a living," Maudie said as she took the necklace and draped it over my head, "it also carries a question with it, as well as an enormous and wonderful power."

It felt cool against my skin. "Maudie, is this the one you thought was meant for me?"

"I was absolutely sure of it, Louisa."

We heard the screen door slam. Mary Etta was home. I slipped the pendant inside my shirt, for some reason hoping that she wouldn't notice the beads. But I could almost feel her eyes on the back of my neck as she clomped into the dining room in her high-top sneakers.

"Well, well, it seems we've had a graduation. Mm-hm. Mm-hm." She stepped in front of me, pulled me up by my hands, cupped her hands around my cheeks, looked me straight in the eyes, and grinned. "Sweetie, you little bit of dynamite you," she said, and kissed me on the forehead. I was already slightly dazed from the light that had expanded me out beyond the beyond for the flash of an eternity. This approval from Mary Etta, if that's what it was — I mean, I hadn't really done anything — was all I needed to make me fall back onto the chair. "Nuh-uh, nope, no way," she said, pulling me up again. "You have something to take care of, and we have something to discuss," she said, throwing a meaningful glance at Maudie. "Up, up!! Oh! Wait just a second." She waved a pointed red-nailed finger over the objects on the table, narrowing its scope until it landed on the little leather medicine bag. "This might come in handy at some point later in the day when you're handing out gifts." She slipped it into my pocket. "Now, begone with you, messenger of mercy, or suffer the consequences!"

Brought to my senses by her imperious order, I straightened my back. "Aye, aye, sir," I saluted her, then turned on my heel and marched stiff-legged out of the room.

* * *

"Hi, Mrs. Jameson, I hope I'm not interrupting anything?"

"Oh, Louisa, do come in!" Jeely's mom opened her door wide. "Just wait right here in the hall for half a minute," she told me, and in a few seconds she returned with a kitchen towel. "I just want to dry you off a little, dear. There, that's better. This nice rain we're having does get things a little messy. You can leave your shoes right here next to ours." I nudged each sneaker off, toe to heel. "Now come on in here, Jeely told us you'd be back, and oh, I want to thank you for inviting him to dinner last night, he had us laughing about the great time he had, that was just so thoughtful of you and your uncle, and I guess the ladies who have moved in next door must be real nice, from the way he described them, so, here we are then, here's Louisa, Julie, you two just sit tight while I go round up Jeely, he's probably in his room, I'll go get him and we'll be right back!"

Julie was sitting in her wheelchair, in a pink and green flower-printed dress, and without even looking at the arrangement of their living room, I went right up to her with a great sense of urgency, as if the exchange we were about to have needed to happen before Jeely's mom returned with her son.

"Hi, Louisa." Julie's voice was tiny, like that of a much younger child.

I put a finger to my lips, and she smiled weakly at me. Reaching into my pocket, I pulled out the silver and blue salt bowl with its miniature spoon, and placed them in one of her hands, and folded her other hand over it, between my own two hands. I kept my hands on hers and looked into her eyes. I wanted to see her real self, just as Maudie had encouraged me to do, so I looked with all the appreciation I could muster. It wasn't hard. She suddenly seemed more beautiful to me than any other girl I'd ever known, and she was opening up to me, I could see it in her beautiful hazel eyes. She had soft, fine, shoulder-length gingery hair, and freckles, and a delicate nose, and such a sweet expression that she looked like a saint.

"Julie," I said quietly, remembering how Maudie had described what she was giving to me. "This bowl and spoon, they're like you, they hold the salt of the earth. And even though..." I wasn't sure what I was about to say, but the words just flowed from me, "...even though you weren't born with a silver spoon in your mouth, which is what they say when they mean you're rich, I think... I think you can be rich now, in whatever way you want to be. And you see how it's silver on the outside, which is so shiny it reflects whatever is around it, but on the inside it's this clear blue, like the sky on a day with no clouds. And even though you might think of yourself as small, you are a treasure. You know that, don't you? You are a treasure."

Suddenly the same thing happened that had happened when I'd checked with Maudie to see if I could pick up the whalebone-seahorse-fish-hook. For a second the world disappeared in a flash of white light, or the universe was suddenly available to us, or something powerful and electric, but also ever so subtle, was charging through us, and between us. Maybe it wasn't for even a whole second, or maybe it was longer. The same tingly sensation showered through my atoms, and I almost fell backwards a step, but I held on to Julie's hands. Our eyes were still locked into each other's, and for a moment I thought I was looking into the eyes of a wise old woman who was seeing the same thing in me.

Then her eyes widened a little, her mouth dropped open, and she was a twelve-year-old girl again, and I was just Louisa, holding hands with someone I hardly knew, and a girl at that, how embarrassing! I did step back, then, just as Jeely and his mom could be heard coming down the stairs. Julie mouthed the words "Thank you" at me and looked down with glistening eyes at the little bowl as if it were the cause of whatever had just happened. She raised her pale eyebrows in a question directed at me. I reached up to my neck and felt my fish-hook under my T-shirt, and shrugged, but we both knew that we had both felt it.

"There you are, girls, Louisa, you don't have to just stand there, dear, take a chair, and Jeely, you can make your guest feel right at home, can't you, and, let's see, I'll go get us some lemonade, how would that be, would you all like that?"

"Yes, please, Mrs. Jameson," I said, sensing that both of her children were doing their best to diffuse her nervous energy by not saying anything that would bring on another torrent of responses.

"Good, then," she said, and left the living room, which I could now give greater attention to. I sat down on the blue paisley couch, took in the blue and white flowered curtains that hid the front yard from view, noticed the little ceramic figurines of Alpine toddlers and be-ribboned poodles on a triangular corner shelf, the paintings of Jesus and of a vase of daisies on the ivory-colored walls, and came back around to Jeely. He was now sitting on a matching easy chair on the other side of the glass-topped coffee table, underneath which was an assortment of magazines about homes and housekeeping.

"Oh, Jeely, before I forget! Mary Etta and Maudie are the ones who gave me Julie's bowl..."

Julie held it up, her eyes glowing, her cheeks pink.

"...and they had some other neat things, too, and, well, I think maybe they kind of wanted you to have this." I handed him the medicine bag.

"Whoa..." he said in a whisper, examining it carefully. He glanced at the kitchen, then slipped the leather cord over his head and tucked the little bag down into his collared short-sleeved tan shirt.

I was pleased that he hadn't jammed it into one of the zippered pockets in his khaki pants. "I'm not sure what exactly you're supposed to do with a medicine bag. Come to think of it, how do I even know that's what it is? And there's a dream-catcher on the front of it, did you see that? Whatever a dream-catcher is..."

Jeely slipped the bag up, tilted his chin down against his neck, and said, "Yeah."

"I think we could find out more about what medicine bags are used for at the library," I told him. "We could take the bus there tomorrow."

He tucked the bag back inside his shirt as Mrs. Jameson arrived with a tray of glasses and a pitcher of lemonade, which she set down carefully on the coffee table. Was she wearing a different blouse? Hadn't she been in an old loose off-white cotton thing? Now she was wearing a soft orange peasant blouse that matched her hair. She sat down on the couch beside me.

"Mrs. Jameson, I was just saying to Jeely that I need to go to the library tomorrow, and I was wondering if he could come with me."

"Oh, what a nice idea. I'll have to check my calendar... well, no, I won't either, you two just go on ahead whenever it suits you, there's no reason..."

"And I was also wondering," I interrupted her, "could we take Julie with us, that is, if you'd like to go, Julie?"

Julie's eyes lit up. "Yes, Mama, please."

"Oh, my, well, I don't know, dear, you mean the library downtown? That's got to be fifteen or twenty blocks from here, and pushing her chair all that way? And then pushing it up the hill? No, I don't think..."

"Mrs. Jameson, we could take the bus."

"But you're children! Taking the bus all by yourselves? And how would you get Julie's wheelchair on the bus?"

"Oh, they'd help us. I've taken the bus lots of times, Mrs. Jameson, and I've seen people in wheelchairs on the bus, pretty often, actually. Didn't you know they have a kind of side door platform that lowers and raises from the sidewalk to the inside of the bus? And the bus we'd take..." I could see that Julie's mother was not at all comfortable with this whole major shift in her regular way of managing their days, and I also knew that it was about time to break their routine, so I had to find a way to reassure her, and that meant we needed an *adult* in the picture, so I continued, "...the bus that goes into downtown in the early afternoon, well, the driver knows me, he's a friend of my uncle's, and he always watches out for me, which is every time I need to go to the library, you know, especially when Uncle Rim is working." Okay, don't overdo the lie, Looze. Give her some time to let it sink in.

"Louisa, it's a lovely thought, dear, but, you know, you and Jeely can bring some books back for Julie, wouldn't that be so lovely, because, you know, Julie is awfully weak, she can't really take that kind of change in her routine..."

"Mama."

I turned toward Julie. Mrs. Jameson looked down at the pitcher of lemonade she hadn't thought to pour out for us.

"Mama, look at me."

Mrs. Jameson looked up at Julie, and I could feel her terrible sadness wafting off her like a fog. I glanced at Julie, to see if she too would suddenly feel too sorry for her mother to do anything but let her find whatever way was her own safest path to take. But Julie wasn't shrinking. She was... she was beaming!

"Mama, I want to do this." Her voice wasn't tiny anymore, either. "I want to go with Louisa and Jeely to the library."

Mrs. Jameson started to resist, but Julie continued.

"And you're going to let me," she said in an even, calm tone. "Because you love me, Mama. You love me so much."

At that Mrs. Jameson burst into tears. She grabbed a napkin from the tray in front of her and dabbed at her eyes. It didn't help. She covered her face with her hands and sobbed.

"It's going to be okay, Mama," Julie assured her. "Daddy's never coming back, I'm telling you that right now, and it's the truth, I can feel it. So things are going to keep on getting better and better, and you won't have to worry so much any more."

"Julie's right, Mrs. Jameson," I said, putting my hand on her back. I felt her shudder, but not in fear, in a way that was releasing fear. I could tell she was letting herself be calmed, even though if she had looked at this scene from the outside and watched an eleven-year-old girl comfort a grown woman, she would have wanted to make it appear different. Something caved in inside her, some wall of strength that had been shutting her away from her own realness collapsed, and she softened. She looked up at Julie, and she smiled, even though more tears were spilling onto her cheeks. Then she looked more deeply, as if she hadn't really seen her child since she was quite small, and she took a deep breath. "Julie, you're so grown up!" And despite Julie's thin arms and motionless legs, she did look like she had filled out somehow. "If you want to go with Jeely and Louisa to the library, if you're sure..."

"I'm sure, Mama."

"Then, Louisa, I'm going to trust you to take the best care of my daughter."

I nodded my head at her. "I will."

"Look, Mama," Julie said, "Louisa brought it back, the gift she gave me."

"Oh, thank you, Louisa." Mrs. Jameson looked like she was about to cry again. "And Jeely, I know you will help, too, you always do help. I don't know what I would do... what I would do without you!" And she did start crying again.

I looked at Jeely. His eyes were brimming as well. But he wiped at them with the heel of his palm, and scratched the back of his neck, and then said, "I think I need some lemonade, and like, seriously, Mom, what's up with that, no cake?!"

Jeely

After having met our new neighbors at Louisa's Uncle Rim's house, I was pretty sure it was Maudie who'd wanted me to have the medicine bag, but Louisa assured me it was Mary Etta, who had also called to Louisa as she was about to knock on our door the next afternoon. She'd handed Louisa a paper bag, which we were not supposed to examine until we were at the bus stop, but the contents of which we were encouraged to make good use of. Louisa waited until she and I had rolled Julie down the sidewalk, all of our repeated assurances to my mother behind us, before peering inside it, and then rolling her eyes. It contained three hats, one for each of us.

I placed the fedora that Louisa handed me onto my head, balancing it on my ears, and tilted it forward. I was quite convinced by the raised eyebrows of my companions that I looked like a small grown man. Julie put on the bonnet, tying its ribbons under her chin, pleased that it matched her pale blue sweater. She batted her eyelashes at us, and we both grinned, nodding our approval. Louisa was left with the headpiece that resembled a rainbow cluster of cloth worms which dangled down around her ears. She wore beneath it an expression that stated quite clearly that she was not amused, but it was my opinion that it was a perfect fit!

So there we were at last, the three of us, on the bus, flushed with excitement, flashing sparks of ecstatically conspiratorial mischief at one another, while behaving outwardly as if this were the most normal of daily events, taking the local public transit to the downtown library, dressed like escapees from the circus.

How had this happened? How had Louisa infected not only me but my frail yet transformed sister with this totally unfamiliar but exhilarating mixture of are-we-really-doing-this? and we-are-most-definitely-doing-this!

It was all I could do to contain myself, the urge to shout out a victory cry competing with an almost irrepressible hilarity. Facing Julie in her wheelchair, with Louisa next to me, in the section of the bus near the rear door, I had to be careful not to catch either's eye too frequently, for fear of bursting or sputtering or making highly improper sounds in a public setting. I looked up at the ceiling. I looked down at my shoes. I clamped my lips together, rocking slightly to hold down the bubbling sensation. Louisa glanced over at me, and scowled. That didn't help. Frowning furiously over her own compressed lips, she elbowed me in the ribs. Well, that did it. A cascade of high-pitched laughter broke away from my control. Louisa was aghast. At the sight of her horrified expression beneath a nest of bobbing worms, I laughed so hard and so loud and so long, each outburst refreshed simply by looking at her again, that Louisa herself found it impossible to hold in a few muffled snorts, which rapidly became an explosion of screechy laughter. Throwing her head back and stomping her foot, she brayed. Which of course caused Julie to join in. My sister's rippling giggles, tinkling from behind her hands, as modest as the bonnet that shaded her sweet face, were the finest music I'd ever heard. My own laughter reached a crescendo of exhilaration, a celebration of freedom from everything and anything that had ever limited me before. I doubled over laughing. Tears streamed from my eyes. Some of the other passengers began to smile and chuckle, too, and then a few of them had to laugh out loud as well. The whole bus felt charged with benevolent electricity.

Julie wiped her own tears with the edge of her cardigan sleeve and looked around at the people sitting nearby. She lit up at the sight. They were delighting in her, being moved by her, enjoying her sweet joy. Her shining eyes went from person to person as the bus rumbled and wheezed down the street. I took a deep breath and turned to look at them, too, a variety of ages and sizes and colors, all of them smiling at my sister in her wheelchair and then needing to look away, but unable to stop smiling.

After a few delicious sighs, we three settled back down into the pure and simple pleasure of our freedom, looking out the windows at the buildings, the trees, the cars, the side streets, the pedestrians, taking in the sights with no less a sense of adventure than had we been on a riverboat in jungle country.

Mary Etta, I decided, was a genius. Louisa was a hero. My sister was an angel. And I had the marvelous privilege of being an escort to all of this fiendishly fresh vitality!

It wasn't until we were in the library, though, that I caught my first glimpse of what other magic might be brewing beneath the surface of luminous happiness. Having stowed our hats back into the paper bag, we'd wheeled Julie in through the front door in silent reverence, drawing no attention whatsoever from the person behind the front desk. After searching the aisles, I sat down at one of the wooden tables with a book about Native Americans in front of me, with Louisa across from me, perusing another, while Julie wheeled herself along a tall shelf of books perpendicular to our position. She had already deposited one volume in her lap, and, tilting her head, was reading more titles.

I almost didn't see it happen.

In my peripheral view, I caught sight of Julie sitting back down.

A jolt of shock went through me.

Had she stood up? No. How could she have? But she had just lowered herself into her chair, so she must have been standing...? A prickling sensation crept through the roots of my hair.

I examined her profile. She'd opened the book she'd just grabbed and was scanning the first few pages. There was no indication that she had done anything out of the ordinary. And then, as if the electricity raising bumps on my arms had conveyed itself to her, she turned and looked at me. I closed my mouth but couldn't erase the surprised question on my face. She looked down at the book, then up at the empty space on the shelf, which was a foot higher than she could have reached from a sitting position. Now her mouth dropped open.

"What?" Louisa looked up from her book. "What's happening?" She rubbed her arms. Julie and I looked at each other again, and then at the space on the shelf. Louisa seemed to catch on instantly. She got up and walked the few steps over to Julie, took the book from her, read the alphabetical name on the spine, and checked the names of the authors on either side of the space, which was at a height that Louisa herself could just barely reach.

All three of us were frozen in a moment of silence.

Louisa glanced around the library. "Julie, do you want to check this book out?" she whispered. Julie nodded. "And you want this one, too, right? Okay, Jeely, grab those two books on the table, and let's get out of here."

I wanted to stop right there and clarify what had just happened. How could Julie have stood up when she'd been wheelchair-bound for a year? Could she walk now? Did wearing weird hats cause miracles? But the urgency with which Louisa was getting us to move was contagious.

We wheeled Julie to the front desk, and despite my internal whirlwind of confusion, I placed the four books onto the desk with external aplomb.

"Do you have a library card, young man?" the middle-aged woman asked me.

I maneuvered my brain into making a complicated calculation: she wanted an answer. "I'm uh puttem, uh, no mer, missus, I, uh... what?"

"Here, I have one," Louisa withdrew hers from her jeans pocket and placed it on the pile of books. "Don't mind him, he has a speech impediment."

A horrible look of shame and sympathy washed over the poor woman's face as she glanced from Louisa to me and then at Julie, who was emitting a strange species of strangled snorting.

Louisa noticed the framed portrait directly behind the librarian. "Lucky for us we have Jesus watching over us, huh?"

"Oh, yes, dear," the woman replied, running the card through a slot, stamping the inside of each book, and then sliding everything toward us. "You take care now."

We made it out of the library just in time. Julie's snorts turned into gasping laughter.

Trying to prevent the books from sliding out of my arms, I sputtered, "But, what... what just...? How can...? What's a peach imbediment?"

Julie laughed even louder.

Louisa pulled out the hats, plopping the fedora on herself, the bubbly nest of colorful cloth worms on Julie, and the bonnet on me.

"Hey!" I whipped it off. No way was I going to walk back to the bus stop wearing a blue bonnet with ribbons!

"Okay, here," she said, handing me the fedora and taking the bonnet.

"Wow, now you look like a *serious* spy," I commented as she began to tie it under her chin. She gave me a why-don't-you-just shrivel-up-and-die look. "Fine!" she exclaimed. "Here, Julie, this looks best on you anyway."

"And this looks so perfect on you, Louisa," Julie said, handing her the rainbow of springy cloth curls. "It matches you. You know, the way you can make things be more exciting and alive. The way you can make things *so much brighter.*" The two of them looked at one another, and something passed between them. I could see Louisa visibly soften. "Here, Jeely," Julie offered as she tied the bonnet on, "let me hold those books on my lap." I was glad to oblige. I should have brought my backpack. It was such a relief not to carry books to and from school, to keep everything I needed in my pockets, that it simply hadn't occurred to me. Louisa must have felt the same way. "I think maybe we're all a little confused, or even scared a bit?" Julie looked at each of us. We didn't even have to nod to show our agreement. "Can we go somewhere to talk?"

"That's a great idea, Julie," Louisa said, obviously relieved. It occurred to me that she often felt responsible for whatever situation she found herself in, and I knew personally how difficult it could be to have to try to figure things out all the time. It wasn't just a relief, though, it was closer to a miracle that Julie was taking charge. Come to think of it, she'd already started doing that when she'd told our mom that she was going with us to the library. This whole business was entirely too confusing for my ten-year-old brain, I decided. I looked to Louisa for an answer. "There's a little park right over there," she pointed out.

We parked Julie's wheelchair in the shade of a giant mimosa tree, next to a green-painted iron bench. I took the books from Julie, laid them on the bench, and sat down beside them. Louisa plopped herself down on the other side of the books. A mother pushing a stroller walked by on the macadam path, glanced at us, and smiled to herself, reminding me that we were quite a sight, but apparently a happy one, although my own energy was flagging after all the excitement of the day. I didn't even want to know any longer if what I thought I'd seen in the library had actually happened. I was just completely spent. I leaned back, pulled my fedora down over my eyes, let the soothing breeze allay all concerns, and then I must have dozed off for a few minutes, because the next thing I knew, the bench felt like it had been kicked and I was jolted awake.

Louisa

As we sat there in the shade of the mimosa tree, Julie in her wheelchair still wearing that blue bonnet, Jeely slumped on the bench under his fedora, I didn't know whether I'd be elated or frightened by whatever answer I was about to receive when I posed the question. "Julie, did that book jump into your hands?"

She sighed. "I don't know. I don't think so."

Okay, what other possibility was there? The one that was even more awesome, and even more terrifying. "Did you stand up to get it off the shelf?"

Julie shook her head slowly. "I just don't know, Louisa," she said, her innocence so pure she looked almost transparent. "I just know I wanted to see that book, and then there it was, in my hands."

This was a problem, as far as I was concerned, that needed to be solved right away, or I would be awake all night. "Well, can you stand up right now?"

"Oh."

We looked at one another for a long few seconds. Then Julie put her hands on the armrests and leaned forward.

I held my breath. What if she was healed? That would be too crazy. I didn't want Maudie to have given me that much responsibility, if that's what she had given me along with the necklace. But what if Julie could walk now? Would her mother think it was because of me? Would Uncle Rim look at me differently? Wasn't I already too different? And it wouldn't be because of me, it would be because of this necklace. Would I have to explain about the necklace, and Maudie, and... No. What was I thinking? Wouldn't it be amazing if Julie could walk? Wouldn't that make everything better for her family?

"I don't think so, Louisa."

"What?"

"I don't think I can."

"You can't stand up?"

"No."

What? She wasn't healed after all? Nothing had happened except maybe a book had fallen off a shelf? There weren't going to be any answers? Suddenly I was overcome with a confused flurry of fury and disappointment and resentment. Why did Maudie even give me the stupid necklace? Why did Mary Etta give us these ridiculous hats? I had *had* it. I tore that absurd bundle of bobbles from my head and flung it away from myself in a rage verging on tears.

It disappeared. It didn't land on the grass in front of me. Julie and I frowned at one another, and then she thought to look up, and there it was, hooked by a twig, hanging from a branch directly over Julie's head, and she stood up and retrieved it and sat back down and handed it to me.

Both of our faces fell open.

Julie let out a long, slow breath. She reached into the pocket of her cardigan and pulled out the little salt bowl and spoon. "What *is* this...?"

"Wait, wait a minute, wait just a minute," I said, putting my silly hat down on the bench beside me. "Julie, stand up again."

She looked at me with a pained expression and put the bowl and spoon back into her pocket. She leaned forward again, bracing herself on the armrests, and lifted her body up an inch, but sank back down into her chair. "I can't, Louisa."

"What do you mean? You just did it! You can do it again!"

She shook her head. "I can't do it when I think about it."

"Why not?!" I wanted her to just *do* it! If it had been me, I would have let *nothing* stop me from standing up again.

Julie untied her bonnet and tossed it over to the bench. There were tears in her eyes. "My mama needs me to need her. If she wasn't taking care of me, she'd have too much time to feel sorry for her own self. That's what comes into my heart when I think about standing up." She looked at me apologetically. "So I think you better take these back." She pulled the bowl and spoon from her pocket and held them toward me.

"No, Julie! That's not why this is happening! It isn't because of your bowl. It's because of this," and I pulled the necklace up from beneath my T-shirt.

She looked at it and shook her head. "But, Louisa, when you handed these to me, didn't you see the light? Didn't you feel it? Like something magical and powerful was happening?"

"Yes, I did, but it wasn't the bowl." I explained to her what had happened when Maudie let me choose the necklace. Or when the necklace chose me. Whatever.

"So, then... how... no, I guess I just don't understand any of this at all," she sighed, her tears shimmering. I took her hands in mine and looked into her eyes, and she looked into mine, and suddenly it happened again, for less than a second but longer than time, the world vanished in a flood of light, and I saw her, not her face, not her body, not the paint covering the grain, but her true self, the self that was whole, the self that wanted to be whole and could be whole and was whole... and magnificent... and I was seeing her through the eyes not of an eleven-year-old girl but of someone... grand.

"Oh!" she exclaimed. "Oh!" She looked out somewhere beyond the park. "She might not..." she pondered, "because he's not coming back..." her eyes wandered over an invisible scene, "so I could, now that..." Her voice drifted.

"Yes," I said, not recognizing my own voice, "it's about time." I pulled my hands away and leaned back. As completely as the world had vanished, it now returned in full color, the lush foliage and neatly mown grass of the park, the sprawling mimosa tree shedding its pink and white blossoms around its base, the dark green bench on which I sat next to a sleeping boy with a million freckles on his folded arms, the young girl in her pale blue sweater with her soft ginger hair and hazel eyes sitting in her wheelchair in front of me.

Julie blinked. "It's about time," she said.

I wasn't sure what she meant. I wasn't sure what I had meant when I said it. "It's about time for you to get better?"

"No, it's about *time*." She brought her focus back to me. "It's about the time it takes for changes to happen, and for us to get used to them, whatever they are." Her earnestness pleaded with me to accept what she was saying. "I need time. My mama needs time."

I understood. I needed time, too. I needed time for everything that was happening to slow down. "You're right, Julie." I stood up. "I think it's about time... we were getting back?" She nodded, and we exchanged an unspoken understanding. We didn't really know what was happening, so there was no need to talk about it any further, or to mention it to anyone else. I turned around and shoved the bench with my foot. "Hey, sleepy head! Let's get going."

Jeely jolted awake, rubbed his freckled face, yawned, and seeing both of us hatless, removed his fedora and put all three hats back into the paper bag.

We handed the bag and books to Julie to hold on her lap as we wheeled her out of the park and past the library to the bus stop. We were all three of us silent on the way home. We didn't look at anyone on the bus, and no one looked at us. It took both of us, me and Jeely, to push Julie's wheelchair up the slope of the sidewalk toward their house.

"Are you coming in?" Julie asked me as her brother opened their front door.

"No, I don't think I… I'll see you later, okay?"

"Okay." She handed me the bag of hats. "You'll want to give these back. Oh, and Louisa?" I stopped in mid-turn. "Thank you so much for an absolutely *amazing* day!" There was a trace of that conspiratorial sparkle we'd all shared earlier, which eased something in me, and reminded me of why we'd gone to the library in the first place.

"I want to know what you find out about medicine bags and dream catchers, Jeely," I told him.

"Okay," he said. "So," he added, "did anything…?"

"Nope."

"Oh. Okay." He scratched the back of his head. "See you later."

After they'd closed their front door behind them, I stood under the avocado tree and considered my options. I could go home. Uncle Rim probably wouldn't be there until supper time. So I'd be left to my own devices, which meant, watch a video, read a book… darn! I hadn't brought any books back from the library for myself. Or I could return the bag of hats to Mary Etta. But then I'd have to tell her and Maudie how the day went. And I didn't know exactly how the day had gone. As usual, I'd gotten myself into a situation that was more upside down and inside out than I could manage. Which made me feel very small and completely drained and in great need of comfort. And the only available person I could think of who always somehow made everything seem okay was Maudie.

* * *

"Louisa, honey, what in the world could be making you feel so deflated?" Maudie asked me in a tone of such sympathetic concern that I tried to stop the tears by looking up at the chandelier and around the dining room, but my lips were quivering, and when she took me into her arms, I melted and flooded and shuddered, sobbing into her chest with my hands over my face. "That's right," Maudie whispered. "That's right." It was as if she could hear thoughts that I wasn't even thinking. About how hard it was never to have had a mother. About how worried I was that my dad might never return. About how exhausting it was to ride the roller coaster of my own emotions. About how unpredictable everything was. I felt so alone, and so very tired. "I know, honey," she said softly, gently rocking me and caressing my hair. More tears and sobs poured out, all the self-pity and anxiety I'd always tried to cancel by getting furious or by summoning my fierce independence. "It has been one hell of a long road for you, hasn't it, sweetheart?" At that I wailed for a long minute before finally pulling back and wiping my face with my hands so I could look at her deeply seeing eyes and her fine white hair and her soft wrinkled cheeks and her tender smile. She was so beautiful.

"You said hell," I observed.

We both laughed.

"Well, hell, I guess I did," she remarked. "So what are they going to do, send me there?" She sat me down in one of the straight-back chairs and plopped herself onto another. "Do you want to talk about any of it?"

I shook my head no. "I think I'm going to have to give this back to you, Maudie," I said, pulling the necklace over my head.

Maudie accepted the string of beads with its whalebone carving. "I understand." She rested her hands in her lap, fingering the beads. "It's a shame, though. Power is so easily misused. It's unusual for it to find those who will handle it in ways that are beneficial not just to themselves." Her look told me that she considered me to be one of those who would take that responsibility seriously.

"Maudie, I don't understand."

"Hmm. It is a little hard to grasp. Let me see if I can explain. True power is everywhere, available to all, but not everyone senses that. Some do, because the awareness of it is taught, or passed on, or the memory of it is rekindled by some event. Because it's not an everyday kind of power, true power can be a little overwhelming when it first demonstrates itself. But when it has chosen someone to open up to it, it's because that person already has, deep inside, a strong desire to make things better than they are."

I considered that. I remembered what Uncle Rim had said about me. Who had urged him to dress more suitably? I had put Mrs. Pritchard's pansies back in order. But that was different. The best way to make things better, to my way of thinking, was the way Maudie had asked me about at Cooper's when we'd gone for ice cream. Didn't you ever want to do something nice for someone without them knowing about it, that's what she'd asked me. It was better if they didn't know that I was involved at all. "Oh! That's what went wrong today."

"Did something go wrong?"

"Well... no, not exactly."

"Did anything go right?"

I had to smile at the memory. "Yes." I told her about how we'd felt so hilarious wearing the hats that Mary Etta had given us onto the bus that our laughter had tickled everyone around us.

"Oh, I would have liked to have seen that! Did anything else go right?"

"Well, in the library, Julie stood up."

"Oh, my!"

"And then she did it again in the park!"

"Oh, my goodness!"

"And we saw the same light again!"

"Of course!"

"And Julie knew that she wants to take her time."

"That makes total sense."

I stopped to catch my breath.

"So, everything went right?"

"Yeah." I thought about that for a moment. "I guess it did."

"Bravo!"

"But I still don't totally get it, Maudie. How does the necklace make these things happen?"

She smiled sweetly. "Well, I guess the answer to that doesn't really matter, does it, since you don't want to keep it."

I looked at the necklace in her hands. Whale energy that is enormous and fluid. Fish-hook energy that reels in what you need. Seahorse energy, so you can camouflage yourself. And the upside-down question mark.

"Or do you?"

I shrugged. "Why not?"

Jeely

Even though Louisa had denied the occurrence in the library, leaving me with a vaguely discomforting question about the accuracy of both my sight and my memory, and even though when I'd stumbled over my words in front of the librarian, Louisa had worsened my embarrassment, I couldn't hold a grudge against her, because without her appearance in our lives, well... let's just say, my sight had not let me down after all. This was to become apparent during the remainder of our summer vacation. Even if the only improvement had been the change in routine, it would have been worth celebrating. Instead of having to watch my mother plod in quiet desperation through her days, I witnessed, even on our return from our first adventure with Louisa, the difference it had made for her to have entrusted her daughter into the care of someone else. That the someone else was only eleven years old seemed not to have triggered her customary anxiety in our absence. She greeted us, Julie and me, not with the relief of having one's worst fears proved false, but with a light-hearted eagerness to hear how our outing had gone. She was so moved by Julie's description of how the people on the bus had responded to her daughter's happiness, it was no surprise that she was quite willing to let us return to the library every few days. She might have assumed it was the library, I suppose, although our further explorations included the ice cream parlor and the pier and a larger park further along the bus line. As long as we would return within two or three hours, we were free to follow Louisa's suggestions.

It was still to the library, though, that we went on our second outing, as I had learned what I could about medicine bags (and had decided to be on the lookout for sacred items to keep in mine), and was ready to return the books we'd borrowed. This time our bus ride was less public. In fact, it was quite private. It was Julie who motioned to Louisa and me to huddle closer.

"I want Jeely to know," she said, "because I want to try again, Louisa."

"Are you sure? Already?"

"Mama is readier than she lets on. She needs this to happen. So do I."

I was about to ask if anyone would like to clue me in, when it hit me what they must be talking about.

"Well, then, there's something I want to say to Jeely first," Louisa said, and I figured that if I stayed silent long enough, someone might eventually notice my actual living presence and address me directly.

Louisa turned to look at me. "Jeely, I'm sorry."

I could have made it more difficult for Louisa by asking what exactly she was sorry about, but I imagined it had taken her some deep thinking to arrive at the obvious benefit of an apology. So I said simply, "That's okay."

"You were right."

There was only one thing I needed to be right about, so I looked at my sister for confirmation.

Julie leaned in closer. "I did stand up."

I knew it!

"Twice."

"Twice?"

They told me what had happened in the park with the hat.

By the time we were rolling Julie's wheelchair down an aisle between two tall shelves of books, I was so eager for what we all wanted to have happen that I was shivering inside.

"So, how do we do this?" Louisa whispered to Julie. "Do you want to get another book?"

Julie looked around. No one could see us. "First we need to get you in on this, Jeely," she said in a low, secretive voice. Oh. I thought I was already in on it. She reached into the pocket of her cardigan and pulled out the tiny bowl and spoon which Louisa had had to give to her twice. She returned the bowl to her pocket. "I want you to keep this in your medicine bag." She placed the little spoon in my hand, folded her hands over mine, and looked into my eyes. "This way we'll always feel the bond between us, Jeely. We're part of the same set. If I'm the container for the salt of the earth, you're the one who can dip into it and make good use of it. You have a big heart, and you're smart, and you're wise, and you're kind, and you're precious to me. I love you so much." She smiled at me with so much affection and appreciation, more than I'd ever had aimed at me so directly in all my ten years, that something dissolved, something opened up, something inundated my being, and filled me with light, until the light became what we were made of, and I saw Julie's original self, and I knew

I was seeing her through the eyes of a part of me that was immense, and I understood our agreement.

As she pulled her hands away, I wanted to cry. But I also wanted to be strong for my sister. I looked down at the tiny spoon in my hand. I reached into the neck of my shirt and pulled out my medicine bag, opened it, and slipped the spoon inside.

Julie rolled herself back a bit from where I stood next to Louisa, engaged the brake on her wheelchair, glanced around to make sure no one was in sight, and leaned forward. She stood up, a surprising half-foot taller than me, beaming, and then sat down again. She had stood up while thinking about it!

Each time we three took the bus to yet another destination, Julie took herself a step further, literally. First one step, the next time two. We never needed to confirm our exchange of light again, although Julie and I talked in the evenings about everything that was happening. She caught me up on the full story of the little ritual of Louisa's that had inspired her own with me. She told me what she'd believed about our mother's needs, and what she thought about taking the time to experience and enjoy every step. And each time she did take a few more steps than the time before, the three of us would look into one another's eyes, sparkling with anticipation and certainty, and we'd laugh with delicious delight when she succeeded. By the time our summer vacation was drawing to a close, Julie had proved to herself, and to us, that she could walk.

The day after she showed our mother that she no longer needed her wheelchair, she and I were both eager to share our family's complete transformation with Louisa.

But Louisa was gone. Her Uncle Rim's house was deserted. She had disappeared. We never saw her again.

Addie

It was all I could do to quell the questions that had formed after hearing Jeely's version of what had happened that summer so long ago, but I did, of course, hold them at bay, because I wanted to hear what Gran was telling me without disclosing the present proximity of her childhood friend. For now, while Gran was on the phone with one of her lady friends, I was sitting with my mug of tea on her couch, in front of her walnut slab coffee table, which I now knew she had helped pick out for her Uncle Rim.

If his house had been deserted when Jeely went looking for Gran's childhood self, how had the coffee table remained in her possession? Where had she and her uncle gone? What had happened to her father? Why hadn't she stayed in touch with Maudie and Mary Etta?

The questions kept arising, most insistently, but I would not give them voice, not yet, anyway, not until Gran had offered what she remembered. Other thoughts and feelings were surfacing as well: an eagerness to find my own furniture, to settle into my new house, and to follow through on something else that had taken seed; the anticipation of getting to know Jeely and his daughter Karen better, and to learn more about Julie's life, which had not ended until four years ago. Like an impatient child, antsy with a lack of trust in the way things always manage to unfold in the best possible ways, I set the mug down on the coffee table, stood and stretched, walked over to the bookshelf and perused the titles, peeked out the window at the darkening day, and finally plopped back down onto the couch with my knees pulled up to my chin. I pulled my necklace up from inside my blouse, the one Gran had given me when I turned eleven. She had said very much the same things to me that she had heard from Maudie, and we two had also experienced the ignition of an awareness of universal beingness, undivided and yet infinitely multifaceted. Holding the whalebone-fish-hook-seahorse in my hand, I took a deep breath and allowed myself to disappear into a flood of light and supreme love. All is within and beyond, all is forever changing and recreating, all is miraculous beyond comprehension, electrifying, animated, peaceful, serene, mystifying and mystified, and so in love with every facet of itself that it bursts into a cosmic ecstasy.

I sighed, settling into an indescribable comfort and a wonderful sense of belonging. This awareness has been growing into global prevalence since the shift. But Gran lived through those years of chaotic transition from four-dimensional density into actually living and cooperating in multi-dimensional consciousness, and her memories of how things used to be have made me sad, but also so in awe of the human beings who made it through those most difficult of times. Their capacity to invent and to overcome and to take action and to feel compassion has recreated a way of living with this entity we call our planet. We love her now.

"That was Malama," Gran said, returning from her phone call. "She's organizing a full moon dance on the beach. Do you need more tea, Addie?" She had brought her own refilled mug in with her.

"Oh, no, I'm fine. You must be coming to the end of your story, yes?"

"Well, let's see. Where was I?" She sat down on the other end of the couch.

A gentle breeze crossed the room from the open windows into the kitchen. Crickets had started their songs. Miniature violin players in concert, is how I thought of them as I listened to their familiar chirping. "Julie had been progressing, each time the three of you took off on one of your adventures."

"Oh, yes. She was walking by the end of the summer. And not only that. She and Jeely were seeing auras, too. How could they not? All three of us kept radiating pinkish glows and sparkly shimmerings so often, it was a wonder we didn't draw more attention to ourselves. But, you know... in those days... Anyway, we all went to Maudie and Mary Etta's a few times as well, and Mrs. Jameson joined us on one occasion. After spending a little time with Mary Etta, Jeely's mother took to dolling herself up a bit. She was inspired to get herself a paint set, and although her first attempt was hardly a masterpiece, even I could see that she had talent. The three of us children had been avid readers all along, so when Mrs. Jameson showed an interest in our selections, we were happy to share books and conversations with her." Gran took a sip of her tea. "So the summer had been a turning point in all of our lives. Even my Uncle Rim, who'd given Mona another chance but found himself in an on-and-off affair, seemed content."

"But then…?
"Oh, yes, there was indeed a 'but then'!"
"Something happened that left an unsolved mystery."
"Well, one unsolved mystery, yes. And one solved mystery."
"Oh, do tell!"

Gran put her bare feet up on the couch. I did the same, settling myself in to hear what was left to tell before we would open the letter in the little gold silk box.

Louisa

I couldn't wait for Uncle Rim to come home so I could demand that he *do* something! It had been four days since no one had been home at Maudie and Mary Etta's. No van in the driveway, no answer at the door. Where were they? What could have happened? Four whole days without a word?

I couldn't open a book. I couldn't watch a video. I paced. I straightened up my room. I went into the bathroom to scowl at myself in the mirror, and noticed the little white ceramic duck that Mary Etta had given me the week before. "Now you have something from each of us, to remember us by," she'd said. "Ducks always let everything just roll right off their backs." It had never occurred to me that it might have been a going-away present. Did they know they wouldn't be sticking around? Why hadn't they said anything? "Don't be gone," I pleaded to the duck. "Please don't be gone."

I heard the front door open, and I zoomed down the hall. "Where have you *been*, Uncle Rim?" I was about to pour out all my concern and frustration, but I stopped dead in my tracks at the sight of his face. His jaw was set, his brow furrowed, his eyes unfocused. "What's wrong?"

He shuddered a little, refocused, tossed his briefcase onto the couch, and took my shoulders in both hands. "Looze, pack yourself some clothes, we have to leave right away."

"What? Why? What's happening?"

"I'll tell you on the way to the airport."

"No! Tell me now!"

"Louisa. Do as I say. Right this minute. I'll explain everything later. We don't have any time. We might just make our flight if we are out of here in five minutes. I mean it. Pack a bag. Take enough stuff for a week. Go!"

A horrible shivering took hold of me, but I ran back to my room, tears welling up in my eyes. I opened my backpack and stuffed into it a couple of shirts and a pair of jeans and some underwear.

"Toothbrush!" Rim yelled. I could hear him pulling the zipper on his wheeled suitcase.

I ran into the bathroom and grabbed my hairbrush and toothbrush, and in a moment of undefined panic, I stashed the little ceramic duck into my pocket.

"Okay, let's get out of here," Rim said when I appeared.

"Will I need my coat?"

"No. Come on, kiddo, we have to get moving." He refused to say another word until we were in his car, out the driveway, down past Sycamore Street...

"Rim! I have to tell Jeely and Julie that we're leaving!"

"No time. You can let them know later."

"But where are we going? When are we coming back?"

He didn't answer until we were on the highway. "I can tell you where we're going. I don't know when we'll be back."

At that disclosure, it felt as if a trapdoor had opened up beneath me. I was in free fall. I couldn't stand the thought of Jeely and Julie feeling the same way I was feeling about Maudie and Mary Etta just disappearing. I couldn't get my head around having to rush off this fast not knowing for how long we'd be gone.

"I haven't had time to figure out how to tell you this, Louisa, so I'll just give it to you the way I got it about an hour ago."

"Okay." I heard the smallness in my voice and knew I was resigning myself to being dragged along by whatever was happening. I slid down on the seat and put my feet up on the dashboard.

"A special delivery envelope addressed to me was brought to the office. The guy who brought it said it was urgent and he'd been instructed to make sure I opened it up in his presence. Inside were two plane tickets to Honolulu..."

"What? That's in Hawaii!" I sat up again.

"Yes. And there was a letter enclosing a check for a pretty sizable amount of money."

"Who was it from?"

"Some law firm downtown."

"Oh." I waited for Rim to go on, but he looked like he'd locked up his face, and it wasn't just because he was concentrating on driving. I gave him another minute. "What did the letter say?"

"This is the hard part, Looze..."

I waited again. Maybe I didn't want to hear this.

"Clay has been released..."

"Daddy's free?"

"He's been released, but he's not in good shape. They transported him to a hospital in Honolulu, but they didn't dare take him any further. His condition is critical. They thought his best chance would be for family to be with him."

I couldn't speak. *Daddy! Oh no no no, please be okay! We're coming! Please hang on! Wait for us! Don't die! Please, Daddy, you're going to be okay. You have to be okay.* The evening traffic shimmered and wavered through the blur of my tears. I tried to control my voice, but I knew he could hear the tears in it when I said, "Uncle Rim?"

"Yeah, Loozey?"

"Thanks for hurrying."

"I called the airline and told them we'd be there. They'll push us through security... anyway... arghhh... I just want my brother to be okay." His voice had the same catch in it. He drove on in silence.

This was taking too long. Why didn't they tell us sooner? "Uncle Rim?"

"Yeah, Loozey?"

"Who was the letter from? Who was the 'they' who thought Daddy needs us?"

As we took the exit to the airport, a low flying plane slid by overhead.

"All I know is it came from that law firm. I called them right away. The attorney who'd signed the letter wasn't available, but the secretary gave me the number of the hospital in Honolulu. She said if I needed to, I could cash the check at the bank around the corner from my office. And she told me to look at the flight information on the tickets. Holy moly! I had to get moving! But I called the hospital first. Clay's there. Everything was legit. I cashed the check. I've got our tickets. Okay, here we are, long term parking. Are we going to make this flight?"

I took a deep breath. I put my hand up to my heart and felt the whalebone carving beneath my shirt. I thought about how Julie had been healed, and her brother had turned out to be happy and clever and fun, and their mother had rediscovered life. I thought about Maudie telling me that when true power chose someone, it was because that person already had a deep desire to make things better. There was nothing I wanted *more* right at that moment than to make something in particular way way better.

"Yes, Uncle Rim. We are."

Addie

Gran had to wipe her eyes at the memory of why she and her uncle had disappeared so quickly from the lives of her friends. I gave her a moment to come back to the present. Resettling myself into the couch cushions, I pulled her bare feet into my lap and rested my hands on her ankles.

I suspected that this part of her story would end well. I'd never had the impression that she'd lost her father at an early age. So it didn't seem uncaring to satisfy my curiosity about another point. "Gran, before you tell me any more," I said, "did you ever let Jeely and Julie know what had happened?"

She took a sip of her by now cooled tea. "I did. As soon as I had the chance, I sent them a postcard from Hawaii. I remember exactly what I wrote to them. 'I'm with my dad. I'll never forget you.' Because by the time I was able to do that, I knew that I'd be going home — not to my uncle's, but back home, with my dad. And as it turned out, all three of us moved away from the west coast." She set her mug down on the coffee table. "How I ended up back here a year ago is another whole story. No need to go into that."

"But I still want to hear about what happened in Hawaii! I'm so relieved that your father turned out to be okay."

"Well, he wasn't, not at first. But what happened in Honolulu made sense of everything that had happened before. As if it had all been orchestrated so that I could do what I did."

"You healed him."

Louisa

We arrived in Honolulu after midnight, and I wanted to go straight to the hospital. I didn't have to convince Rim. He wanted the same thing. He wasn't going to let anything or anyone stop him from getting us in to see his brother. And so we stood at my dad's bedside in the middle of the night, looking at an ashen, slack-jawed, emaciated man with tubes all around and in him, connected to a monitor. His closed eyelids looked bluish and papery. The nurse had told us he was in a coma. Her attitude seemed to convey that she would give us time to say our good-byes.

No way was I going to let this be the end of my father's life.

I glanced at Uncle Rim, at his bloodshot eyes and unshaved jaw, and decided that he was just going to have to be ready for this.

But how was I going to get us to share the light, my dad and me, when his eyes were closed? And what could I give him to hold, if he could even hold anything, because wasn't that how it had happened before? I'd put the bowl and spoon into Julie's hands and told her how it was like her, that she too was a treasure.

When my skin prickled at a spot inside my jeans, I remembered what was in my pocket. I took out the little white ceramic duck. I opened the slightly curled fingers of my father's left hand, slipped the duck into the nest of his palm, and closed both of my hands around his. "Daddy," I began, not knowing quite what I was going to say. I closed my eyes and pictured my dad as I remembered him, healthy, vital, handsome, strong. "This duck is to remind you that you can just let it all roll right off your back." I took a deep breath, and then the words just eased themselves out of my mouth in a calming stream. "You're like a duck, Daddy, because you can feel at home in three different kinds of places. You can walk on land. You can swim in water. And you can fly in the air. And from the air you can see where you're going and where you want to be. You can see where your family is and decide to be with them. Because they love you. I love you. I love you so much, Daddy."

Suddenly we were awash in the light, floating in a beautiful golden white space filled with vast peace and infinite love. We were together in translucent forms, looking at one another with beams of joyful love flowing between us. We were surrounded by love, so much love, and perhaps even by other beings who loved us. I sensed two forms nearby. Vague forms, people, maybe, people my dad's age, a male and a female who seemed somehow familiar, or were they angelic assistants who were intensifying the love, focusing it toward us? My dad looked down, so I did too, and we could see, far away but also right below us, two people standing by a hospital bed, one of them holding the hand of another person who was lying motionless beneath a sheet, just barely breathing. We looked up at one another again, and without words, an agreement was made. A cosmic understanding of perfection and joy and power was exchanged in a harmony of souls. Then, as wonderful as it had felt to be surrounded and inundated by such tremendous love, it was even more incredibly amazing to feel an enormous surge of energy pulsate throughout our ethereal forms, rearranging invisible molecules, charging cells made of light with a rush of revitalization, electrifying the spaces within and among the subatomic information particles of our being. We became one with the universe, an infinite realm of potential, a myriad of choices of timelines, an ongoing, ever-flowing, infinite and eternal experimentation with creation. And then, as we began to narrow our focuses back into two separate individualities, each of us knowing that we were implementations of divine experience, the very spark of life itself, we surrendered and accepted and received what was vibrating our very essences into something in true harmony with the whole, truly willing to trust and to participate in the ultimate perfection.

Gradually the sensation faded, and I felt myself return to my body. I began to withdraw my hand, but it was grabbed and held. I opened my eyes. My father was looking at me, holding the duck in his left hand, holding my wrist with his right. We gazed at one another in bewildered wonderment through our tears, and then I leaned down into his arms and sobbed with incredulity and elation and self-pity for all that I had worried about, and he held me to his chest and stroked my hair. For a long few minutes we remained in our embrace, and then, still not letting go of me, my dad whispered, "Louisa. My angel!" He always called me his angel. "Did that just happen?"

"Clay! You're awake!" Rim came closer, and as I stood up, he leaned into his brother's arms. "Oh my god, you're okay!"

"I am okay." Dad released Rim, and after smiling at him with grateful familiarity, he looked at his own arms. We looked at his face. He was still thin, but there was color in his cheeks, there was tone to his jaw muscles, there was sparkle in his eyes. He sat up. He looked around at the hospital room, the monitors, the tube running under his nose and the one attached to his left wrist. He removed both. Some machine started beeping. He threw the sheet back and lowered his feet to the floor. "Rim, find me some clothes, man." Rim still had his own suitcase with him, of course. He unzipped it and pulled out his own clothes and gave them to Dad.

"Louisa," Rim said, turning me toward him while my dad got dressed. "What just happened?"

"I don't know if I can explain it, Uncle Rim."

"You were saying those words about a duck, and I was just about to say something to you when there was this flash of light, well, no, more like a glow of light, but it was so brief I'm not even sure I saw it."

"Rim, come on, let's get the hell out of here," Dad said.

Rim zipped up his suitcase again, I grabbed my backpack from the chair, and Dad, in his bare feet, led us to the door, where a nurse, the same one who had let us in, startled herself backwards, grabbing for the doorjamb.

"Excuse us, Miss," Dad said.

"But you can't... wha... how...?" she sputtered.

We three walked past her to the elevator. It opened instantly, and we smiled at her distraught hand-waving as the door closed her out of sight.

PART TWO

Addie

"Gran, oh my goodness, you really did heal him!" In the course of telling me this last part of her story, she had pulled her feet back from my lap, set her mug down on the coffee table, and curled her knees up to her chin, then closed her eyes, and finally opened them and sat up straight on the edge of the couch.

"I haven't thought about that moment in such a long time." She looked a little dreamy.

"What an amazing story." I sat up and leaned forward as well. "So you and your uncle and your dad left the hospital?"

"We did. We bought him some shoes at the airport. That's when I found the postcard I sent to Jeely and Julie. We flew back to the west coast, then moved, several times, actually." She tested the tea in her mug. "Stone cold!" She laughed. "I have no idea what time it is!"

"Neither do I!"

"I'm going to take a bathroom break and then make myself some more tea. Would you like some as well?"

"Yes, please."

After we'd settled back onto the couch with our steaming mugs, Gran pulled the little gold silk box toward her and opened it up.

"Oh, Addie, I should have shown you these before I started talking! Look, here they are, the twins who couldn't have been more different from one another." She handed me two of the photos.

"This is exactly how I pictured them, Gran. Your descriptions were perfect."

"And, now will you look at this, when did Maudie take this?"

In the photo that she handed me next, through a haze of surrounding leaves, as if the photographer had put her camera up to an open space between bushes, could be seen three children, one of them in a wheelchair. They were not looking at the camera, so their faces were in three-quarter portrait mode. The girl in the chair was so delicate and sweet, it would have been impossible not to want to do absolutely anything for her. The boy, standing behind her, had determination in him, and tenderness, and willingness, and vulnerability, and the very early traces of wry humor that I knew had continued to develop throughout his life. And there was my grandmother as an eleven-year-old girl, so much prettier than I had imagined from her description of herself. I'd seen photos of her at younger ages, and a few others at older ages, but here was the girl who was transitioning from a stubbornly set chin, a skeptical arch in the eyebrow and a mischievous lift at the corner of the lips — from that exuberant, feisty, moody, altruistic pre-teen — to the calm, comfortable, content woman sitting beside me. The strongest resemblance was in the eyes — deep, soulful, intelligent eyes that never missed a thing.

"I don't have any other photos of them," she said as I handed it back to her. She sighed as she replaced the photos into the box and removed the fat letter. "I wonder whatever happened to them."

Some inner part of me wanted to leap up and start dancing and yelling out *I know! I know where Jeely is!* I quelled the buzzing interference by testing the temperature of my tea. Ouch. I set it down again, and my fingers started drumming themselves on my thighs.

"You're eager to hear what the letter has to tell us?" Gran eyed me, and for a moment I saw a flash of acuity that startled me. As well as I have always thought I knew my grandmother, I was learning so much more about her that it seemed almost impertinent to think that any young person can know what someone with three times as many years of experience might be all about.

"I am," I answered. "Gran?"

"Hm?"

"You've been a healer all your life."

"When I was needed to be one, yes. Although it was never me, this individual person, doing the healing. All I was able to do, really, was to trigger a remembrance."

"How come I never really knew that?"

"You never needed to be reminded."

"Oh."

"You never went through the conditioning."

"Oh."

"Shall we read the letter?"

"Can I have a hug first?"
"Absolutely."

* * *

By the time you read this, my dear Louisa, you will probably have figured out that it wasn't what you received from me that gave you your abilities. But I'll get into that a little later, because the first thing you will be wanting to know is why we left. And the second is, did we find the person we were looking for? And perhaps the third would be, what ever happened to that dog?

Before I answer any of those questions — oh, all right, I'll tell you that Mary Etta called the animal shelter and made sure that poor dog was taken away and would never bother anyone in the neighborhood again. Before I go into anything else, though, I want to address what I'm sensing as I write this. I will be leaving this letter for you in the attic of this house. As I sit here contemplating how to begin everything that I want to say to you, I can see two probable times in the future when you might come into its possession.

One of the two times that show up most clearly is about twenty or so years from now. At that time you will already have found yourself called upon to make prolific use of your ability. If that is the time you are witnessing as you read this, then you know that the need for healers and messengers and reminders of all kinds has been increasing as the shift in consciousness that began some time ago continues to result in an eruption of worldwide fear and resistance, even as the numbers of people living in conscious awareness increases in wave after wave. What you are witnessing is souls arriving in droves to demonstrate the human potential at very early ages. Surges of awakenings such as you yourself have already experienced continue to multiply as the internet connects people from all cultures to one another and provides countless paths to follow, through meditations, music, documentaries, programs, movies, videos, invitations to global prayer — all these and more are enhancing and spreading new ways of perceiving human beings: as self-healers who can reclaim their self-sovereignty, as integral contributors to their communities, as having the right to love one another without the interference of institutions, as ever-changing vortices of quantum energy whose physical experience is influenced by thought and emotion. You are seeing monumental movements toward sustainable practices. People are putting their energies and ideas together to find ways of using sunlight and wind and water for energy, ways of clearing the ocean of debris, ways of replanting forests and preventing further extinctions, ways of eliminating the ignorance and poverty that drive many to cause damage to their environment for the sake of their families.

Some are being called to actively participate in communal or global reevaluations and rearrangements as the old paradigm gradually begins to crumble into ineffectiveness. Others are called to work on a smaller scale, or even simply to work with themselves, to clear their own outmoded patterns of behavior and expectation, to reinterpret the histories and traditions handed down to them. Each clearing, no matter how many people it involves, is adding its music to the resonating field that then vibrates even more people into the same free and joyful frequencies.

Those operating from their lower chakras, those focused on the theory of survival of the most aggressive, those driven to eliminate their competition, to overpower and enslave others, to amass far more material gain than they can ever make use of, are feeling threatened, are in denial, and are on the brink of ego-annihilation. They are free to choose: to resist the resounding rise of humanity's song, to resist opening the upper chakras of compassion, expression, vision, and connection; or to join in the creation of a timeline in which all human beings recognize themselves as members of a global family who seek to live in harmony with all of life on this most beautiful of planets.

If it is at that time, my dear, about twenty years from now, that you and this letter come together, then you will be noticing that the growing numbers of healers and teachers needed to assist others to transform their physical and emotional wounds are being joined by more and more life coaches and counselors who encourage others to exercise their own ability to heal, to listen to their own hearts, and to fulfill their own personal potential.

There is still a widespread and indeed necessary chaos as the outmoded beliefs and institutions fail, but the growing sense of humanity's spiritual, multi-dimensional expansion, as more and more discover how to connect to the divine essence within and beyond, is carrying forward those who have chosen love over fear into an increasingly hopeful outcome. You are part of this transition.

If it is not at that time that you are reading this, then what I'm seeing is another time, when you will be quite a bit older, after the greater part of humanity has chosen their own best outcome. Most of the chaos will be behind you. Your world will be an experimentally creative, flourishing, exciting cooperative of updated cultures and diversity-appreciative communities, sharing what they know and what they grow — a world without boundaries, with no need for defense, with no need for governing institutions, because the majority of people will have had the kind of revelation that you had when you were a child. The greater part of humanity will perceive themselves as facets of the infinite and eternal exploration of consciousness. They will trust that an ultimate perfection is always at work. Almost everyone will be experiencing what once seemed like magic but is finally understood as the natural, unresisted, unforced flow of elements and situations into the masterpiece of one's life. They will be certain that their needs will always be met, and their gifts will always be found by those who need them. Their conversation with the invisible oneness will have become an ongoing exchange of guidance and discovery and delight. Most human beings will know themselves to be as precious and valuable to the conscious universe as a character in a book is to an author who is learning as much about herself through the surprises offered by her inventions as they are learning about sharing the direction that their mutual story is taking.

If this particular time, the present for you, the future for me, is when you are reading this letter, then you know the truth of what I have foreseen. I am thrilled that you are living in such a time, and I am thrilled to have been one tiny element in the woven fabric of such a magnificent creation.

Okay, you have questions.

In the beginning was the question, and the question was, why not?

Now, why did I just write that?

Mary Etta just glanced over my shoulder and harumphed. She pointed out that there is no beginning, nor, for that matter, an end in an infinite and eternal multiverse. She walks away muttering to herself, "...and the question, why not, was with God, and the question, why not, was God, who obviously had a tremendous curiosity about Her Highness, and, come to think of it, Her Lowness..."

I've gotten used to it.

Either way, twenty years hence or fifty, my dear Louisa, you might still appreciate having a few details cleared up concerning the disappearance of Mary Etta and myself. Ah, but let me backtrack first to whether or not we found our niece.

We did not.

She had died before we tracked her down.

But we found her daughter.

Or I should say, you found us.

Okay, I'll give you a minute to flicker back through our first encounter. You're bound to arrive at this conclusion: Mary Etta and I lied to you.

Yes, we did. By omission, by allowing you to make your own assumptions, we did lie to you.

How to explain...

Ten years before we arrived on Sycamore Street, we had already tracked down Samantha — or, as you would have known her, had she lived through your birth, Mrs. Clay Bylander. We were aware of your existence when you were a year old.

If we had given you that information when we met, you would have been furious with us — admit it, you were that kind of girl at the beginning of the summer — half wanting us to have showed up in your life sooner, half wanting nothing more to do with us. We could see that in the ice cream parlor. You might not have trusted us, and what was ignited in you that summer might not have shown up in time for you to open up a timeline in which you and your father would be together. None of us wanted you to have lost both parents. Mary Etta and I have our own gifts, but healing is not one of them. You are the healing catalyst. You were the one needed by your father. It seemed important that you trust us.

So we juggled the truth a bit.

We weren't quite sure how to handle the situation, because we were not alone in orchestrating it. All of our souls' needs and desires and intentions were involved, of course, but as you must know by the time you read this, there are influences at work from an even higher perspective than that of our souls.

So we stumbled through our reasons for being in your neighborhood. We didn't actually know the reason ourselves until we found out that Clay was being held prisoner in China.

How did we find that out? After dinner at your Uncle Rim's house, while you and I were outside getting the lamp from the van, Mary Etta overheard Rim answering a question of Mona's in the kitchen. She was wondering where your parents were, and Mary Etta just happened to be within hearing distance.

We couldn't have brought up the question of your father's whereabouts during that dinner. In that atmosphere of lively exchange and easy laughter, it would have been intrusive, and, as it turned out, quite the downer. So the fact that the information came in its own form was something to be taken note of and appreciated as an indication of what actions might be considered. Isn't it interesting that even Mona, who obviously had not won your unmitigated approval, played such a significant part in what was to follow. And thus do we engage in our often surprising conversation with life, staying alert, noticing what comes into our field, checking it out to see if it opens us up to unexpected possibilities.

It was just a matter of time, then, to contact the embassy most likely to have had the latest reports about your father, until we finally had it narrowed down. Then there were further arrangements to be made with a lawyer — Mary Etta had already been setting up a trust fund for you — visas to be obtained, communications, preparations. Through a series of connections we contacted someone who informed us that Clay would be released only into our hands, under the imperative that no reporters, no cameras, no political officials, nothing but ourselves be present at the clandestine transferral of a heavily drugged prisoner, in exchange for a large sum of money.

When we were alerted that everything was in order, we left immediately. We were hoping to return Clay to the hospital downtown, but as you know, we didn't make it that far.

After hearing from our lawyer and his assistants that you two made your flight, I waited until yesterday and then contacted the nurse who was on night duty in the IC unit at the hospital in Honolulu, just to make sure that what we expected did indeed happen. You have fully claimed your power and are reunited with your father. Mission accomplished. My heart overflows with happiness and gratitude.

So now you know why we left so abruptly. Which gives rise to other questions. Why didn't we stay at the hospital with Clay, at least until you and Rim arrived? Why am I letting this letter find you so far into the future instead of making sure you get it now?

As you must have deduced from the treasures I showed you, Mary Etta and I spent those ten years — in between discovering the fate of our niece and sensing that the time had come to connect with you — traveling the world. What a wonderful world it is. So many courageous, open-hearted people. So much beauty. And such unnecessary deprivation and ignorance. We were being led, during that decade, to various places, and to specific individuals, to do what we did with you — which was not to give you an object containing the power to heal. For, as I mentioned earlier, and as you know by the time you read this, it was not the necklace that imbued you with your abilities.

When you asked me if the necklace was the item I would have thought of as belonging to you, I said I was absolutely sure — because whatever you chose, or whatever chose you, was needed only as a reminder of your abilities. It didn't transfer them to you. You already had them.

Many humans do. Many humans, and indeed, many minerals, plants, and animals are emanations of that aspect of source consciousness that regenerates, revitalizes, and recreates. There are aspects that do the opposite, of course, not in the sense of polarity, but as a necessity in the unfolding of the first dimension, time. Time is what allows experience. Outside of time is absolute stillness, the void of pure potential, the peace beyond understanding. It is within time that perceivable existence is birthed. Time is motion, motion is change, change is the rise and fall of waves, the on and off of pulsations, the solidifying into actuality from potential, the dissolution of now into then. In time, there are cycles and seasons, contractions and expansions, pendulum swings from one extreme to another.

The human population of Earth, as I write this, has become unbalanced in the extreme. This happens during times of change. Snows melt and rivers overflow. Old trees fall and new ones push themselves into the light. And as the seasons change into the blossoming of another spring, life is stirred into a new phase. Sensing that inner stirring, many of us are responding to an insistent urge to counteract the miseducation, disinformation, numbing oppression, and wanton annihilation that has overreached itself. We are feeling the urge to ignite the remembrance of the light, to assist others to empower themselves, and to radiate the frequencies of the upper chakras into the atmosphere.

You know this.

As you read this, you know that you have already spent your life so far making use of your abilities, offering your gifts, and changing people's lives for the better merely by being yourself. You have done this even as you've stumbled through times of forgetfulness, even though you've needed to clear your essential self of limiting beliefs and emotional blockages, even as you were unraveling the patterns of behavior that once served to protect you and are no longer needed. You know that your inmost urges are worth following. You know that you are in essence one with original mind-heart-soul of universal beingness. You know that you are loved for being exactly the unique individual expression of creation that you are. You know that your conversation with life is mutually exchanged through guidance going both ways, gifts going both ways, gratitude going both ways.

And so you will understand, Louisa, when you read this, that Mary Etta and I have to follow our urges. We have done what we didn't even know beforehand that we came here to do. Mary Etta is packing the van as I write this. Jeely and Julie are helping her. We haven't told them anything except that you are with your father and we are moving on. They of course have some sadness over both apparent losses, but what they have gained, their insights into their true natures, Julie's health, Jeely's infatuation with what he can learn from the internet through the computer we're leaving with him, their mother's revitalization (which I suspect was passed on to her directly by Jeely), these gains will carry them forward.

I imagine that by the time you read this, Mary Etta and I will no longer be in physical form with these particular identities in this particular set of dimensions. We will still be, however. We all continue to be. If that's what we choose.

Mary Etta and I will still and always be loving you from wherever the next adventure takes us.

Maudie

* * *

It was dark outside. Gran and I sat on either end of her couch in silence. As she'd read each page, she'd passed it over to me, so now the entire letter from Maudie lay in my lap.

My mind was whirling, as were my emotions. Finally, after long minutes of sorting and assimilating themselves, one of the feelings surfaced as needing to be addressed first. "Gran, part of me is hurting for you — or for the little girl you were who never got to see Maudie and Mary Etta again."

"Thank you for that, Addie." She stretched, arching her back, and then settled back into the cushions. "But you know, even back then, after reuniting with my dad, on some level I understood. I couldn't have put it into words for myself at the time, nor did I have much time to do anything but become completely immersed in the life that my dad and I were creating for ourselves. But later, as I looked back, I could feel only an immense gratitude, almost an overwhelming awe, at the wonderful gift I had been given. To have broken through into experiencing myself as both the dreamer and the dream! It left me in a state of such encompassing love, for myself, and for all of creation, that it outshone everything else. Which was truly a timely blessing, because the changes we all endured were painful, even devastating, for so many."

She set her tea mug down on the coffee table. "I think the best part of Maudie's letter, for me, isn't even having some of those old mysteries solved. Oh, it's extremely satisfying to have all the pieces of the puzzle fall into place, no doubt about it. But what gives me the deepest comfort is knowing that Maudie was able to look beyond what was at that time a critical juncture in the history of the human race. I'm so glad that she could see for herself that life would prevail. She already knew back then that the world we live in today is one that nourishes the soul and challenges only the imagination. When I was young, we were conditioned by society — which was in a way a kindness — to be numb. We could not have coped with what would have been excruciating to our innate sensitivity. We could not have endured what was being done to animals and forests and children, let alone the planet, without having been trained and misdirected to overlook and ignore, to accept and focus only on what was right there in the cubicle in front of us. Our challenges then, unlike today, were to outgrow the conditioning and to reclaim our personal capacity to love, to love fiercely and wildly and hugely."

As I listened to Gran, I thought about how different that time was from this one. The ongoing wars, the cruelty, the disease, the anesthetized robotic plodding necessary for so many to survive. Yes, there had been beauty, art, inventions, scientific advances, but nothing even close to what is happening today. It suddenly occurred to me to ask Jeely what he'd been working on — all those mini-discs on his shelves — what holographic images or stories had he been producing at his desk?

"What Maudie saw back then was going a step further than the common perception of the day's forward thinkers," Gran continued. "They thought that humans alone were responsible for the climate changes. To some extent they were right — the water and air were being poisoned by the activities of humans. But they didn't see the greater cycle at work. There was a galactic seasonal change occurring because of the solar system's orbit around the outskirts of the Milky Way. Humans were arriving at accountability, yes, which was way overdue — but they were also responding to that reawakening life force that arises when the icy blanket of winter thaws, or the sun rises on a new day after a long night." She reached her hand out toward me, and I handed her Maudie's letter. "I think I'm ready for a good night's sleep, Addie, dear." She put the letter back into its box. "It has been a most amazing day!"

We both stood up. Our embrace was long and warm and soothing.

"Your room is all ready for you."

"Thanks, Gran."

"I think I'm going to have to go online tomorrow," she said as she collected our mugs and headed for the kitchen. "See if I can find out anything about Jeely and Julie."

I paused. No! I definitely wanted to be the agent of their reunion! "That won't be necessary, Gran."

"Oh?"

"No." I followed her into her garden of a kitchen, potted plants flourishing on every available surface. "I know where Jeely is."

"What??"

"I'll tell you more tomorrow. It really has been an amazing day. In more ways than you know! But let's save this next part for tomorrow, okay?"

"Well!" A hint of indignation escaped her as she rinsed out the mugs and set them into the drainer. She turned to me with hands on hips. "Fine!" And then, rubbing her arms, she laughed.

* * *

I've tried retracing the trail of events that led me to finding my house. Some of them were so seemingly insignificant and accidental that they could almost be overlooked if they hadn't been added up.

I was in the area visiting a friend, planning on stopping in to see Gran, when Charlene mentioned a park that sounded like a lovely place to catch up with myself. If I hadn't been there in that park just when that piece of paper blew by, if I hadn't picked it up to put it into a trash bin, if I hadn't noticed the same word on it that I'd just heard on the radio on the way to the park — I wouldn't have heard the little ping inside my head when I passed the street sign that had the same word on it: Sycamore.

But what in the first place had made me decide to move closer to Gran? I'd met someone at my local co-op, bumped arms with him actually, as we both reached for the same avocado. We started a conversation that didn't seem to have a natural ending even after half an hour. He was just passing through, on his way back to this area from somewhere north of where I was living, and he decided to stay a few hours longer than he'd intended so we could continue our conversation. By the end of it, we knew we needed more time together. As I wasn't quite ready to share with Gran what seemed to be unfolding, I called Charlene to see if I could stay with her for a few days while I continued my conversation with Carlos. By the end of the third day, he and I both knew we didn't want to have to travel for several hours every time we wanted to spend more time together. It made total sense to me that I be the one to move.

But what had led me to the co-op in the first place? Nothing in particular. I went there frequently. I'd been given a recipe for guacamole by another friend, and since I was there, I decided to pick up a few avocados. Just when Carlos happened to be there. Because he'd suddenly remembered that he had no food with him and knew he'd be getting hungry in the hours ahead. When he pulled off the highway, there he was. There I was.

Why had he not taken some food along? Because, as he told me later, just as he was leaving, putting a cloth sack of groceries into the hovercar, a six-year-old child was passing by the house he'd been staying in, heading up the street to one of the houses further along. The little boy was pulling a small red wagon with a bag of loose groceries in it. He stumbled over a part of the sidewalk that had been pushed up by the roots of a tree, and in his determined refusal to let go of the handle, since he'd obviously been entrusted by his mother to collect the food, he accidentally tipped the wagon over. The bag toppled into the street, releasing its contents into the gutter, and almost all of the fruits and vegetables rolled down into the drain. The broccoli that remained was covered in mud.

Tears sprang into the boy's eyes. Carlos helped him up. "*Ola, nino*, you okay?"

The boy wiped his eyes. "*Mi madre...*" He pointed up the street.

Carlos spoke to him in Spanish. "You know what? You can say thank you to that tree." He himself looked up at the tree and said, "*Muchas gracias, mi amigo.*" The boy watched him, still wet-eyed, but curious. "See how that tree's roots made you fall? The tree didn't mean to hurt you. It's just growing here and needs more room. But it's lucky you fell here instead of somewhere else. You know why?" Now the boy's interest was hooked. He shook his head no. "Because it made you fall in exactly the right place! Look what I have here!" He took his own sack of loose groceries from the back of the car and put it into the wagon. The boy looked inside and grew wide-eyed at the sight of even more fruits and vegetables than he'd lost. "And you know why else I said thank you to the tree?"

"*Por que?*"

"Because of the tree, I got to meet you! And I got to help you. And those are the two things I love doing more than anything. Meeting people. And helping."

The boy looked up at the tree. "*Muchas gracias, mi amigo*," he said. Carlos lifted his hand, and the boy, now bright-eyed and smiling, gave him a high-five.

When Carlos told me that story, we'd already met at his place near here, and I'd already found my house. I just had to ask. "Do you remember what kind of tree it was?"

"Oh, yeah. It was a sycamore."

So, for how long can one follow the trail back before it circles around? I gave up after that. I'm just glad it all happened exactly as it did.

* * *

It was two days later, after I'd told Gran all about my visit with Jeely, had told her about Julie's passing four years ago, and had checked with him about visiting, that she and I emerged from my house. Gran had wanted to take a slow, nostalgic walk through it, and was happy to see that the day before I'd found a bed and a few other items of furniture.

Carlos had helped me. I think the reason I wasn't mentioning him yet to Gran was because of what was about to happen in her life.

I closed the door behind me and followed Gran down the wooden steps. We passed beneath the old oak, which was casting dancing shadows from the late afternoon light, and crossed the driveway to knock on my neighbor's door.

Jeely opened the door. He was wearing a pale linen tunic over the same colored pants, his feet bare and his face wide open in a welcoming smile. He gave me a warm hug and then let me step aside so he could take in the full view of my companion. Gran was in a muted rose dress, a peach-colored shawl draped over her shoulders, and an equally radiant smile on her face.

"Louisa!" Jeely breathed out, opening his arms. I had expected them to stand for a moment to take note of all the changes that fifty-some years had wreaked on their features, but as if magnetized across the space of no time at all, they moved into one another's arms, blending into one another. He was only a few inches taller than she, so their hearts were aligned, their cheeks touching, and their mutual deep breaths relaxing them into sharing silent memories and the closure of a life-long distance. It was beautiful to witness these two beloved people — for I had already come to love Jeely — holding one another for so long, with so much being exchanged, that my eyes, like theirs when they finally pulled apart, were shining with emotion.

"Jeely." Gran put her hands up to wipe her cheeks, and then she smiled through her fingers. "Whew!" Her eyebrows lifted and her hands went to her heart. She couldn't speak.

"Hard to believe, isn't it?" Jeely asked, putting a hand on each of our shoulders. He seemed more subdued than he had been while he was telling me about their mutual childhood. "Come in, come in, my dear beautiful friends." He led us into the house. "There's so much to catch up on. Louisa.

The last time you were here, my mother's love of blue flowery things dominated the living room. As you can see, I've made a few changes."

While Jeely ducked into his kitchen to fetch tea, Gran looked around at the furnishings that were so very different from her own style of decor. I could see that she was somewhat surprised, and even a little confused, by the black couch and chairs, the brushed steel coffee table and desk, the shelves of mini-discs. There were no live plants, like the ones crowding her kitchen. No soft earth-colored fabrics, like those thrown over her own furniture. She glanced at me, and I shrugged, hoping to convey the wait-and-see attitude I knew she was perfectly capable of adopting once she decided to eliminate any pre-judgements. She seemed to catch my thought, and with a wry smile, seated herself on the black couch. I sat down in one of the single-pedestal chairs and tucked my feet up under me, preparing to be, once again, not a participant, but a listener and an observer, as these two old friends decided which parts of their histories to share with me and with one another.

Jeely returned with a tray holding a teapot and three black ceramic mugs and set it on the coffee table. I was about to point out to Gran that Jeely grows his own tea, when Gran and Jeely both spoke at once.

"Jeely, would you tell me about Julie?" said Gran.

"Louisa, I'd like to tell you about Julie," said Jeely.

When they looked at one another, something, some memory, perhaps, seemed to flit across the space between them, a miniature lightning bolt of meaning.

He nodded, went to his desk, buzzed open a drawer, and retrieved the little silver and blue enamel salt bowl with its miniature matching spoon. "Louisa, I'm sure you remember giving these to Julie." He handed them to Gran, his eyes still aglow with the soft fire left by the bolt of lightning.

"Oh, yes, of course I do," she answered, accepting them. She couldn't help but glance up at him to return her own soft glow.

"And do you remember when she gave me the spoon?" He sat down in the other chair.

"It was the day she passed the remembrance of the light into you. She wanted you to keep it in your medicine bag."

"Yes. You do remember. Do you remember what she said to me?"

"Something about the bond between the two of you?"

"Yes, exactly," he said. "You haven't forgotten." Something was going on inside him, but I couldn't tell what it was. "And she also said that if she was the container for the salt of the earth, then I was the one who could spoon it out and make good use of it."

Gran and I waited to see where he was going with this.

"Julie had had a lot of time just sitting in that wheelchair before you came along, Louisa," he continued. "So she'd exercised her imagination and fine-tuned her memories, of her own life, of scenes from the books she'd read, the videos she'd seen, even before you healed her."

"Or she healed herself, because she believed I could."

"Yes, as we now know." Jeely poured himself some tea, lifted the teapot toward us with raised eyebrows, and at our nods, poured for us as well. "So, we have a young girl with a vivid and disciplined imagination, and we have a young boy who was given a computer by two remarkable ladies. Maudie and Mary Etta left theirs with me when they took off." He of course didn't know that Maudie's letter had already informed us of this fact. "And that computer led that boy down the path of experimenting with each new advance in technology as it came along." He drew himself into a lotus position, holding his mug of tea in both hands, and took a deep breath. "Fast forward a few decades, when the first neurotech devices became publicly available, and you have two siblings playing with what could be produced by interfacing imagination and memory with that technology. Our first attempts were hazy at best, disconnected, jumbled, but we got better at honing our skills." He tested the temperature of his tea. "So, there was Julie, salt of the earth, with a rich inner world, and there was me, spooning her dreams and memories through the headpiece into the electronic equipment that would translate what she could see with her inner eye into something visible to others." He looked at each of us to emphasize his next words. "What she said to me turned out to have been prophetic."

Again I saw something cross the space between the two of them.

Neither Gran nor I was familiar with how to make creative use of the technology he was referring to, but his metaphor made it easier for me to understand what he seemed intent on conveying.

"So you two stayed close all those years?" Gran asked then.

"Yes, we did. We both had our own lives, but because we ended up living quite near to one another, we made a point of getting together for the specific purpose of recording what Julie was able to see and experience." He waved a hand at the stacks of mini-discs on the shelf. There might have been hundreds, it was impossible to count them all at a glance.

"Oh!" Gran and I both exclaimed together.

"I have them all digitally stored, but I rather like seeing the volume of Julie's output, and it's always good to have a back-up. There's one I'd like to share with you today, if you're interested?"

"Oh, yes, of course," Gran said. "Yes, I would love that."

"Only one?" I asked.

Jeely smiled. "They vary in length." He sipped his tea. "The one I have in mind is short, so we could view more than one today, if you'd like. And if you enjoy the first one or two, there are obviously any number to choose from."

Again I was struck by the difference between the energetic, outgoing man I'd met a couple of days ago, and this intentionally calm person sitting before me.

I have my own electronic devices, for practical purposes, and I've seen what some people have done with holograms, but I've never tried my hand at creating anything, so this was going to be a new experience for me, watching in 3D something that Julie had dreamed up. Gran, too, has seen the holograms available online, and she has her communication devices, but her creative skills, as far as I know, have more to do with plants and environments and interactions with people. Neither of us had any idea what we were about to be introduced to.

I was curious about why Jeely was moving us along like this, away from personal conversation and into his obvious fascination with the work he'd been doing, but I sensed that there was a purpose to the particular way he must have planned this encounter. Maybe this was the best way to lead into telling us more about Julie's life? And then his own?

"If you'll scoot your chair over here, Addie," Jeely said, setting his mug down on the coffee table and moving the chair he'd been sitting on closer to the desk, "and Louisa, you can sit here. Best to leave your tea there." He arranged our chairs to be on either side of the one he lowered himself into, which was set back far enough from the outward curving desk so that we could all see one another.

Gran touched him on the shoulder, and when he turned, she handed him the salt bowl and spoon.

"Ah, yes," he said, returning it to its drawer. He looked at her, and suddenly he seemed full of electricity, almost unable to contain himself. I thought it was because he was so excited about what we were going to be watching. He looked up at the ceiling, grinning, and then, glory be, with his hand over his mouth, the man bent forward as if he were a ten-year-old boy trying not to laugh out loud. Gran frowned at him, and then elbowed him in the ribs, and they both burst out laughing.

"Jeely! Stop!"

"Louisa!" He looked at her with an impish sparkle in his eye. "Do you remember that hat?"

Gran compressed her lips in a futile attempt not to be amused, narrowing her eyes and jutting out her chin in warning. "Which hat?"

Apparently he was more than satisfied with her denial of any such hat. Was that a pinkish glow wafting from his shoulders? "Shall we proceed, then, milady?"

"We shall."

All three of us aimed our attention at the empty space in the center of the desk, with big fat smiles on our faces.

Jeely clapped his hands three times, and the silvery drapes pulled themselves closed, dimming the light. "So, picture a young woman sitting here where you are, Addie, wearing an intricate headpiece." He pointed to a delicate contraption on one of the shelves above the desk. "She starts to tap into a memory, it gets transmitted into the neurotech equipment, and later I get to see it as I do some editing. And this is the result." He tapped the surface of the desk.

A mist of colors appeared on the desk against the concave backdrop, gradually congealing into forms. I didn't know if that was how Julie's inner vision had transmitted itself, or if it was an effect added later by Jeely. The holograms I'd seen had popped instantly into focus. As the forms took shape, my breath caught. I recognized them from Gran's photo. Julie in her wheel chair, ten-year-old Jeely, eleven-year-old Louisa. They were in an ice cream parlor, two of them peering at the selection of tubs behind the glass-fronted counter. We could see the whole room, the wooden tables behind the children, the young man behind the counter.

"Come on, Julie, you have to pick your own," piped up the holographic version of Louisa. I'd forgotten about that higher tone of voice in pre-teens.

"I'm having the pistachio chocolate chip," young Jeely decided.

Julie wheeled herself closer. She probably could have managed to see into the tubs of ice cream by rolling her chair sideways alongside the counter, but clearly that was not her intention. She engaged the brake, and facing the counter, stood up, took a step forward, and put her hands against the glass. The details were so clear, I could see the look that passed between Jeely and Louisa behind her. There was a flash of conspiratorial but suppressed glee. The secret agents who had spied on one another were now in cahoots, and their mission was not impossible.

Wait a minute!

It was amazingly impressive to see what degree of focus and detail Julie had been able to transfer into the hologram from her own memories, but how had she detected and then injected into the scene not only the expressions but the emotions emanating from her companions, when her own miniature version was not turning her head to look at their faces but was peering through the glass at the variety of choices? How could she remember what she had not seen?

Then it hit me.

In order to visualize the whole scene from not just one perspective, she would have had to move her perception into the field of consciousness, the oneness of being. She was no longer focusing through one vortex of information, she was all perspectives at once.

I heard Gran gasp. She must have reached the same conclusion. Neither of us spoke, though, as the scene continued.

After making their decisions, ten-year-old Jeely paid the young man behind the counter. The children took their cones, and two of them walked to the same table that Louisa had shared with Maudie and Mary Etta, the one by the lace-curtained bay window with the speckled begonia on the sill. Julie turned toward them, considering for a moment what to do, and then walked the five or six steps from the counter to the table. Meanwhile, the soda jerk — I remembered Louisa laughing about his title — scratched his head, obviously wondering why the wheelchair was still parked in front of the counter, or perhaps why one was needed at all.

So this scene must have taken place closer to the middle of the summer, when Julie had already taken enough steps in previous outings to have gained the confidence to take a few more. Jeely and Louisa were obviously delighted. Their scheme had worked! Jeely pulled a chair out for Julie, and the three of them started licking their cones with considerable pleasure.

I looked at Julie more closely, and as I did, I had the impression that I was able to zoom in, or that her face was in close-up mode, and yet the whole scene seemed to remain otherwise intact and unchanged.

The smile on her face was not what I was expecting. She wasn't experiencing only the innocent pleasure of her own accomplishment. Her expression betrayed a hint of sly awareness of her own contribution to what was happening for all three of them. She knew, it was obvious, that her own role was as significant as those of the two children who believed that they had been arranging opportunities for her to exercise her gradual healing.

She knew. She was still taking her time, on purpose.

The slurping of ice cream dripping from cones continued, punctuated by conversation and laughter. As I watched the hologram, my mind stumbled, shifting from having believed, because of both Gran's and Jeely's accounts, that young Louisa had been the agent of change in the lives of her friends. But no! All three of them, including Julie, had participated in a mutual evolution from the despair and frustration felt by each of them into the joy and humor being demonstrated in this holographic ice cream parlor.

The scene ended with Julie having returned to her wheelchair and her brother turning it around to face the door. As he wheeled her out, she glanced up. I was startled. Was she looking at us? Impossible!

I sat back, not having noticed that I'd been leaning forward, in a state of astonishment. Not only was the transference from mind to visual projection, in such vividly intimate detail, more dazzling than anything I had ever witnessed before, but layers of insights were still clicking into place.

Jeely tapped the desk and the hologram flicked off. He clapped his hands twice, and the drapes parted, flooding the living room with light.

I looked at Gran. She sat with her hand to her heart, her eyes brimming.

Jeely's face was a fluid palette of gentle satisfaction, infinite affection, and hopeful anticipation as he awaited our responses to this enormous gift he had just given us.

"Omigod." Gran managed to say, wiping her eyes. "Jeely! This is simply brilliant! Really! To capture someone's memory so that others can see it! And so accurately! It's just as I remember us. You and me thinking we were luring Julie into taking more steps! But she was taking her time on purpose! For our sakes as well as for her own — so we three would continue to have good reason to go off on our secret adventures together. We were three interlocked parts of the same experience..." She looked at Jeely with what seemed to me a nostalgic mixture of sadness and longing and sweetness. "I'm just blown away! And how did... I don't have any idea how... I mean... was there an instant when the focus zoomed in on Julie's face? Did you see that, Addie? Did that happen?"

Jeely was obviously pleased. "I knew you'd get it, Louisa." He motioned her to the couch as he and I slid the chairs back toward the coffee table. "Even though this was one of our earlier attempts, Julie already had the overview perspective down pat, and she could already infuse her scenes with that dreamlike tendency to neglect spacial conventions. Now, to tell you the truth, I don't know if she was aware at the age of twelve of what you just saw, or if her thirty-something self added that feature. She and I discussed it, and we decided it didn't matter, because don't all of our ages exist at once? Aren't we constantly able to be in touch with our younger selves and our future selves, and don't they influence one another, back and forth?"

"That was amazing," I told him.

Gran narrowed her eyes at him. "Talk about becoming the ultimate spy, Jeely Jameson."

He laughed out loud, with relief, it seemed, as well as amusement. "You're right. A far cry from hiding in an avocado tree, but not far from the driving force behind it."

Gran and I posed the silent question of "Which was?" with our expressions.

"Insatiable curiosity." He considered something for a moment. "Speaking of which," he said, almost hesitantly, "are you going to tell me, Louisa," a ripple of pained need flickered across his features, "where you disappeared to at the end of that summer?"

"Of course, Jeely." It was clear that she needed to tell him as much as he needed to hear why their friendship had ended so abruptly.

As Gran began the part of her story that I was already privy to, I sipped my tea and watched their exchange. How would they have been relating to one another without that childhood summer as common ground? If I'd met my new neighbor without the story that the silk box had opened up for me, would I have thought to introduce the two of them? Would I have known...?

As soon as my mind began to highlight again all of the coincidences that had led me to the very house that figured so prominently in their story — and to this reunion — the luminous connections brightened, disappearing my tiny thoughts into universal mind, where any number of luminous connections formed patterns that seemed to be alternatives to the single story my smaller self had been listening to. A grandly gratifying peace, a liquid light of quiet delight gentled its poetry into the spaces among the stars and galaxies within me, and I billowed into a fully fulfilled cosmic smile, enjoying the tender affection I was feeling for my creations and their creations, and then I dissolved...

...and all was light...

...and all was love...

"I don't think she's back yet," was the first thing I heard.

I returned to my body and opened my eyes.

Gran and Jeely were sitting on the couch, at opposite ends, with their bare feet almost touching. My mug of tea was on the coffee table.

"Oh."

"Welcome back," Jeely said. "Thank you for that."

"Hm?"

"Just as Louisa was telling me about leaving the hospital with her father and her uncle, I noticed that your mug needed rescuing. And once I was up, well, the couch looked rather inviting." He looked at Louisa with a gratitude that must have had something to do with her account of why there had been such an abrupt ending to their childhood time together. "We could both feel the glow of the energy you were emanating, Addie, so we joined you."

"That was so lovely," said Gran.

"Mm."

We three sat in restful silence for a little longer.

"And now, before you offer us anything more, Jeely," Gran said, and his evident eagerness to do so settled back down, "I want to thank you. For filling up my heart to overflowing. I am so inundated with wonderful newness that I need to go back to my own space, for now."

Jeely nodded. If he felt at all disappointed, it didn't show beneath his acceptance of her decision.

Their parting embrace, however, was even longer than the first one.

"Can I invite myself and Addie back sometime to see more of Julie's holograms?" she asked as we stepped off the porch.

"As if you have to ask, Louisa."

Louisa

I walk with Addie back across the driveway to her house, wanting to make sure she has food in her refrigerator even though I know she can walk down into town while I borrow the hover-car. It has been a while since I've needed to drive, as the community I live in has everything I could possibly want right within walking distance, and there are plenty of friends with borrowed cars if I ever feel an urge to travel further. Which, I'm noticing as I lift out of the driveway, I am feeling right now.

I park near the pier. It has since been rebuilt, but it still reminds me of the time that Jeely and I shared our family situations. The edge of the planet, that vast horizon of ocean, will soon be blocking out my view of the sun, but for now the blue sky is paling into honey green and rosy peach beneath a few scattered clouds as I walk barefoot along the thin line of foam curling and receding into the next wave. The beach is almost deserted, only a few couples strolling along in the distance. I sit down on the sand, my arms around my knees, and gaze at the beauty before me, inhaling the colors and the scent of salt and seaweed, listening to the crashing of the waves pierced by the cry of a seagull, feeling caressed by the breeze, and I begin my examination of all of these emotions. So many of them. More than those elicited by my memories of that summer. More than those generated by Maudie's letter.

Some of them are related to awe — what Jeely and Julie accomplished is just stunning. And there is sorrow — because Julie is gone. But the ones I need to address, the ones dancing and dodging inside my heart, playing hide and seek, peeking out from behind one another, these are all about the man I have just met. Oh, yes, I knew him as a boy, but who is this all too familiar stranger whose sudden presence in my life is somehow fragmenting me into an inner crowd of vying personalities?

Here is eleven-year-old Louisa, of course, noticing how much she missed her friends, innocently excited about a renewed friendship. She's feeling a feisty conspiratorial playfulness that I must say I have been missing. Okay, my dear, you're fine, you can stay right where you are.

Here is the widow of twenty years who has settled herself into a contented independence for so long that the prospect of even considering adjusting to another person's lifestyle or expectations is actually alarming. Look at her waving her red flag to get my attention! You, my dear, can benefit from a little reassurance, yes? Who says you have to adjust? Who says anyone will be allowed to have expectations of you? You are self-sovereign, still and always, so relax. That's better.

Who is this over here? Some flirtatious younger woman eager to lure an obviously enchanted man into wherever her wiles can entice him? You, my dear, into the thrill of dangerous games, how long have you escaped my notice? I haven't been aware of you in decades. We're needing an update here. We do not endanger our heart, and we most certainly do not endanger the heart of another, so do you change or do you leave? Oh, you were unsure of your own power and longed to test it? You are so much more powerful than you know. And your power increases when you become protective, especially of another. Will you put down your guises and your shield and let yourself be alert but open, discerning but authentic? Good, then you can stay. I need you.

Here we have someone calling herself an old fool for being ready to crumble, melting at the warmth of this man's genuinely affectionate openness, longing to be held again the way Jeely held me to himself for so long, not once, but twice… My god, woman, are you going to cry? Oh, cynical self, you're here too? Scoffing at the part of me that has every right to accept the same kind of nurturing that she has been so good at providing? So interesting to have you reveal yourself! Where have you been hiding all these years? And what purpose will you serve if I let you stay? What's that you say? I can't hear you. Oh, I guess you've left. Good choice.

Who is this romantic teenager dying to find out what Prince Charming has in mind, reveling in the glow in his eye, luxuriating in the prospect of becoming his princess? Well, since cynical me has departed, there's no one here to tell you that you can't dream.

Are we done here…? Nope. Who are you? You say you've lost enough people? You say you don't want to become attached to someone who might leave his body before you leave yours? An interesting fear, considering how well you know that we do not die. You do have a point, though. It isn't easy to become accustomed to the physical presence of a beloved person and then to lose it, even when you've had a lot of practice. So there's a trade-off to be considered. Giving up the possibility of joyful and exciting discoveries for the unknown of timing — because you really don't know who will depart first, do you. Is that what you want, to avoid possible pain by relinquishing just as possible happiness? Could you speak up, please? You're willing to take it one step at a time? Ah, a wise decision indeed, as that's really the only way to take it.

And who am I doing all of this investigating? I'm the one who is on the verge of tears because every time Jeely said my name, it felt as if he has been loving me forever. Here is this stranger of a man, no longer the boy I knew, and yet so familiar that I feel seen to my core, seen by consciousness itself, seen with more love and secret elation than I've ever known. He made me feel, even though he was clearly pacing himself, that he has been waiting a very long time to let me know how much I am loved. How can this be happening?

Can I allow it, not resist it, not force it, but allow it to happen?

Can I love this man as much as he deserves to be loved?

I do love him.

Not fully, not completely, not yet.

But I do.

How can I not?

How can I not love the beauty that is unfolding right before my eyes?

The sky is blazing now with scarlets and magentas and golds and lavenders and indigos. What an awe-inspiring reality. The air is so soft and cool. What a beautiful world. What miracles! What have we created here, the unnameable You who is beyond the beyond, the me who has funneled your awareness into this vortex of fluid sensations, what a marvelous dream we are tasting and touching, what a cascade of surprises and delights we are sharing! So, yes. Let us surprise ourselves. If you are looking into my core through the eyes of this man, then I am looking into you by seeing him for who he truly is. We are you, you are us, loving yourself through us.

The sun has disappeared from view. I am no longer in pieces. I'm in peace.

Jeely

In the two days since Louisa's and Addie's visit, I have been in paradox mode. Jittery calmness. Vulnerable certainty. Speeding in slow motion. An inundated arid desert. Upside down on steady feet. Reading an invisible map.

Paradox mode is at least a bit more manageable than what happened as soon as Louisa and Addie left. I brought the tea tray into the kitchen and began to rinse out the mugs, trying to ignore the tears that were surfacing, when suddenly I was at the mercy of an outpouring of sobs. I rested my hands on the edge of the sink and cried, loudly and messily, cried out all the pain my ten-year-old self had never allowed himself to cry at the loss of his best friend, his champion, his rescuer, his beloved Louisa. And then I cried out the years of loneliness I'd never acknowledged, especially these last four years without my sister to keep me focused on our work together. After a few wailing cries of grief, I went back to rinsing out the teapot, still crying, but this time with disbelief and wonder and gratitude. I cried because I'd lost touch with how much we are loved, as Julie always said, by Great Mystery. I cried about the miracle that had just happened. Louisa!

And then I started laughing. I laughed until I could hardly catch my breath. I laughed at myself for being so unsure of what to expect, even though Addie had told me that Louisa is unattached and would very much like to reconnect with me. I laughed because Louisa is still herself, real, and present, and... do I dare think it? Still in cahoots with me? Still flashing looks at me that see right into me.

I finally finished cleaning up and went back into the living room.

And I still can't seem to decide which hologram will ease Louisa into what I know and want to share with her. I don't want to overwhelm her. I don't want to lose her. Again. I don't want to have any expectations!

I just want to be in the moment with her. And it's feeling like it's up to me to decide what that moment will be. I knew as soon as Addie called about their first visit which would be the best hologram to introduce her to a lifetime of exploration. That was an easy choice. Reconnect us to our beginnings. But for this afternoon? Maybe it's not up to me. We'll see.

Two days ago I watched Louisa's face while she was telling me about how her Uncle Rim had torn her from our lives in order to save her father, and I could see that young girl all over again. I was so moved by her anxiety over leaving us without saying good-bye, I felt that little boy in me swell with love again, his heart — my heart — lighting up with the treasure that was being entrusted to it. I couldn't tell her at that moment that I knew some of what had happened, that I'd seen some of what she described, but I will tell her that.

Taking a moment here to center myself.

And there is the knock on my door.

"Addie's not joining us today?" I ask Louisa when she appears alone on my doorstep.

"She's so excited about turning her house into her home," she explains. "And as she said, she is fortunate to have the best possible neighbor available to her from now on."

"I'm the fortunate one," I tell her, opening my arms. Our embrace is even fuller this time, no longer catching up from the past. This one is full of the present, with its promise of a future, as we crest a surge of emotion into deep relaxing sighs of comfort that do not want to end. I don't want to stop holding her. "Let's just stay like this, Louisa," I find myself murmuring into her hair, her soft graying hair, sweet-smelling and inviting. Am I being too quick to make assumptions?

"Okay," she says, tenderness and amusement in her voice, and I ease myself into accepting whatever arises.

"At least Addie's nearby," I say as we finally pull apart and I usher her into my living room. "You won't get to meet my daughter for a while. Karen's visiting her mother in Australia."

"Oh. I look forward to meeting her. When's she coming back?"

"No idea. Her mother's apparently in need of some special attention."

"I hope she'll be okay?"

"I hope so, too."

"Jeely," she says when we've settled onto my couch, "I want to know about how Julie passed."

"Yes. I want to share that with you, Louisa." She has just made my decision for me. "But before I do, I'd like to tell you how far she progressed from that early hologram I showed you." There are other things I'd like to be telling her, but for now… "You saw how she was able to transmit that scene from a perspective outside of her own. It turned out that she could move into that perspective at will, not only to record her own memories, but to remote view other times, other places, other experiences that were not her own."

"What do you mean?"

"Well, for instance, she went into the mind and body of a specific dolphin and recorded its perception of its undersea world."

"Oh, so something like taking a shamanic journey? But wait, how would that translate into a hologram on your desk?"

"Oh, no, no, by then we'd moved on from that limitation. I made some changes to what used to be the den. It's now our own, well, my own private hologram theater. As you know, we'd perfected transmitting the video and audio of a scene, but then Julie began to fine tune her ability to convey that dreamlike quality of space and time elasticity. And you saw a hint of picking up on the emotions being felt by the people in the scene, but that was mostly conveyed through visible signals. She got to where she could translate an inner reality clearly enough that when you're in the theater with the dolphin recording playing, you get to be the dolphin. You feel the water on your skin. You see both the visual and the echo-location images around you. You sense the speed you're achieving to break through the surface and leap into the air. You feel the ecstasy of that, the rush, the pure joy of being alive. You eat and breathe and dive and spin as a dolphin. You understand your communication with your fellow dolphins."

The expression on her face is wide open, in awe.

"So, I can experience being a dolphin? Is this what you're going to show me?"

"Well, no, not today. Yes, sometime, of course. But I'm trying to prepare you for… How can I…? Okay, a few more examples. For one recording she entered the consciousness of a redwood tree. In another, that of a luna moth. Her curiosity was equal to mine! So there's that, the shift of focus into other lifeforms. But then there are visits to distant locations. And there are time leaps. She could go to a moment in past history and bring it to life." I pause, waiting for Louisa to catch up. This is a lot to take in all at once.

"Omigod, Jeely. I mean, literally, oh my god, as in, omniscient, omnipresent. Not just lifting into moments of recognizing our own divine expansiveness — that seems almost abstract in comparison to what you're describing."

"Oh, it's nothing new, really. Shamans have been doing it for ages. Indigenous peoples have had the ability to shape-shift and remote view and interact with beings from other dimensions for as far back as their traditions have been passed along. There are people who remember past lives, and near-death experiences, people who can tell you what you dreamed last night, people who can levitate or be in two places at once, who can communicate directly with animals, or with those who have passed on, or with interstellar entities. It's amazing, really, what we humans are capable of. The only thing different about what Julie and I were able to do is to make a personal experience directly available to another person who might not be as open to the field in that way. She could have described in words to me what she remembered about our moment in the ice cream parlor, but when she gave me the actual scene from an overview, my own memory was deepened and enhanced by a different interpretation. A mentor can try to convey a concept, but personal experience is always the best teacher."

"You've made it possible for anyone to share directly any kind of experience."

"No. I tried transmitting, myself — you know, focusing on a memory wearing the headpiece. I couldn't even edit the jumbled mess that came through. I can see what I'm remembering, but I can't send it. It's probably something like the talent of an artist. Some have it — they can portray a face or a landscape or agony or bliss — and some can barely draw a stick figure."

"Julie had it." Louisa nodded. "Have you published any of these online?" She indicated the shelf full of mini-discs.

"No. At this point I'm not sure how they'd translate, beyond the early ones that were still confined to the desk, and those were mostly personal and private. Checking in on our mother, or on my daughter when she was traveling. Julie never had any children of her own…"

Louisa puts up her hand, palm toward me. I stop talking. She's forming a question. I think I know what's coming.

"Jeely, did you and Julie ever check up on me?"

I tell her the truth. "Only once."

"Oh." She considers that. I can see her mind working.

Do I want to tell her how often I thought about her, wondered what she was doing with her life? Maybe. But not yet. Do I want to ask her if she ever thought about me? Yes. But not yet.

"When?" she asks.

For a moment I think she's heard my thoughts, but then I realize she must be asking about when Julie tapped in and transmitted what she saw so that I could share it. "Before I tell you about that, Louisa," I reach over and rest my hand on her arm, "can I show you something?"

She puts her hand on mine. The way she looks at me makes me feel transparent. Seen into. I have been missing this, being seen into, exactly like this. "Of course," she says.

"Come, then." I help her up and guide her to the hologram theater. "Wait here." I go back into the living room, take a long deep breath to calm the quivering, make a choice from the memory bank, and carry the remote with me back into the theater. It's a bare white-walled room, with only the transmitter equipment installed in the upper corners and three overstuffed chairs along one wall. We've only ever needed the three, for me, Julie, and Karen. I've never shown anything to anyone else. I direct Louisa to a chair and sit down next to her.

"Four years ago," I tell her, "Julie felt finished."

"Oh, Jeely." She puts her hand on mine.

"No, it was okay. I understood." I turn my hand over and take hers into mine. "She had been out of body so many times, for so many years, she wasn't all that interested in returning to it any longer. She knew she could lift out and just not come back. And she was ready to do that." I'm so very aware of holding Louisa's hand. "But before she did, she hooked up and forwarded herself to the moment of leaving her body for good. That way she knew exactly what she was in for, and she left a recording of it for me." I intertwine our fingers, not expecting the jolt of electricity that doing so sends through me. I wait until our hands feel comfortable, almost familiar, before I ask her, "Are you ready for this?"

"If you think I am."

"It's Julie's gift to us."

"Then I'm ready."

* * *

Twenty minutes later, although time has been immeasurable for those twenty minutes, we sit in silence for a long time. Louisa's cheeks are wet, although she seems not to notice. She's just emerging from the same luminous dream, the indescribably loving presence, the infinite perfection of the greater reality, that moved me into unforgettable knowing the first time I experienced this recording. There can be no fear after this knowing. There can be no sorrow for the one who has entered that realm.

"I'd like for Addie to experience this sometime," she says, still unfocused, still gathering herself.

"Of course."

She blinks and takes a deep breath and squeezes my hand and lets go of it so she can wipe her cheeks. "Jeely, don't you want to share this with the rest of humanity?"

"Oh, it's already out there, the same kind of thing. Theaters like mine. Larger ones, too."

"But I mean, each person who transmits their own experience is offering something different. For those of us who can't transmit, let alone envision, it's such an incredible gift, the opportunity to take such a personal, tangible journey through another set of the eyes of god, all the way into *being* god."

"How do you know you can't transmit?"

"Jeely! You're changing the subject."

I shrug.

"You're not ready?"

"I've never really considered it."

"Will you?"

"Consider it?"

"No, play canasta on Tuesday. Duh! Yes! Consider it!"

How does she still do this to me? "Will you consider seeing whether you can transmit?"

"Oh, you have not changed one iota, Jeely Jameson!"

I have to grin. "Can I ask you something?"

"What?"

"What's a peach imbediment?"

A burst of surprised laughter escapes her.

I sit here grinning like the winner of a championship. But I really do want to know. "Will you consider it?"

"I'll consider hearing about that one time that you and Julie checked up on me."

If the same sparkles that I see in her eyes are what she is seeing in mine, we've closed some of the distance that time inevitably placed between us. I don't mind taking all the time we need to close that gap, and then — and this determination surprises me — to see what we can do about whatever distance still remains.

I catch my breath when I see something around her shoulders. She looks down and sees it, too — a pinkish glow. Then her eyes move to my shoulder, and I see my own aura wafting off me like wisps of sparkly rosy morning mist. We look back into one another's eyes, and I am being seen, not just by this woman who means so much more to me than I can tell her, but also by the unfathomable vastness of consciousness, and I am seeing the same. This is why we are here. This is the original intention. To know and to be known.

I take her hand and raise it to my lips. "As your ladyship desires." I release it again, reluctantly. "I will tell you about the time that Julie and I checked up on you."

"You didn't record it?"

"We did."

She lifts her shoulders and a raised open palm as if to say, **Well**?

"Oh. Quite. Yes, your majesty."

"No." She grabs my arm as I begin to get up to see to it that her every wish is my command. This thought tickles me so much I have to snort out a half-laugh. "Are you laughing at me?" She feigns indignation.

"Heaven forbid."

"Why not?"

At that I have to laugh for real. I love this woman. I don't know what we're in the middle of, I don't know how this came to be, but I do know this: I love this woman. "You know, I forgot to offer you tea, or...?"

"No, no, nothing. I just realized that I can't handle another direct dose of multi-dimensional reality right now, so you're right, just tell me about that time. If you want to. Your lordship." She is smirking. Confound you, woman! You haven't changed! The effect you have on me hasn't changed a bit.

I extend my hand to her. She accepts it, and rises, and I place her hand on my arm, lead her back into the living room, and usher her to the couch. But she waits until I'm sitting, then seats herself close, leaning against me so I can put my arm around her. She leans her head against my cheek, and if this wasn't feeling so utterly beyond anything I've ever known, it would be feeling like the most familiar thing in the world.

"We were in our late 30's," I begin. "It took a few years, after the equipment became available, for Julie to experiment with more than her own memories. Once we'd had some success with whatever spontaneously occurred to her, we realized we could ask questions and get them answered. What was it like to be a samurai? What do elephants communicate to one another? What happened that brought Louisa and her father together?"

"Mm."

"We'd received that postcard from you, so we knew you'd been reunited with him." I don't tell her that I still have that postcard, and its message, the one that dove straight for my heart and locked itself in: 'I'll never forget you.' "But until you told me a couple of days ago all the circumstances around why you and your Uncle Rim disappeared overnight, I never knew any of that, because what Julie tapped into when she went searching through the space-time continuum was the moment you were in the hospital with him and your father." How can anything feel this wonderful and right, snuggling like old friends who might become…

"You were there."

Oops. Come back to this conversation, sir! "Well, Julie was there, in a sense, and she…"

"No. Jeely. *You were there.*"

"What do you mean?"

"When my dad and I were out of our bodies, about to look down at his bed, I sensed two beings nearby. That ocean of love surrounding us was intensified by the presence of two ethereal people who were not just witnessing, they were adding to the love. They were part of the healing."

I can't speak. I'm remembering how much love I was feeling when I sat watching Julie's hologram, seeing the young girl I had known so long ago put something into her father's hand while telling him how much she loved him, seeing them lift out into a brightness so brilliant that everything else disappeared, knowing that something powerful was taking place. "When you and your father left the hospital, I knew you were both going to be fine. The same thing happened after Julie left her body for the last time. When you know that someone you love is in a good space, happy, moving on, you don't feel any more sorrow. You miss them, terribly, but you can only feel happy for them. That's why I never asked Julie to check on you again." I think I might have just told Louisa that I love her. I hope that's okay.

"Jeely, you're not listening." She sits up so she can twist around and face me, and takes both of my hands in hers.

"What?"

"You were *there*. Even though you didn't do the remote viewing, or astral traveling, or whatever, yourself, when you were in your theater watching the hologram, part of you entered the same space that my dad and I were in. I saw you."

"Are you sure?"

"I didn't know it was you, because it was your adult selves. At that moment in time, I knew you only as children, so when I sensed a man and a woman who seemed somehow familiar adding love to the light, I didn't get it, not until this minute. It was you and Julie."

I am speechless. Neither of us can talk. We're rubbing the goosebumps on our arms.

"Do you know what this means?" she asks me.

I'm beginning to be blown away. The holograms are not just multi-sensory movies. They're interactive. "The holograms are interactive."

"Is that possible? I mean, did it happen just that once? Maybe it happens every time."

"I don't know. I never went down this path before. Does what you're suggesting make any sense?"

"It does. Think about it." She swings her feet up off the floor and her legs across mine so she can face me without twisting. Oh, woman, what are you doing to me? "You said that you and Julie didn't know if she was aware, in the ice cream parlor, if her 12-year-old self was aware of… or if her older self was… can you help me out here?"

"Only if you move about a million miles away." Oh, no, I didn't mean that the way it sounded. What can I say to…

"I love you, Jeely Jameson."

My heart explodes so wide open I'm in danger of falling into it. I think it's called being gobsmacked.

"I love you," she says again. "I love your mind. I love your soul. And if I don't back off right now," she rearranges herself on the couch so that she's sitting cross-legged, her dress draped over her knees, facing me from a foot away, "I'll be wanting to love the rest of you." Her breath catches. "And I'm not quite ready for that."

"That's okay."

"It's been twenty years for me…" She doesn't finish her sentence.

Oh, how hard it is for me to hear that and not want to do something about it. And how easy it is for me to hear that, because it's been at least that long for me, too. "I understand."

She gazes at me from such a deep place of longing and reaching that her holding back is all the more beautiful to me.

"I've always loved you, Louisa."

"You have, haven't you."

The way she says it, accepting years of love from me, and years of emptiness, melts me down to my core. "There's something I want to say to you, but I don't want you to take it the wrong way."

"I can only take it the wrong way if it's a one-way street. And it's not."

How does she know exactly what I need to hear? Who is this woman that I've loved for so long, the thought of it almost hurts. And doesn't hurt at all. Not at all. "I don't ever want to spend another day, let alone fifty years, wondering where you are."

She shakes her head slowly, and the look in her eye tells me that my confession has hit home. She gets up and pulls me to my feet, and our embrace is difficult to break away from. "You won't have to, ever again," she says. "I promise."

Louisa

It's not that I *had* to leave Jeely's house when I did. Well, okay, yes I did. For both of our sakes. Knowing when you're filled to the brim, to overflowing, with so much to savor in hindsight, well, that can be part of the pleasure — letting it settle into your bones, inhaling every essence of its sweet flavor, allowing its nuances to trickle through your bloodstream and feed your soul. My soul is so exquisitely fulfilled right now.

It's only after I've meandered through my house, nibbling at some bits of food that couldn't interest me less, talking to my plants as I water them, sitting on my couch hugging my knees and feeling liquid inside, sending astonished gratitude out into the universe, that I'm able to think back to where we left off... right before I couldn't hold in any longer what this beautiful man was igniting in me... so, where we left off...

Oh, Jeely, what are you doing right here in the middle of my heart? Or have you always been hiding here? You simply amaze me. You can lead or follow with equal grace. You can expand into the infinite and retract into the little boy you were, in an instant. You have so much respect in you, for knowledge, for human beings, for me, for timing, and, despite your modesty, for yourself. You are funny and sweet and accomplished and spontaneous and so utterly authentic. How can we have moved so quickly into this reunion of souls unless they have always been united, despite the distances of time and space?

What was it Maudie said? When true power selects you, it's because deep down you wanted it to make good use of you. This is true of love, too, then, isn't it. Love knows — even if you yourself do not — when you have been waiting to become an instrument of its music.

What an amazing creation is this universe. It's tangible and intangible, perceivable and beyond perception. It's mere information and it's solid to the touch. It's in constant motion, and in absolute stillness. It's holographic — in any of its smallest parts resides its entirety.

Oh!

That's it!

That's what was almost within my grasp. The holograms *are* interactive! Because everything in the universe is interactive, constantly influencing and being influenced by another part of itself. There's no limit to what can be influenced, in space or in time, because it's all interrelated.

So when Jeely appeared to me when my dad and I were above our bodies, it didn't matter that Julie had sent her perception — no, her ethereal self — ahead in order to record what he would then see later in time. The time that we perceive as a one-directional flow is an illusion. Of course it is! What Julie and Jeely have made accessible isn't just the facilitation of interactive observation, it's the facilitation of interactive influence across space and time. They each went back in time from a different starting point, but they arrived at the same place in time, and added to the love that restored my dad to health.

Well, of course. What am I saying that I don't already know. We're all part of the same infinite and eternal consciousness, and being omniscient and omnipotent, it can do anything it wants to!

So of course we can go to another moment in time — even if we aren't what Julie was, a remote viewer or an astral traveler who could translate her awareness into a form perceivable by others. We can at the very least go back in our memories — to earlier parts of our own lives — and not just witness but influence what happened. When we send anger back, when we interpret the actions of another as harmful, we make it so. When we send love back, when we interpret the actions of another as beneficial, we make it so. And it shifts who we are in the present. If we want to be empowered by having had the universe do what it did for our *benefit*, we can simply observe it to be so, and so it is.

Can I apply that to myself in every instant? Checking in… yes… yes… oh. Ouch. Oh, no! What is this pinprick of pain? A capsule of tearful loneliness, a child's longing for the mother she never knew. I thought I'd cleared that area.

I don't know if I want to go there right now.

Where's my phone?

"Jeely?"

I can hear the surprised smile in his voice when he says my name.

"I've been thinking about how the holograms can be interactive," I tell him.

"Quantum entanglement."

"What?"

"I've been thinking about it, too. You were right. Quantum entanglement is one possible way to think about it. Everything's connected, in a kind of wave pattern of ripples and influences, but two particles, if they've already been connected, remain connected and continue to specifically influence or mirror one another, no matter how far apart they are."

"Really? That does explain a lot. Wow. And then there's this — time is fluid."

"Yes!"

"And it goes both ways."

"It goes all ways! Every moment in time has the potential to influence any other moment in time. Especially if there's a conscious intention directed at it."

"Yes! I was thinking the same thing. The hologram was your time machine..."

"Whoa. Now you're spooking me big time. Oh, wait, did Addie tell you I've been interested in time travel?"

"No. You're interested in time travel?"

"Wait. Go back to what you just said."

I think for a second. "Oh. The hologram was your time machine."

"I never thought of it that way — because I never had any confirmation that the place or time or creatures I was witnessing in the holograms had become aware of or were influenced by my presence. So, wait a minute... if I was traveling in time... it didn't matter what time I left from. I went to the same time that Julie did."

"My conclusion exactly! And you influenced that time. With your intention, you added love to it."

"I wasn't aware of having an intention, though, Louisa. I just couldn't *not* love you."

"I am so grateful to you, Jeely. I am so thankful for you."

"Louisa." There's a pause. "This is all so much bigger than us. I hardly know how to hold it all."

I have to let that sink in. It's true, there *is* a ripple effect happening here... But I don't want to lose my train of thought. "So I was also thinking..."

He's silent.

"I was also thinking... No! Not what you're thinking right now, Jeely Jameson!"

"Huh? Wha...? Library card?"

I'm laughing.

"What is it you were thinking?" I can hear the sly satisfaction in his voice. He loves this. I love this.

"I was thinking that even without the vehicle of a hologram, we can go back and influence a different time."

"You're right. Back, forward, sideways. We can influence our pasts, our futures, our parallel lives…"

"You blow me away."

"The feeling is mutual."

He has to know, how can he not, that he is elevating my happiness quotient right off the charts. "I came across something, though, that I don't know what to do with."

"I'm listening."

Yes, you are, aren't you, you amazingly beautiful man. "I found a place inside myself that must have somehow stayed untouched even when I was inundated with the light. It's small, but it's there."

"Tell me, Louisa."

"Well, part of what I believe is this — if we allow that the universe loves us because we are it loving itself, then even though we have the free will to make choices about our experiences, ultimately everything eventually returns us to source consciousness, so everything that happens to us is for our benefit… or our education, or our entertainment, or our evolution…"

"But?"

"But. How could not knowing one's own mother not leave an emptiness?" And, it occurs to me at this very moment, "How could having had the father you had, how could that have been to your benefit?"

There's a silence on the other end of the phone.

"Louisa." He pauses. "When you asked me if Julie and I had ever checked up on you, I told you the truth. Just the one time. But there's something I didn't tell you."

I'm not sure what to expect.

"I didn't know what Julie was doing — it was her own need to offer something directly, I guess, just in case — because she had benefitted so much from watching our mother's transformation and then sharing a lifelong friendship with her — our mother was a major part of our lives until she passed."

"What are you saying?"

"Or maybe she knew that someday it would be possible."

"Jeely, what are you talking about?"

"Julie made a recording of your mother She left it as a gift for you. In case I ever found you again."

"What?" I'm overwhelmed.

"She loved you as much as I do, Louisa."

I don't know what to do with all the gifts this man is giving me. "How can you be so incredibly beautiful?"

"How can I be so incredibly blessed?"

I make a decision. "When's a good time for me to come over and see it?"

"Now."

I laugh.

"Or tomorrow."

"I like now."

"I do too."

"You do realize that we parted ways less than two hours ago?"

"Feels like years to me."

"You're incorrigible." I'm grinning.

"Did you say I'm porridge-able? As in mush? How astute of you, your royal loveliness. I am indeed an absolute mess of mush."

"And I suppose you're going to say it's all my fault."

"You're a mind reader. I knew there was *something* intriguing about you."

"I'm coming over."

"Please do."

* * *

I borrow a hover-car, and zoom over the streets with their sun-powered lights glowing above me in a blur. Addie said we live twenty minutes apart, but I make it to her neighbor's house in fifteen, and into Jeely's arms in under a minute. So much for savoring in hindsight.

We can't seem to let go of one another. It just feels too good to be held by this man. "We could just stay like this forever," I suggest, resting my head in the crook of his neck, loving the strength of his arms around me. We're still just inside his front door.

"That works for me." He moves me away a little so he can take my face in his hands. "Or not."

I have never been kissed with so much tenderness.

"Have you eaten?" he asks when he releases me. He brushes a strand of hair from my brow.

"I might do so tomorrow. Or maybe next week."

He smiles and shakes his head. "Is this a dream?"

"Or a dream come true?"

"Maybe you don't need to see that hologram this evening."

"Oh, no. You're giving me a choice."

"This is true."

"I would rather not be required to make any decisions in this condition."

"So you want me to decide?"

I look up into his eyes. They are full of so much contentment. He doesn't need anything to be any different from the way it will unfold, however that may be. "I think you already have."

"I think I'd like to take you over here," he leads me into the living room and pulls me toward the couch, "and just hold you, Louisa." He sits down, leaning against one arm of the couch, and pulls me down alongside him, and I lean back and sink into him, loving the clean smell of him, loving every freckle on these arms that are wrapped around me.

"Jeely."

"Hm?"

I just wanted to say his name, but then a question occurs to me. "I never asked you about your father. I remember hearing arguments from your house before the day I fell into your yard, but I never saw him."

"The day you fell into our yard." I can hear the smile in his voice. He kisses my hair. "No, he left before then, and Julie was right when she said he was never coming back."

"Was it awful when he was around?"

"He drank. He was a very unhappy man. He liked to get his point across with his belt. Just on me, though, fortunately, not on my mother or Julie."

"No! Oh, no, Jeely, I can't stand the thought of that. I can't... oh my god." I'm inundated with regret, a need to apologize for what I once thought of him, a desire to have been able to protect that little boy from such abuse.

"It no longer matters. I thanked him in absentia a long time ago for the role he played, for the gift he gave me. The gift of knowing exactly what kind of man I never wanted to be."

"But, Jeely. I had no idea. I thought your circumstances were difficult. I didn't know they were out of control in the cruelty department. It's no wonder you seemed so unhappy and withdrawn."

"I was. Until you showed up."

I can't let go of how awful it's feeling to think of that sweet, funny boy I knew being belted by his father. I sit up and turn to face him. I touch his cheek, for just a moment. And then I blurt it out. "I am *so angry*!"

He frowns a question.

"I'm enraged! I want to rip that belt out of that man's hands and use it on him. How dare he! How dare he hurt you!" I'm so angry the tears come. "I *hate* that you had to endure that, Jeely. I hate it!" Tears are shining in his eyes now, too. "You were such a sweet, beautiful, caring boy. I never knew. I would have..." I want to say I would have killed him, but I know that isn't true. "I don't know what I would have done..."

"You would have done what you're doing right now, Louisa. You *did* do what you're doing right now." He puts a hand on my cheek. For just a moment. "You made me feel seen."

"But I never saw you as angry as you had every right to be."

"No, that came later. I was angry for the teenagers who gravitated to me for help because their fathers weren't much better than mine had been."

"But you never felt angry for yourself?"

He shrugs.

"You still have some anger inside, Jeely."

He looks at me, pained. This is hard, but it could be worth it.

"You said you've thanked him in absentia for showing you the kind of man you never wanted to be."

"He was awful. He was the reason my mother was such a bundle of nerves. He was the reason Julie was shrinking away. I hated him."

I wait.

"I dreaded his coming home. I couldn't do anything right. I couldn't stop him from yelling and getting into such a rage that he'd whip off his belt and come after me. I was terrified. It wasn't even the pain so much as the fear and the rage."

He's on the verge, I can see it. "Tell him, Jeely."

His face contorts into a silent scream. He pulls his knees up into his arms. And then he lets it out, a roar of outrage and anguish. "*Leave me alone*!" he shouts. And then in a quieter voice, "Leave me alone." The tears are flowing. On both of our faces. The air is heavy with grief and sorrow, not just for ourselves, for our generation, for all of humanity when it was still locked up in suffering.

He takes a deep breath. He relaxes, stretches his legs out again.

"That's it?" I ask.

"I'm realizing how much pain he must have been in. He must have had the same kind of treatment from his own father. It was as if there was a demon inside him that took over. It must have killed him to have turned out the same way. No wonder he drank."

I wait again. The insight will come.

"I feel sorry for him." He looks at me and sees me loving him. "Why would a soul choose such a life?"

I know what we're both thinking.

"You said that ultimately everything happens for our benefit."

"If we choose to see it that way."

"I wouldn't have been able to understand or help those teenagers…"

"Those of us who were right in the middle of the worst chaos, before the shift, were prepared, in whatever way was needed, for what we'd have to do to make it through, and to help others make it through."

"So he deserves my genuine gratitude."

I raise my eyebrows.

He nods. "And we were also led to be with the people who would make it easier to move on," he says.

I'm thinking back to when Maudie and Mary Etta told me to look for people who might need our help. "They knew what they were doing."

"Who?"

"Maudie and Mary Etta. They're the reason I fell into your yard that day."

"They may have been behind it," he says, taking my hands, "but you're the one who changed our lives, Louisa. I went from years of dread and anger and grief into days of sparkling sunshine and laughter and adventure because of you." He pulls me back down to snuggle against him. "Do you know what you did for our family?"

"Maudie and Mary Etta asked me to check out the neighborhood to see if there was anything that we could do in secret to help anyone."

"Maudie and Mary Etta hadn't even arrived on our street when you fixed Mrs. Pritchard's pansies."

"What? How did you know about that?"

"You weren't the only spy in the neighborhood." His arms are wrapped snugly around me, his cheek is resting on mine. "But the things I saw you doing in secret around the neighborhood were only confirmation of what I already knew when you put Mrs. Forger in her place."

"Mrs. Forger? Our fifth grade teacher? Oh, you're kidding me. You remember that? I was so pissed off!"

"I could tell. You were as angry as I was. But the way you handled that situation… that was the moment I fell in love with you. For all time."

I am zapped. Direct hit. Liquified. I am loved. I have been loved for a long time. Foolish self-pitying happy tears. Silly shuddering sigh of sorrow and relief. It has been so long. So very long. Lifetimes ago... Never before... Never like this. I'm sinking into this man. I raise his hands to my lips and kiss them. Something opens between us. Our surfaces disappear. Our energy is one electrified, ecstatic, joyful merging. I feel you, Jeely Jameson. I feel your beautiful essence. I hear you wanting me to accept your gift of love. I feel you needing to give this to me. I do. I accept. I love you. Totally. Entirely.

A quivery breath escapes me, and I relax. I feel Jeely doing the same.

We sit here on the couch, me leaning back into him, for a long quiet moment.

"I didn't know," I tell him.

"And now you do."

"Yes."

"It has always been you, Louisa."

I feel a surge of pride. In myself. That I have had the love of this gentle, conscious, centered, quietly powerful, brilliant, modest man must mean that I somehow deserve it. "Why only now?" I ask. "Why didn't I try to find you sooner? I'm so sorry, Jeely. So sorry to have kept you waiting."

"Life happened."

"Yes, it did, didn't it. We got married to other people, raised families..."

"I never married. We had a child together so we tried to make a go of it. Didn't work out too well." He moves his cheek against mine, and liquid ripples of desire course through me. "You'd think that when we received the light — Julie from you, me from her — it would have stuck. But the chaos during those decades was intrusive. We had to keep our focus on the positive, and that wasn't always easy."

"I remember."

"When Karen's mother left — took Karen with her, actually — my daughter came back on her own when she was in her twenties — when they left, I was lucky I had Julie and our ongoing project. I was fairly content, actually. Busy. So much innovation, so much technology to keep up with, so many ways to communicate to the world what we were going through and what we could do about it. And then the spread of consciousness reached critical mass, and all the old ways imploded or crumbled, so even more attention needed to be paid to how to rearrange everything so that we could all live the way we do now."

"Of course you were involved in the changes."

"It was a debt I felt I owed. I'd been rescued from despair by someone who took charge and made things better." He pulls me even closer into himself. "I wanted to pass that favor on to the people around me."

I feel that surge of pride again, but this time not in myself. I have so much respect for this beautiful, trustworthy man. "And now you're on the verge of making yet another contribution?"

"Is this going back to a conversation we had a few centuries ago?"

"Jeely, you have me thinking about all of the people in our generation who lived through the chaos. Enlightenment has freed up the younger generations. They're coming in clear, they're exercising all of their abilities. But even though there's no more corruption, no more crime, no more poverty, there are still people with old wounds who don't have to be as shut down as they are. I know, because I'm trying to help some of them. What if your holograms, what if interactive holograms...?"

"It's a big what if. What if that one instance was interactive because of quantum entanglement, because the connection between two particles remains so no matter what the distance between them... or the connection between two people... Maybe I was able to find you in the same way that Julie did, directly, because of the strength of our bond. We'd have to do some more exploring to see if that was a singular episode or an expandable possibility." He leans his chin on the top of my head. "So unless you're willing to..."

"Okay, okay." I think about this. "It wouldn't hurt to give it a try, I guess."

"No expectations."

"But I'd have to be totally clear. Nothing smudging my filter."

"Oh, so this is how you're getting around to watching Julie's hologram about your mother."

"You caught me!"

"I am so glad I did."

* * *

Jeely settles himself into one of the overstuffed chairs in his hologram theater, pulls me into his lap, wraps his arms around me, and clicks the remote.

A scene fades in. A toddler walks between two young women about thirty years old whom I recognize instantly. Maudie and Mary Etta! Maudie has brown hair. Oh, no, so does Mary Etta! She dyed her hair? They each hold one of the little girl's hands — she has to be Samantha. Their niece. My mother. The girl who grew up to be a woman known to my father as Samadhi. The child is gleeful, demanding to be swung into the air every other step. The women are accompanying the swinging with exclamations of "Wheeee!" They're crossing a lawn in front of an old house painted white with green trim. Maple trees on either side of it. They swing her towards where Jeely and I are sitting, and flowers appear in the foreground, roses, and they point out a butterfly to her, a monarch. She lets go of their hands and reaches for the butterfly, but her eyes are pulled by something beyond the fluttering insect. My heart is jolted when she looks directly at me. "See, Maw? See, Metta? Angel!" Her little mouth gapes open. She brings both of her chubby little hands to her mouth and blows me a kiss. I smile, tears prickling my eyes, and blow her a kiss back. She chirps with delight, and turns to her aunts. "See? See angel kiss too?" Maudie and Mary Etta are looking at me now. If they can see me, they're looking at a graying-haired woman... and suddenly I realize I'm not in Jeely's lap. I'm standing on the other side of the rose bushes, and love is pouring from me toward them. Toward all three of them. "Yes, honey," Maudie says. "She's your angel. And you're her angel." "Bye, angel." Little Samantha waves as the scene fades out...

...and fades in to a backyard with a child's plastic picnic table placed beneath a maple tree. A corner of the house shows it to be the same one as in the first scene. A girl of about five is sitting at the table, serving imaginary tea to the two dolls and a teddy bear propped on the bench across from her. She has soft brown curls, a little frown of concentration as she makes sure not to spill any of the invisible tea. "There!" She sits back and smiles. "Here, Bollie, you pass the cookies." She laughs. "No, silly, you can't have *all* of them all by yourself!" She is about to reach for the paper napkins, when a slight breeze blows the top one off the table. She turns into my direction to grab for it but stops when she sees me. Again I find myself standing at the edge of the hologram. This time I notice that I'm not solid. I'm made of light. But I can see the shape of my hand. "Angel! There you are again! I remember you!" I can't speak. I can't move. All I can do is beam love at her. She does it again, she blows me a kiss, and I do the same. She is still watching me as the scene fades.

I'm aware of being on Jeely's lap again as the next scene comes into focus. It's a schoolyard at recess, third-graders jumping rope, playing ball, raising the noise level with shouts of excitement and arguments. I see Samantha being shoved by a stocky boy who scowls at her. "You can't even catch a ball, dumb-ass, so, no, you can't be in the game." She backs away from him and turns into my direction, and I see her tears. I want so much to reach out to her that she feels it and looks up at me. I'm in my light body again. I say to her, "Never mind him, Samantha. You're my angel." Her sweet face is full of hurt and confusion, but she smiles through the pain and nods at me. The scene fades out...

...and changes into a moving panorama, a country road slipping away beneath a small motorcycle as it passes a cornfield on one side and a hardwood forest on the other. Two people are on the bike, young teenagers, the girl's arms around the boy's waist. Even with her helmet on, I recognize Samantha. Suddenly a deer leaps out of the forest and into the road. The boy tries to swerve, braking at the same time, and the rear wheel starts skidding forward. The bike's going to go down. I'm instantly in the scene, putting myself between the deer and the bike, shoving the deer toward the cornfield and keeping the bike from falling. The boy sees the way clear, releases the hand-brake, dips his wrist to accelerate, and they straighten out and surge forward. Samantha is clinging to the boy, but she glances over her shoulder and sees me. And then, even though she's looking ahead again, she raises her left hand high, thumb up, and I have to laugh with relief at her cheekiness.

The next scene opens onto an outdoor cafe in a small mountain town. Samantha is in her early 20's. She's sitting with a young man of the same age, and my heart leaps as I recognize this younger version of my father. So much love pours from me toward both of my parents in their youth that they both look up at me. Samantha glances at Clay and back at me. "You see her, too?" He nods, unable to speak. There seems to be a glitch or a skip in the scene, and I'm looking over her shoulder as she finishes writing a postcard addressed to Maudie and Mary Etta. "Don't worry about me. My angel is with me."

Now we're in a room with white walls and several monitors. Samantha's face, as she lies on a raised hospital bed, is beaded with sweat. The huge mound of her belly is hidden under a sheet. "I just know something's wrong, Clay," she says to the young man holding her hand. He's shaking his head no. His eyes are glistening with tears. "If I die..." she begins, and he puts his hand gently over her mouth, but she removes it and kisses it and holds it in both of her own. "If I die, you tell our daughter how much I love her." He is sobbing, but he nods. "It'll be okay, my darling. My angel will be with you."

As the scene fades, I am sitting on Jeely's lap with his arms around me and his head resting against mine. I'm shaking with sobs.

* * *

It's dark outside. Jeely has lent me a tee-shirt to wear over my underpants, and he's in a pair of boxer shorts. We're propped up against the pillows of his bed, my head on his chest, his arms around me. I'm still shaken. My nose is stuffed up and my eyes feel puffy. I haven't spoken a word since the hologram ended. I've let Jeely guide me to the bathroom and then the bedroom. I've let him help me undress and slip the tee-shirt over my head. I simply can't fathom it all, the gift I've been given, the love that surrounds me, the beauty I have somehow been a part of, the rewiring of my brain as it short-circuits its way into new configurations. I'm so filled up — with gratitude, and questions, and grief, and elation, and more gratitude — that there's nothing I can do but fall asleep in the arms of the man who is holding me to himself as if it's all he ever wants to be doing for the rest of his life.

Jeely

I'm in the kitchen when Louisa enters, her hair all over the place, her eyes bleary, my tee-shirt crumpled and damp. "Good morning, beautiful," I grin at her. And I mean what I say. It is a fantastic morning and she is the most beautiful sight in the world.

"Oh god, you're a morning person." She can barely drag the words down from her brain and out of her mouth.

"Tea, my love?" I can't help it. This cheeriness. It's not how I am in the mornings, either. Awake, yes. Cheery, not necessarily. But sheer delight will out.

"Yes." She yawns. "Please." She seats herself at the table and asks, "What time is it?"

"You slept for a solid eleven hours."

"Unnh. Where's the bathroom?"

She must not remember her visit to it last night. I point, and she gets up and stumbles into the hall. This is the Louisa I have longed to know. When she returns, I hand her a mug.

"Mm." She sits down again and dips her finger into it. Her conclusion is apparently that it's too hot to drink yet, because she gets up again and walks straight into my arms. "I mean it, Jeely." She hasn't yet told me what it is she means, but I'm sure that if I wait long enough, I will be rewarded with illumination. I'm willing to wait until the sun goes down on the other side of the galaxy. Holding her like this, with her arms around my waist, in my own kitchen — this is what I was born to do. "This time I really mean it."

"I believe every word you're saying."

She snorts a laugh into my bare chest.

"I want to stay here like this forever."

"Your wish is my command."

"Or at least until my damn tea cools down."

I'm trying not to laugh out loud out of pure unmitigated happiness, but the effort is making me jiggle her against me.

"Is this what you call dancing?" she mumbles into my armpit, and when the hilarity of it sputters out of me, she leans back, still holding on, and the love and happiness beaming from her eyes leaves me speechless and grinning like a fool.

"I love you more than I thought it was possible to love anyone... or anything..." she yawns again and returns her cheek to my heart, "or any animal... or any plant... or any mountain..."

"I catch your drift," I say when she runs out of steam, drinking in her words, ambrosia for my soul.

"I'm unspeechified."

"*That* remains to be seen."

She snorts a laugh into my chest again. "Okay. Tea." She goes back to her chair, carefully sips at her mug, and then downs about a third of the contents. "How can you look all sparkly and squirrelly-tailed after I've slept for so long?"

I sit down catty-cornered to her. "I didn't sleep a wink."

"Oh, so *that's* your secret." She takes a few more long gulps. "You didn't sleep?"

"Too busy listening to you snore."

"Oh, now that's just not kind."

"You don't snore. Well, other than the occasional pig noise..." Tea shoots out of her mouth back into her mug. "I was just too happy. Didn't want to miss a minute of it."

"Really? Didn't sleep at all?" She's concerned.

"Maybe a few hours, off and on."

She finishes her tea. "Jeely, about last night..."

"Nothing happened, officer, I swear it."

"Jeely!" She gives me a look. "Oh." She refocuses. "I mean about Julie's hologram."

"What about it?"

"Did you ever watch it before last night?"

"No. Julie wouldn't let me edit it or even keep it in the memory bank. She told me what it was, but she taped the sleeve of the mini-disc shut and wrote your name on it. I'd almost forgotten about it until you mentioned the emptiness of not having known your mother."

"Did you see what I saw?"

"What did you see?"

"Could you tell me what you saw first? Please?"

"Okay." I take a sip of my tea. "In the first scene, two women, maybe in their 20's or 30's, were swinging a toddler toward some rose bushes."

"The toddler was my mother, Samantha. The women were Maudie and Mary Etta."

"The women were Maudie and Mary Etta? Wait, how did Maudie and Mary Etta have your mother with them?" A little case of the goosebumps here.

"Oh, that's right, I haven't had a chance to tell you that. Their little sister died giving birth to my mother. She was their niece. They were my great-aunts."

"You're related to Maudie and Mary Etta." Does the great mystery ever stop to take a breath?

"That's how they found me."

"They were looking for you?"

"I'll bring you the letter Maudie wrote next time."

"She wrote you a letter?"

"Yes, but I didn't get to read it until last week."

"Last week." Nope. The great mystery plunges onward tirelessly. "You're related to Maudie and Mary Etta. Actually, that explains a lot. And leaves a lot to be explained."

"Which I'll do, I'll explain all that. Later. I promise. Just please tell me what you saw last night. They were swinging the little girl toward some rose bushes..."

"...and she saw a butterfly, and she reached for it. Then in the next scene..."

"Wait a minute. She reached for the butterfly. What did she do after that?"

"That was it. The scene faded out for a bit, into white, and then it faded in to another scene."

"Did she say anything?"

"The little girl? No."

"Did Maudie say anything?"

"No. What are you saying...?"

"And then the scene changed?"

"Yes."

"Where was I when she reached for the butterfly?"

"Where were you? You were on my lap. You were on my lap through the whole hologram. You don't remember that?"

"I'll get back to that. So in the next scene...?"
"A little girl is serving tea to her toys."
"And what happens?"
"A napkin blows off her little picnic table, and she goes after it, but she stops and looks up."
"Did you see what she was looking at?"
"No. That was the end of that scene."
"And I'm still on your lap."
"The whole time. What...?"
"So then there's a schoolgirl being bullied."
"That's right. I felt so bad for her. She was crying. By that time I'd caught on that Julie was giving you glimpses into your mother's life from early on. Why would she include something that would just break your heart?"
"Julie knew what she was doing, Jeely. Omigod. She knew what she was doing!"
"You're losing me."
"She knew. You were right. It's only possible if there's a bond. There's no connection between you and my mother."
The minute I think I know where this is going, it turns a corner.
"Then there was a scene on a motorcycle," she prompts me.
"Two kids on a bike, and a deer jumped out in front of them."
"And what happened?" she asks me. She didn't see what I saw? She was right there on my lap watching the whole thing with me. Where *is* this going? "The biker swerved and braked, and it looked like they were going down, but the deer kind of jerked out of the way as if it got hit, only the bike didn't hit it, the biker was avoiding the deer and getting the bike upright somehow, although at that angle... it was like a glitch in the matrix or something. I was wondering again why Julie included that scene, but then the kids were okay, and the girl looked over her shoulder, but by then the deer was long gone, and she raised her fist in the air."
"Wow. Unbelievable! Okay, so then Samantha's with a man at an outdoor cafe."
"Right."
"That man was my father."
"I didn't get that until the last scene, when I remembered him from the hospital you found him in."
"Did you see her write the postcard?"
"Yes. It was one of those visual elasticity things."
"Did you see what she wrote?"

I try to remember. I was still trying to figure out the gist of the whole hologram. It didn't tie together somehow. It wasn't like what Julie was capable of. Nothing else she'd done had been this disjointed. "I did, but I'm not remembering what it was."

"That's okay. Just tell me about the last scene, and I'll tell you why I'm asking you all these questions."

"The last scene — no wonder you were sobbing by the end of it. I was crying myself, it was so hard to watch. That poor young man. Your father. But you weren't just crying, you were going deep. I didn't know you still had so much grief over losing your mother, Louisa. I could hardly bear for you to be feeling all that pain, even though I know it's the best thing to do, express it, clear it out. I was just glad I could be there with you while it was happening."

"I couldn't have handled it without you, Jeely. You knew just what I needed — no comforting words, no pushing me through it, just holding me until it was all out, and then helping me to bed. I'm so, so glad you were with me… and that we saw it together." She takes my hand to her lips and kisses it.

"At least you got to hear your mother say that she loved you."

She nods. "Yes. But that wasn't what Julie was giving me, Jeely. I saw what you saw. But I saw something more. And I did something more. Because I stepped into every scene. Not this physical me. My ethereal self. My light body. When the toddler reached for the butterfly, she saw me, and blew me a kiss, and I blew a kiss back to her."

"You left your body? She saw you? You were interacting with her?"

"The same thing happened when she was a little girl. We blew kisses at one another. And then in the playground? Samantha saw me, she recognized me from the earlier times in her life. She thought I was her angel. And she heard me when I spoke to her. In the motorcycle scene? I got between the deer and the bike. Samantha wasn't looking for the deer, she was looking for me, because every once in a while, three times in her life up to that point, she had seen her angel. She figured it had to be me who saved them, so she looked back to see if she was right, and she gave me the thumbs up!"

I'm trying to take all this in. Louisa was sitting on my lap the whole time, but I was so engrossed in the hologram, I didn't notice… When people leave their bodies, don't their bodies go into still mode? "You were out of body each time. You were your mother's angel. You visited her from her future."

"Yes! What *you* saw, Jeely, that's what Julie set up, like a framework. But she also set it up to be a time machine for me."

I'm brain-swoggled. "Wait. How's that possible? It doesn't make logical sense."

"I know. I couldn't get my mind around it either. I was completely overcome. Not with grief about the loss of my mother. With awe. The gift that Julie gave me — not just the opportunity to see my mother at different ages, but to interact with her? To use the power of my love to reassure her and even rescue her? That's why I was crying. Out of gratitude and joy and incredulity. That, and the enormity of it. What are we talking about here? Different timelines? Impossible paradoxes? I don't have a clue. All I know is that Julie's gift not only gave me back enough of my mother to fill me to overflowing with love, she gave me a whole new set of dimensions, and a huge mystery to boot!"

I wrap my hands around Louisa's hands. "You gave Julie her life. *You* did, Louisa. Yes, it came through you from source, but it came through *you*. You are the facet of the universe that was chosen and then was willing to be the agent. Because of who you are. She wanted to give you something back. I know how she felt."

"You know, Jeely, when Maudie gave me a glimpse into the all-pervasive and never-ending love that is creation, and when I passed it on to Julie, and she passed it on to you, I had *no idea* that the universe would be giving it back to me a thousand-fold."

Hearing that fills me to the brim. Spiritually, anyway. "You know what? I'm getting really hungry."

She fake-punches me on the arm, trying not to laugh.

"Ow."

"Have I told you yet today how madly and wildly and passionately I am in love with you?"

What am I going to do with this woman? "Not *nearly* enough."

She climbs onto me, straddling my lap, and I know I'm in deep trouble.

"I think it's about time we remedy that," she says.

I lead her back to the bedroom. I think I'm going to enjoy being in deep... trouble.

*

You see, the thing is, even after the shift, people still thought they needed technology. Oh, there are people like me, millions of them, who can do out-of-body, but even those, like me, always come back in. When you're in, you need a purpose, you need a story, you need to be making discoveries and perfecting skills, whether they're physical or creative or interpersonal or whatever. Humans are wired that way. Look at any baby learning to crawl and walk and handle a spoon. That's how humans are different from other species. Without that personal ongoing evolution, they begin to stagnate, which is slow death. But for those that don't do out-of-body — which many don't, because even after the shift we're still human, we still focus our intentions and abilities into specific areas — well, technology had taken what we can see in detail out beyond the solar system, and what we can hear from one side of the planet to the other in less than a second, so why shouldn't technology be able to counteract gravity and transfer power without cables and capture remote viewing directly from the viewer. So the technology kept advancing, and that was giving purpose to people like Jeely.

I love my brother. So much. His consciousness is as expanded as anyone's on the planet. He is the essence of the divine masculine. Kind, protective, forward-thinking, able to organize creative solutions when something needs improvement, respectful of everyone's contributions, gentle, strong, willing to be seen for exactly who he is and what he's feeling. But he can't do out-of-body at will. He can do it when he's not thinking about it — or at least he did once — but he loves using his mind. And why not. He loves accumulating knowledge, unraveling mysteries, putting the pieces of the puzzle together.

So when I told him what I was "learning" from joining my light body to that of a snow leopard or a mango tree or a storm, he got excited about figuring out how to make it possible for me to share my experiences with him. He was in it for the learning — never guessed he'd be taking mini-vacations! I'm not saying you don't learn. A lot. But for me it's all about the experience, the sensation, the otherness, the pure thrill of communicating with Great Mystery — oh, you are this! and this! It's like being in love with one who is always surprising you and offering you yet another gift of appreciation. Funny, that. How I feel appreciated for being open to experiencing even more.

Or that's what I've grown into, anyway. It didn't start out like that. My earliest out-of-body's were to escape. Every time the man whose sperm contributed to our physical existence — it was hard for me to put him into the category of parent — every time he took his miserableness out on the little brother I loved more than anyone in the world, I felt it double. I felt the pain his poor little body was crying out against, and I felt my heart being torn and stabbed. Since there was nothing I could do to stop it, I just left. Lifted out. At first only up through the ceiling and above the house. Then up over the town. I was one of those earthbound astral entities suspended in purgatory, but that was better than what I was escaping from.

For the longest time I refused to even think about that man. Now, of course, I can only love the soul who agreed to play the role of male parent to me and Jeely. He went through so much pain himself — unbelievable pain, before and after — in order to set us up to do what we'd incarnated to do during the shift. How much love did it take for him to do that for us?

Anyway, eventually I found out that I could visit other places beyond our part of the country. Jeely assumed, when we started transmitting and recording, that some of those early desk-holograms were memories from books I'd read. I didn't correct him. I didn't want to tell him why, or how, didn't want to go back there. No need. When you get the big picture, all the puzzle pieces fit. And you know that eventually, whether it takes lifetimes or eons, everyone gets the big picture.

Anyway, before Louisa came along, I'd been out-of-body so much — got addicted, in a way, even just my mama's emotional pain was sometimes too much for me — that my poor physical body was suffering the consequences.

When Louisa gave me the bowl and spoon, that was the first time I left the astral plane and met Great Mystery. Love at first sight! I don't know how long it lasted, seemed like hours, days, of lusciousness and freedom. In the presence of Great Mystery, everything is full of love and light. Nothing needs to be questioned or understood or judged. It's all about experiments and choices and explorations. Each projection of Great Mystery — each human being, animal, plant, avatar, star — is Great Mystery's way of discovering and experiencing Itself.

So some of us are sending back the message, this hurts too much, we need change here, or it's okay for this to hurt because I can make good use of it, or this is super wonderful so let's do more! And without any single one of us, Great Mystery would be missing that unique experience. So I'm a gift to Great Mystery. It took me a while to come to that.

Of course there's an infinite measure more to it than what we in human form can offer. All those interfacing influences, the cycles of change, the ricocheting of information among all the worlds within all the galaxies… see what I mean? Stupendous!

So, anyway, this whole new sphere opened up for me. And with the changes in my mother and my brother after our summer with Louisa, I wanted to take care of my physical body, so I was choosing carefully when to leave and where to go. And that's when I discovered I could blend myself into a kangaroo or a chameleon.

Sharing those adventures with Jeely — getting him to take time away from advocating and implementing necessary adjustments to the social structure — I mean, my brother is either out there doing something for someone or for the community, or he's in his house living like a monk — it has been such a joy for me to engage him in some fun! We both benefit.

I've been left with a lot of time on my own, though, to explore even further than what it's like to be another sensate aspect of Great Mystery. I discovered that I could make a difference. The first time was when we visited Louisa and her father in the hospital. I could feel the love intensifying through us, quickening the process, like a laser beam of intention. What a rush! We had a desire to know something, and there we were, at the moment of the answer. Time travelers! Another explosion for me into the next larger sphere. That's what this love is like. The initial entry into a new realm is staggeringly beautiful, and then you get to explore it for however long you want to, and eventually you wonder how else you can get to know each other, you and Great Mystery, and then, wow, another spherical bubble dissolves and another arena of play is revealed. Don't you just love it?

So I'm coming back around to the technology thing. The technology is like the silver bowl — it's a reminder, a tool for focusing intention. But it's not what causes external changes. It resets the mind to expand itself. Reality is totally malleable. Mind is the conduit for power. Love is the power itself. Love can bypass a single mind's intentions, or a single mind can align itself with love, and they can work together. As soon as I absorbed this truth, a whole new way of playing opened up for me.

By the time I made the recording of her mother for Louisa, I knew that using the technology to put her into moments that would elicit love from her would reset her mind. It would let her get out of her own way, allow her to react spontaneously, leave ordinary reality behind — because that was the only way she could express the love that wanted to come alive between herself and her mother. She thought she missed her mother's love, but even more, she missed loving her mother. What daughter wouldn't want her mother to be loved? What daughter wouldn't see to it that her mother felt loved, if she could make that happen?

So how did I know that Louisa would someday have the opportunity to make use of that recording? You can see where I'm going with this, right? I didn't record everything I was finding out. Which means that my sweet beautiful brother has no idea that he isn't the only spy in the family!

You don't have to do out-of-body, though, to know what's going on for someone else. I didn't have to come across the postcard from Louisa that he'd saved to know that there was a hole in his soul. I'm not into interfering, just looking to see what wants to happen. So, what wanted to happen? I needed more information. So I did some exploring through time. And there they were, together, in the future, dancing! Beautiful. I mean, really, really beautiful. On so many levels. Great Mystery was doing it again! Making me so happy!

I'm loving it here, but sometimes I feel so ready to take the next leap into whatever happens when you no longer feel the urge to return to your body, because you've run out of purpose and story.

The only thing holding me back is Jeely. So I'm thinking I'll record my departure <u>before</u> I lift out for the last time. Share it with him. So he'll experience it with me and know where I'm going. You can't miss someone you love when you know they are incredibly happy. Besides, a connection of love never dies. Imagine that! Infinite and eternal love!

Anyway, I thought you'd like to know all that before you continue reading…

Louisa

I can hear Jeely in the kitchen. Smells like he's baking something.

Has it been six months already since Jeely and I found one another? Has it been only six months? Time is so elastic! How is it possible that we still just can't get enough of one another?

On our second morning, I was in such a state of euphoria, having been unable to sleep until almost daylight, not wanting to miss a minute of being able to watch the man I love sleeping the sleep of the fully satisfied, that I came into the kitchen, where Jeely was busy at the counter, without my usual sluggish cloudiness. I wrapped my arms around him as he chopped fruits and veggies for the blender, and I could feel him smiling right through his whole body.

"Jeely," I said as I poured myself a mug of tea from the urn. I just wanted to say his name, but since it sounded like I was going to ask a question, I came up with one. "Why did your mother name you Jeely?"

"I think she meant to call me Jelly, but it got misspelled on the birth certificate," he said, not turning around.

I sat down at the table. "Jelly?" I said, a hint of glee in my voice.

"Do not even go there," he warned. I could hear the chopping continue. "Loozey."

"Loozey? I haven't been called that since I lived with my Uncle Rim. Hey! How did you know about that?"

"Spies will not reveal their secrets even under severe duress."

"Oh, I have my ways."

"You most certainly do, woman." He stopped what he was doing and leaned over me from behind, put his arms around me and made some beasty noises into my neck. I stretched my arms up around him, luxuriating in delicious memories, not one iota reluctant to create more such.

He turned on the blender, poured us each a glass of thick green juice, and brought them to the table. "You most certainly do." He took my face in his hands and looked at me. How can so much love be passed through the air without anything but the light in one's eyes transferring it? It was as if we were both saying, *I see you, all the way into your beautiful soul*, and meaning even so much more than that.

Finally sitting down at the table, he asked, "Whatever happened to your uncle, anyway?"

"Uncle Rim." I had to smile at the memory. "He asked me again in the taxi what had happened at the hospital, and again I told him I couldn't explain it. But I knew then what I had to do. So when I saw the miniature ukulele on a keychain next to the rack of postcards in the airport, I bought it. I waited until we were in the air. He was sitting by the window, and I was in the middle, with my dad in the aisle seat, all three of us in a state of heightened excitement. I gave him the keychain and then closed my hands around his. 'Uncle Rim. This ukulele is like you.' His eyebrows went up. 'You make cheerful music for everyone around you. You're upbeat and fun and different, and you hold the keys, you hold all the keys to everything, and I love you. I love you so much.' I looked into his expanded self, and it happened, right there in the plane. He got it." I'm remembering that look of awe and confusion and comprehension on his youthful face. "And you know what, Jeely? Everyone on the plane was so calm for the whole trip. None of the babies cried. Maybe they were all relaxed from their Hawaiian vacation…" I shrugged. "Anyway, a few months later he found a really wonderful woman. Perfect match. They had four kids. All boys."

"Louisa! You kept passing it on, didn't you."

"I did. Mm, Jeely, this is delicious." I could feel my body loving this green drink. "Did you — keep passing it on?"

"I'm glad you like it." He drank down half of his own. "I did, to my mother. And then once more, when Karen came back from Australia. But you didn't stop with your uncle."

"It was part of my calling." I finished my drink.

"So, you have cousins. Do you still stay in touch?"

"We grew up together, more or less. I was fourteen years older than the oldest, so I was more like an aunt to them. Yes, we still get together for family reunions."

"And you got married and had children."

"Mm-hm. My son and his wife and their children come to the reunions when they can. Addie is my daughter's girl. She's the oldest of my grandchildren." I looked down into my empty glass. "My husband died about twenty years ago."

"And your father?"

"He remarried. By the time my two step-sisters came along, I was off to college, so I didn't get to see too much of them. But he was happy." I didn't see the need to go into why Clay had never contacted the aunts that Samantha had sent postcards to. At the age of twenty-two, he'd simply never thought to get their address from her as they were traveling. He'd never met them, so they were nothing more than vague background figures in the wake of a devastation, and he had an infant to take care of. Our talks about that past were brief, and I was okay with that.

That was all that Jeely asked about my past. Other details occasionally came up during the reunion we attended three months ago, but for the most part, all of us were very much in the present. Of course everyone thinks the world of Jeely. How could they not? So he has a large family now, if he wants one.

I go into the bathroom before heading for the kitchen to find out what that delicious smell is, and I see an almost youthful woman in the mirror. Or maybe I'm just not minding the wrinkling and pouching because I'm loving all those signs, of life being lived, on another face. Well, as if anything so trivial even matters when your whole existence is overflowing with magic.

I feel so at home here now. Who would have guessed? It didn't take even a month for us to decide that I'd let my house go ahead and draw in its new occupants, and move in here. Jeely welcomed all my plants and gave me the freedom to change anything I wanted to. We moved his couch into the theater and mine into the living room, along with some of my earth-tone throws. We kept my coffee table instead of his. The shelves of mini-discs and the desk and curtains remain as essential parts of Jeely's work. Strangely enough, it all blends together somehow.

Sometimes I just want to burst out of my skin with happiness.

Now there's a thought.

We could do that. Together. He's done it once. I've done it once. We could do it together. Why not?

I come into the kitchen. When he decided to update it from its older version, he had a similar penchant for the brushed-metal look that used to dominate the living room. Can hardly tell now, as my plants have jungle-ized the room, hanging from the ceiling, cascading down the shelved stands Jeely built for them. I wanted him to keep as much counter space as he needed, since he likes concocting things in the kitchen, but after he'd seen what my kitchen looked like, he wouldn't let me relegate a single potted plant to his back yard garden. "These are your friends," he reminded me when I said we didn't have to find room for all of them. "You want your friends close by." He was right. And they have flourished in here, blossoming even in the cooler months. The spotted begonia is drooping with pink clusters. The gardenias smell heavenly. And so does whatever Jeely is pulling out of the oven.

"Don't look," he says. "Go away." He sounds like a three-year-old up to some mischief.

"Why?"

"Because."

I open the back door and step into the sunshine and mild air, stretch my arms high, breathe in the glory of the morning, and send this overflow of elation and affection out into the world. What a beautiful world it is, full of peace and cooperation among all living things, at long last. I'm halfway through admiring out loud each individual tea bush and herb and vegetable plant when Jeely calls through the window, "Okay, you can come in now."

A miniature carrot cake sits on the table. Two oversized birthday candles have been stuck into the middle of it, so close together, with their wicks purposely bent inward, that they seem to have but one flame.

"It's our six-month anniversary," he says, and I see that ten-year-old boy shining through that sixty-two-year-old face, the one who couldn't believe my eleven-year-old self was inviting him to dinner, the one who laughed with such liberated exuberance in the bus that he infected all the other passengers. I'm flooded with incredulous gratitude. I kiss his cheeks, his eyelids, his temples, his smile. He clicks the remote that I hadn't noticed he was holding, and as he puts it down on the counter, music wafts in from the living room. He takes me in his arms and slowly sways me to the lilting rhythm and light melody. Have I heard these lyrics before? "You came along, just like a song, and brightened my day... and now I can't smile without you..."

I melt into him, my heart overflows into his...

...and we are awash in a golden-white, rainbow-flecked light, slowly swaying in our embrace, and at the same time holding hands as we walk through a space filled with the most delicate blend of music and fragrances and balmy caressing breezes. There's a figure emerging from the misty light ahead. My heart bursts open. I recognize her adult self from the photos Jeely has shown me. Julie approaches us, and Jeely breaks away to offer both his hands to her, which she takes, beaming love at him. Then she reaches her hands toward me, and I am looking into the eyes of an angel, a saint, a sweet, gentle, all-knowing goddess. All three of us join hands. A circle of pink and gold and aqua mist, entwined with visible ripples of sparkling music, wafts around us. "Don't you just love Great Mystery!" she laughs, beaming again at Jeely with incomprehensibly infinite love, the same then at me, and as she fades away, so do we, finding ourselves in the kitchen again, still dancing slowly as the song ends.

We pull apart, just enough for me to see the stunned question on Jeely's face. My mirroring expression is my answer. Yes. That did just happen.

When I had the thought in the bathroom that we could do this, I didn't know it would happen so soon, so spontaneously. I didn't know it could happen while our physical bodies were in motion. And I didn't know that for a moment the three of us would be together again.

He pulls me close again, and we hold one another for long minutes, still floating, still absorbing into the spaces among the subatomic particles within us this divinely buoyant, jubilant sensation of oneness with Great Mystery itself.

When we turn to the kitchen table, the candles are still burning. Jeely opens a drawer and comes back with a third candle. He lights it from the single flame and sticks it into the cake a half-inch away from the other two.

I love this man so much.

* * *

We're in the garden, watering the plants, when Jeely asks me, "Louisa, when did you move into your house?"

I know he means the one I no longer consider mine. I think back. "A year and a half ago?"

"I thought maybe it was about then."

I wait to hear more.

"About a year before Addie brought you to my door, I started having an irresistible urge to find you, to see what was going on in your life. You'd shown up fairly frequently in my thoughts before, but this was an insistent longing. Of course — because you were so close!"

"And I'd had an irresistible urge to move back to this area," I remember. Things had happened, other things had fallen into place, and the move was smooth and easy. I didn't know why, though. I'd driven past the two houses I'd once known on Sycamore Street, but the Jamesons' house was utterly unfamiliar, and Maudie and Mary Etta's was obviously occupied. I settled in, made friends, and got caught up in my new life, never suspecting that I'd moved back to the west coast for an even greater life-altering reason.

"I went searching online, but I didn't know your married name. The only thing I found was a high school group photo from way back. Louisa Bylander, senior class of whatever year that was."

"Oh, how awful! I was such an awkward teenager!"

"I don't know," he says, spraying a fine mist over the herbs, "considering how homely you were as a fifth-grader, I thought you'd turned out to be quite pretty." He twists the nozzle on the hose to stop the flow.

I open my mouth in disbelief and delight. He called me homely! "Well, at least I wasn't cross-eyed like the kid I sat next to in class."

At the sound of some strange guttural grunts, I turn to see him lumbering toward me, his eyes crossed, clawed fingers raised, and with a tiny shriek, I unintentionally swing my hose around at him.

Oops.

Drenched to the bone, white hair plastered to his head, droplets hanging from his eyebrows, he shakes his head slowly. "Oh, you are *so* in for it now, woman."

I am screeching with laughter, trying to duck, as he slings his wet arms around me, but I can't resist, have no desire to resist, when he draws me close and smears his wet cheeks all over mine.

Addie

As always happens when you're in alignment and trust the way things are unfolding, the timing of everything that happened six months ago was perfect for me. If I'd heard the stories of their childhood from Gran and Jeely without certain other events having taken place first, I might have longed for some childhood friend of my own to find me, because their obvious ease with one another, even during the first week of their meeting again, seemed based on the familiarity they'd already established long ago. It was as if they'd never parted. They still seem to me to have known and loved one another for a lifetime. I suspect there's an unspoken game in progress — which of them can move the other to tears of joy or hilarity before being caught off guard by another unexpected expression of love from the other. I am in awe of their happiness.

I know now, however, because of the timing, that a mutual history is not a necessity. The familiarity was there between Carlos and me from the moment our arms touched reaching for the same avocado. It's true that we spent time catching each other up on our pasts and confirming the overlap of our ideals and interests, but those exchanges were simply embroidery on the fabric of what was unfurling between us — a mutual recognition, one that seemed to come complete with its own history.

When he told me how he'd turned that little boy's interpretation of the spilled groceries into noticing what else there was to notice about the tree and his presence, I loved hearing the story. But I already knew — he is that perceptive and thoughtful and loving a man. When I shared with him the sequence of events that resulted in my grandmother's happy reunion, he laughed with delight at the story. "That's such an amazing story, Addie. You should write it down!" he said. "I'm not surprised, though, you know? That you had such a big part in it. I have to look to see how things fit together, but you just know that they do, so you go along with whatever's happening. I'm not surprised, because it's like I knew that about you as soon as we met." Did I mention that we shared that avocado right there at the co-op?

Gran and Jeely grew up in the early years of this century, when conditioning and unresolved emotions could cloud the initial perception of another's essence. Carlos and I have been clear all along. And each story, theirs and ours, is beautiful in its own way. They continue to be so, as the four of us frequently get together, taking picnics along when we explore the coast or the mountains, going to gift-and-trade gatherings, watching the sunset from the beach.

I've discovered that I am, like Julie, a transmitter. Gran — I hear her called Louisa (as if the name itself contains a world of love) so often now that I'm tempted to think of her that way myself — Louisa found that she could move out-of-body easily, but like Jeely, her experiences didn't translate through the headpiece. I hadn't known about myself that I could do either until I'd shared a few out-of-body's in Louisa's company and then accepted Jeely's offer to try transmitting. He gives me free access to the equipment. It has been so exciting to see what I can do when I tap into other places around the world. I hadn't yet tried different times, though, when I received a phone call a few days ago that nudged me into that direction.

"Addie, this is Karen. Have you got a minute?"

"Karen! Of course."

"So sorry I haven't been in touch. Been in Australia the last six months. Just got back."

"Yes, I knew... no problem. There's been so much going on around here, I don't know if I..."

"There certainly has been! Addie, I want to thank you from the bottom of my heart for what you've done for my father."

"Oh! You're welcome. But really, I was only the agent..."

"The agent that brought a happiness into his life that I didn't even know was missing. Your grandmother has brought out sides of him I've never seen before. It's actually quite miraculous. She is wonderful! I love her! Can't wait to spend more time with her. We've only been introduced, really — I've been so busy resettling. Did you ever expect them to hit it off so well?"

"I hoped so. There's actually a long story behind it. To condense it, though — they knew one another as children. Your father never told you about that summer?"

"What summer?"

"Did you know that your aunt Julie was in a wheelchair before she turned twelve?"

"Now that you mention it, I might have been aware of that. When I came to live near my father about fifteen years ago, Julie and he were well into creating their holograms. None of us ever talked much about the past."

"Well, if you want to know something about your father and my grandmother when they were children... Karen! You've just given me an idea."

I could hear the teasing in her voice when she answered. "Oh, didn't mean to, so sorry about that!"

"The perfect inspiration! I'll tell you all about it. Everything okay in Australia?"

"Oh, yes. My mum was in a bit of a bad way, but she pulled through. She's fine now. Wouldn't have left otherwise."

"I'm glad to hear that. And I'm glad you're back. I'd love to meet up with you at some point. Share some news."

"More news? You *have* been a busy little platypus, haven't you!"

"You have no idea!"

"Right, then. Free tomorrow?"

"Come to my house. Noonish?"

"Will do. Can't wait to hear!"

Karen and I caught up with one another — how her time with her mother had gone, how I'd met Carlos — and then I filled her in on some of that childhood summer. She was delighted to hear that I'd been using Jeely's equipment, and loved the idea that I'd come up with. Later, when I took myself to their last afternoon together that summer, I knew I wanted Jeely and Louisa to be able to experience it again. And I knew that Karen would see why her father and my grandmother are so happy together.

The five of us enter the hologram theater. Karen makes herself comfortable in one of the chairs, while the rest of us settle onto the couch that has been added, Louisa snuggling with Jeely, me leaning back against Carlos.

Carlos has seen several of Julie's recordings. His favorite was experiencing himself as an Andean condor. He loved the sensation of opening his huge wings like giant fans before dropping from the edge of a cliff, feeling that rush of chilly wind across the bare skin of his face and tingling through every single downy feather in the white ruff around his neck, sensing the motion of each widespread wing feather as the current of air shifted their position in his flesh... the dip of free-fall eliminating gravity's effect on internal organs... the odd sensation of two separate visual fields combining as one on either side of the rubbery comb cresting his head… the visual acuity shifting perspective into distance and detail almost simultaneously… the stretch of immense wings catching a thermal and riding it effortlessly in spiraling circles above a broad pale-green and rock-speckled valley. He was so stunned, so exhilarated, that when it was over, he sat in silence for several minutes. And then he stood up and began circling the room with his arms stretched wide, a high piercing cry turning into laughter. He had us all grinning.

He has joined Louisa in advocating distribution of at least the animal recordings to a wider audience. He and Jeely have been discussing how that might happen.

I check to see that everyone's relaxed, with a special acknowledgment to Karen, as she's the only one who knows what I've prepared. She secretly rubs her hands together in anticipation. I click the remote, knowing that the scene we are about to view will also ignite our other senses, so that we'll feel as if we are right there with the afternoon sun warming our shoulders, smelling that salty ocean air, hearing the background sound of waves. We're at the pier, as it looked fifty years ago. We've entered the past.

A wheelchair is parked at the juncture of the wooden planks that lead out over the sparkling water and the top of a sandy slope leading down to the beach below. Julie, standing in front of the wheelchair, her ginger hair being blown gently across her face by the breeze, can't take her eyes off the expanse of ocean and sky before her. She is slender, graceful, rosy-cheeked, wearing a pretty orange and yellow printed dress that ripples around her sturdy legs.

"Here, Jeely, hold this," Louisa says, pulling a paper bag from her backpack and handing it to him. Her lavender tee-shirt flutters across the top of her jeans as she sets the backpack onto the seat of the wheelchair and rummages around in it, looking for something.

Jeely puts whatever he's examining into one of the many pockets of his khaki pants, takes the bag, and peeks inside. The way his eyes light up at what he sees is matched by the way the sun catches the shades of gold and orange in his rustling curls. He glances at his sister, the excitement evident on his freckled face, and then at Louisa, to see what else she's brought along for this adventure.

"Julie, these are for you." Holding a pair of bright neon-pink heart-shaped sunglasses in one hand, Louisa is pushing things aside within the backpack with her other hand.

Julie turns away from her appreciation of the broad horizon to see what she's being offered, and as she accepts the absurd glasses, her smile dimples her cheeks. Louisa turns to see how the glasses look on her friend and is rewarded with a flourish of theatrical exaggeration as Julie raises her pinky fingers, settles the glasses on her nose with careful finesse, lifts her chin into the air, and purses her lips prudishly. "I say. Rather! Indeed! Quite!"

"Perfect!" Louisa grins. "And these are yours, Jeely."

He's handed a pair of state trooper shades, the kind that reflects a purple-blue sheen that completely hides his eyes. He puts them on and turns his head slowly from side to side. Through downturned lips, attempting to lower his voice menacingly, he utters a warning. "I don't want no funny business from nobody." Louisa high-fives him, grinning at his willingness to get into the spirit of things. She puts on the last pair, fake-diamond-studded cat's-eyes glasses, purple with green lenses and up-sweeping corners, that make her look like a secretary with a terribly unfortunate sense of fashion. Jeely takes one look at her and practically chokes on his attempt not to laugh. Louisa, her mouth an open square of indignation, gives him a shove.

"Now, now, children," Julie says in a falsetto voice, "we don't want no funny business from nobody." She too is having a hard time not laughing at the transformation of her friend from familiar to ridiculous.

Her admonition comes too late, as Jeely has already shoved Louisa in return, causing her to nearly fall backwards down the slope. In an attempt to save her, he grabs for her but is pulled forward a step by her momentum and tumbles down on top of her. The two of them are lying in a heap. A moment of stunned silence is broken by an outburst of laughter, Louisa's horsey gasps accompanied by Jeely's uncontrollably gleeful giggles. Jeely tries to get up, but one look at Louisa in those ridiculous glasses and he collapses on top of her again, helpless squeals of laughter convulsing him. Julie by now has her hands on her knees, overcome with hilarity.

"Get offa me, you leprechaun!" Louisa yells, kicking her feet and gasping with laughter.

Julie is bent over double laughing, and when her heart-shaped glasses drop off her face, she finds this, too, utterly hilarious, and points at them, unable to speak.

Finally Jeely manages to roll himself off Louisa. He gives her a hand to help her up and brushes the sand off her back. When he sees what Julie is pointing at, he picks up her fallen glasses and hands them to her, and then removes his own to wipe the tears from his eyes. Louisa shoves him again, but gently, and he just grins as he replaces his state trooper blues.

"Jeely, where's the paper bag I gave you?"

He looks around, spots it, and hands it to her.

She reaches into it and pulls out a gold cardboard crown sporting plastic rubies. "For you, your royal highness," she says, smiling as she hands it to him. His eyebrows go up as he takes it. He perches it on his head, but she adjusts it for him with both hands. "There."

Satisfied with the effect, she reaches into the bag again, retrieving a wide-brimmed floppy straw hat with paper flowers clustered around the band. "And for your ladyship," she says, placing the hat on Julie's softly blowing hair. Julie smiles at her, her eyes almost invisible behind the heart-shaped glasses, her dimples conveying her pleasure. Louisa smiles back, affection emanating from the way she settles the hat at a slightly sideways tilt.

"And for me…" She's about to pull her own headgear out of the bag when she changes her mind. "Jeely, if you laugh at me…" Her hand on her hip is accompanied by a fierce scowl.

Jeely looks around. "I think he left. Nobody here but us royal highnesses."

She narrows her eyes, visible behind the pale green of her secretarial cat's-eyes glasses, and stares at him as she reaches again into the bag. He crosses his arms over his chest, lifts his chin, and stands with his feet apart, the very image of masculine self-control. She pulls out a gray furry cap with protruding donkey ears and watches him, challenging him with a tight-lipped glare, as she pulls it down over her head. He slowly turns around, facing away from her, and crumples over his snorts and giggles.

Julie starts to titter. Louisa spins and points at her accusingly, her donkey ears flopping above her purple glasses, and Julie loses it. Jeely is collapsing to his knees and holding his stomach, laughing till it hurts.

Another round of gasping hilarity, renewed each time they look at one another, leaves them all catching their breath, but finally they're ready to descend the slope. After they remove their shoes, Jeely and Louisa each take one of Julie's hands, and the trio maneuvers their way down to the beach — the king in his state-trooper blues, the elegant lady in her heart-shaped glasses, and the donkey-eared secretary. They let go of one's another's hands only when Julie experiences her first rush of foamy salt water curling around her bare feet. She chirps with delight, dancing backwards, stepping forward and sideways. Jeely is splashing along the water line, running zig-zag, spinning around, feeling so wild and free that he removes his crown, cocks his arm, and sails the golden cylinder frisbee-style out over the waves, sunlight glinting off the rubies as it spins. The girls watch it fly, and suddenly Julie does the same, winging her straw hat out to sea, leaving her arm in the air as it soars and is caught by the wind and carried even further than the now vanished crown.

Louisa reaches up to do the same, but Julie puts her hand on her arm. "Are you sure, Louisa? It's a really great hat."

Louisa takes it off and hands it to Julie. "It *is* a really great hat! You keep it."

"Okay." Julie stuffs it into the pocket of her dress.

Each of them lifts her pair of sunglasses off her face and pushes her hair back with it as they stand gazing at the sunlight sparkling on the waves.

"Thank you, Louisa. Thank you for all of this," Julie says, looking around at the stretch of beach to the north, the seawater splashing around the posts beneath the pier. "Thank you for everything." She turns and looks at her friend. "I love you."

"I love you, too, Julie."

The girls hug, an orange and yellow dress wafting in the breeze against a pair of jeans and lavender tee-shirt, bare arms around each other's shoulders. When they pull apart, Jeely is standing next to them. He has removed his sunglasses and tucked them into his shirt pocket.

"I love you, Jeely," Louisa says, turning to him and smiling into his eyes before she hugs him.

He hugs her back. "I love you too, Louisa."

I don't mind the silence when the hologram ends. I was filled with emotion myself when I retrieved the memory from the field. I don't have to wonder what the two people on the couch beside me are feeling. Carlos kisses my cheek in silence. Karen has her hands in prayer position in front of her mouth. Her eyes are glistening.

And then I hear Louisa say softly, "I love you, Jeely."

"I love you too, Louisa."

"I've always loved you!"

"I've always known that."

* * *

I've gained a new confidence. My recording of their last outing is as accurate as Jeely and Louisa themselves remember it. I really did travel back in time to witness, and to bring to life again, a moment that appears no longer to exist — but still does! What a thrill it was to have given such a gift, to the two of them, and to Carlos, who loves them both as much as I do, and especially to Karen, whose understanding of her father has deepened immeasurably.

As we all emerged from the private theater and returned to the living room, Jeely went to his desk and buzzed open the drawer that holds the little silver spoon in its bowl. He took from it something I recognized, although I hadn't seen it before: a small medicine bag. He opened it up in front of the rest of us and let spill into his hand a plastic ruby.

It was Karen who exclaimed, "You kept one! Dad! I couldn't believe you'd just throw that crown into the sea. It had to have meant so much to you to be crowned king by one of the two people you loved most in the world! You sly old dingo, you! I never saw when you removed this." She took the fake gem and examined it.

"I felt it come off in my hand just before I sent the crown out to sea. It was almost as if I could not throw away all of what I'd been given. It felt like a sign — no, an instruction. Keep this. Remember this." He took the ruby back and smiled at Louisa, and then at each one of us. "At the time, yes, Karen, that crown was given to me by one of the two people I loved most in the world. But then along came a third." He shook the medicine bag again, and out fell a perfect little baby tooth.

"Dad!" Karen's eyes overflowed as she hugged the father she had been forced to leave when she was a little girl. "You've had so much loss in your life."

"And now look at it! Full of the people I love!"

Carlos stepped up to him and threw his arms around him. He couldn't speak, but the length of his embrace spoke for him. We three women watched with so much gratitude and respect pouring from our hearts at the sight of these two beautiful men acknowledging their love for one another... that for a moment the room was filled with light.

* * *

As much as Carlos is right about my inclination to trust my intuition and flow with the magic, I do like following the trail of events back through time to consider the influences and connections that were occurring beyond my personal input and intake. There's something about the path of development that catches my interest. So, to satisfy my own curiosity, and because I now have the confidence, I want to try an experiment.

Carlos and Jeely are planning a tour. In the month since I showed them that hologram, the four of us have chosen several of Julie's recordings to project at various theaters around the world. I'm so excited! But for the moment, while the men are contacting prospective hosts and Louisa is sharing specific holograms with people of her generation whom she believes will be expanded beyond their emotional residue, I've retreated to the attic of my house — our house, Carlos' and mine. We both love this spacious room with its simple furnishings, two recliners, two small tables with lamps, a couple of mats on the floor. It's here that we often spend time, together or alone, reading, thinking, meditating, doing yoga.

I make myself comfortable on one of the chairs and close my eyes so I can formulate my intention. Even though Maudie's letter described those years, I want to go back to the second and third decades of our century, when the polarity between life-threatening and life-enhancing influences was peaking and then gradually shifting the balance into favoring the latter. I want to see it for myself. I'm not quite sure how to do this, because instead of taking my awareness to one specific time or place, I want to tap into an overall view of both sides. Oh. Maybe that's all I have to intend. Maybe I need simply to remain open to the impressions that will present themselves in order to give me an overview of how those bent on self- and world-destruction were being counteracted by those who were riding the rising tide of an indomitable life force toward an inevitable evolutionary quantum leap.

Okay, my intention: an overview of conflicting human influences in the second and third decades of this century.

Deep breath. Relax. Let go of personal awareness. Move outward spherically, into ever-expanding spheres... planet Earth within... solar system within... galaxy within... galaxy clusters within... dissolving all sense of the dimensions of space and time into one all-inclusive infinite whole... the ultimate peace...

...and refocusing... narrowing down into galaxy... solar system... planet Earth... into a point of perception...

...inundation of overlapping images and sounds...

...recalibrate into images alone...

...recalibrate into clusters of images and their meanings.

Whew. What I'm confronted with first is the small but power-holding number of world leaders who are so delusional, so outwardly arrogant and self-righteous in compensation for their inner terror, confusion, rage, and loneliness, so shut down on their own humanity that they are willing to fight one another with planet-destroying missiles and bombs.

In the next layer beneath them are men who believe that the amount of material wealth they have accumulated through corrupt and inhumane actions actually confers upon them the regal privilege of ignoring how they enslave, deceive, pollute, annihilate, demean, and suck the life force out of anyone they consider beneath them.

Okay, this is hard.

The military. This is really hard. The killing, raping, torturing, dismembering... the invention of ever crueler and more effective means of denying life to others... the seduction of innocent men into fighting for what they believe is a worthy cause and don't have a clue that the only presumed benefit goes to the ones behind the desks. Thousands of lives wasted. Oh, what horror, what grief, what pointless sacrifices.

Beneath this layer are the institutional people who have succumbed to the distorted beliefs promoted by medieval rulers and propagated by those running the modern corporate world. They believe themselves to be serving a good purpose, because they don't question the methods set up before them. These medical people, religious leaders, teachers, law-makers and law-enforcers, government officials and tax collectors, bankers and insurance agents and production managers, they have good intentions based on false premises. Oh how that must weigh on the souls of those who turn to every form of escape but the real one.

There's another layer below that one. These are the walking dead, the bulldozers of forests, the raisers of animals in deplorable conditions, the child-labor factory bosses, the ringleaders of the sexual exploitation of women and children, the organized criminals, menacing, stealing, murdering. They destroy what is outside of them, and in so doing, destroy themselves.

And the barely breathing dead, the victims of all that weight of all those layers above them. They are suffocating. They are numb. They no longer care. They might as well be in their graves.

I shudder, and proceed, altering my intention. Before I am shown the opposite of what I've just seen, I want to know if there is a neutral zone.

I am relieved to be shown that such a large portion of humanity is simply doing their best to provide for and nurture their families, participating in their communities, promoting creative endeavors, exchanging personal and global information on their version of the internet, living simple lives in villages, more complex ones in cities, with open hearts and open minds.

There's a subtle undercurrent of fear, but the courage and determination to remain hopeful, to help one another, to combat outmoded ways of viewing those who are different from themselves, to bring forth the best that their ancestors left them, these qualities of so many human beings, billions of them, warm my heart and gladden my soul.

Okay, I am more than ready to be shown the concentrated efforts of those inspired by their own best-envisioned future.

The images again inundate my awareness to such a degree that I have to slow them down and take them in a few at a time. There are no layers here, the movement forward is global at a grassroots level, harmonious, interactive, mutually respectful and encouraging and cooperative. Oh, it's good to see this gestation period, when our present world was already shaping itself. So many innovations in so many fields.

Environment is forefront in the minds of many. I'm seeing countries agreeing to reduce pollution and focus on sustainability; innovators cleaning up the ocean with garbage-eating trawlers; sunlight being used to provide energy even in remote areas; plastic being recycled into highways; trees being cloned to give new life to those fallen; forests being replanted by dropping seedlings from planes; wind turbines, from tall towers to small tree-sized sculptures erected in parks to generate local electricity to personal-sized ones that collect water from the air in arid locations; an island of wind, water, and sun devices in the Baltic Sea providing clean energy to five countries; city populations growing their food on their rooftops and along their sidewalks and in their empty lots; eco-friendly homes replacing slums; genetically modified food companies being defeated; organic farming increasing; species of animals being rescued from extinction; animals being provided with safer, wider roaming areas. In some ways, these all look like baby steps from here, but baby steps lead to giant steps, and transformation becomes exponential.

What a surge of intentions and experiments is going on here — thousands all over the world are frequently gathering to pray for peace, to celebrate love, to reconstruct social exchanges, to demonstrate solidarity against outmoded cultural practices, to protest unconscious behavior. Information is being shared globally, reaching hundreds of millions, through retreats, conferences, documentaries, through the internet, about alternative medicinal practices, self-healing, self-sovereignty, self-awareness. Innumerable books about the upcoming shift! Uncountable videos that offer meditations, binaural beats, solfeggio tones, healing music to release the old paradigm, to clear blockages, to balance the inner divine feminine and masculine aspects of oneself. There is a couple in India giving

Oneness Blessings; each person they touch, and then teach to touch others, is healed or enhanced in some way, physically, emotionally, intuitively, spiritually; I see them already having reached millions of people. Reports of near-death experiences, an upsurge of interest in shamanic journeying, a heightened respect for indigenous peoples' wisdom, all of these are in a burgeoning state of growth.

There are experiments in revising local economy — time banks, hour exchanges, locally printed money; community focus is distancing neighborhoods from being governed by politicians thousands of miles away, and returning them to taking care of each other. The seeds are being planted right here.

And the young people! The decrease in youth problems has nothing to do with enforced laws and everything to do with the young people themselves. As those attached to old prejudices, fears, and ignorance die out, and they are doing so, the young people are coming up behind them more than tolerant, they're appreciative. They're more aware, less easily manipulated, able to see through the false facades of the old order. They're arriving with new abilities, changing the ways they need to be taught, teaching their teachers to become more human. What talents, what authenticity, what insistence on a better world. This is the generation that opens the floodgates! My heart is soaring!

It's like watching the snow melt after a long, dark, hard winter as the first green shoots appear. It's like a long night's fever breaking with the dawn.

I love the time I'm returning to, where all of these beginnings have matured into this creative, harmonious global family. There is still some healing that needs to happen, there are still more ways to share what we have and what we learn...

...and that thought snaps me back.

Jeely

I no longer recognize my life. Eight months ago I was content. Master of my own private time. Willing to offer assistance when needed. I thought I'd done all my traveling, both physically and via holograms. I thought the practice of tai chi and runs along the beach were as satisfying as I needed any activity to be. I thought the absence of the fear of death and the occasional longing and the excitement of learning new things comprised the totality of my emotional landscape. I thought meeting occasionally with friends or with my daughter for conversation was more than enough of a social life. I thought welcoming my new neighbor in for tea was going to be just another pleasant exchange before getting back to my comfortable routine.

Could anyone be happier about being so wrong?

This trip to New Zealand — my first — has already been a chain of unprecedented experiences. Traveling with Louisa is a shifting spectrum of pure happiness, delicious laughter, intriguing exploration of ideas, physical ecstasy, profound comfort, and simple ease. Having Addie and Carlos along revitalizes and entertains us no end. Knowing that Karen is taking care of our homes and gardens is an extra bonus.

And here we are on the verge of yet another completely new adventure.

This theater is so much larger than the little one at home — maybe 40 meters in diameter, with seven tiers of seats surrounding an open circle in the middle. I've been asked to introduce the four holograms we've chosen for our first public presentation, and it's with a new level of excitement and anticipation that I address the filled auditorium, almost 200 people, mostly adults, a few teenagers. I explain the level of proficiency attained by my sister in her transmission of the experiences we are all about to share, and as I speak of what Julie accomplished in her lifetime, I can almost feel her presence, which makes it difficult to keep my voice even.

"As you'll have noticed," I conclude, "I've given very little information in the program about the holograms you'll be experiencing, other than the titles. I'd like to say about the first one, *Soar*, that the subject was once an endangered species and is now, as are they all, thriving in its native habitat. The next two, *Energy* and *Flow*, don't really need any words of introduction, as they will be self-evident. There'll be about a five-minute break in between each. You're free to remain silent, or not, as you choose. Before we project the last one, I'll be giving you an explanation of its origin and the reason it was created." I turn to include as many people in the audience as I can. "Thank you for welcoming me and my family. May this experience be as much of a gift to you as it has been to us."

I bow my head to the applause, and when, surprisingly, it continues, I bring my hands together in a greeting of namaste. I am moved almost to tears by everyone in the theater silencing their applause in order to return the gesture. And now the tears do surface as they all hold their palms up toward me in a blessing that lasts for a full thirty seconds. I turn slowly in a full circle, receiving smiles from so many beautiful faces of all shades and shapes, receiving all of this acknowledgement. For Julie.

I return to my seat next to Louisa, who beams at me as she intertwines her fingers with mine, and catch the proud gleam in the eyes of Addie and Carlos. As I take a deep breath, I feel a communal resonance. The entire audience knows to breathe, to become centered and calm. So beautiful.

It was Carlos who suggested we start with the condor. He wanted as many people as possible to know this sensation of pure freedom, soaring high above a deep valley, between rippled foothills and craggy mountains. We share with everyone in the theater fifteen minutes of knowing what it feels like to have wings. It was a good choice. The whole audience is silent when it fades out, basking in what they didn't know to expect, not just a visual rendition of flight, but flight itself, the silent mind of the bird, the direct assimilation of every bit of information absorbed from its own body and from the wind and from the earth below.

Louisa squeezes my hand. Her tears of joy reflect my own.

The four of us contemplated several choices for the second hologram, including the recordings Julie made of her alignment with the consciousness of a whale, an octopus, and a cuttlefish. In the end we agreed that while they are all fascinating, for the first-timers in this audience we'd like to offer something easier to relate to. So for the next fourteen minutes everyone in the theater has the opportunity to experience being a dolphin.

There is such a rush of exhilaration in the bursting forth from the sea into the air, such an ecstatic explosion of the life force itself in the speed and power summoned in order to exit one density and enter another, again and again, leaping and twisting, arcing through the air in synchronicity with a companion, that our heartbeats seem to increase as seawater streams along our bodies, our breathing seems to align with the rhythm. As in shamanic journeying, Julie managed somehow to reproduce the sensations while not actually requiring the body to undergo the differences. Because she was out-of-body herself, we in the audience have the privilege of shape-shifting without actual physical consequences.

As the hologram ends, a multi-voiced cheer arises from the tiers of seats, whoops and cries and whistles, shouts of joy accompanying a long round of excited applause. This thrilled reaction shouldn't surprise me. But it does. Louisa was right. Carlos was right. It was unfair of me to keep Julie's gift from the world. I reach across Louisa to rest my hand on Carlos' shoulder. He turns to me, his eyes glistening, and offers me a high five. Addie is grinning. Louisa is beaming. I am grateful beyond measure.

The audience makes good use of this break between holograms. People are talking, exclaiming, comparing notes, discussing both experiences, and from what I'm hearing, planning on passing the word.

For the third projection, I chose one of Julie's favorites.

How she did what she did, I can't even come close to imagining, nor do I know which river she chose to merge her consciousness with. The river's consciousness doesn't include visual or aural awareness of its surroundings in a way that interfaces with our own modes of perception, so she overlaid both, in the same way a musician adds different vocals and instruments to one recording, but she also somehow infused a sense of time overlapping itself as well. What we perceive with our senses as the hologram unfolds accompanies what we get directly from the river's sense of itself.

The early trickle, dripping and bubbling, is joined by other trickles, becoming a thin stream, gaining momentum, burbling and splashing, as we experience the sensation of flowing around and over smooth stones, lapping at the banks in the shallows, cascading over multiple levels of rock bottom, splashing, rushing, tumbling over heights into free-fall with a dull roar, splintering into droplets and mist, settling into deep quietude, feeling other life forms floating and swimming within us, rippling our mud-laden muscles between fields and forests, growing in strength and width, spreading and dividing into arms that reach for the sea. Unlike the human experience of having a singular presence in each moment of time, the river is aware of its entirety all at once. It is all-inclusive, its full cycle of evaporating mist rising from the ocean into clouds pouring rain over mountains are all part of its existence even as it swirls its ropes of water over fallen tree trunks, spirals into vortexes, splashes against stones, sways the plants at its edges, lingers over smooth pebbles in languid slow motion, spreads itself into ponds and lakes, moves again through many landscapes, and returns to the sea. The river knows its connection to all water everywhere, to the storms and floods and tsunamis, to the fog and the dew, to all of life — knows itself to be a vital part of every other living thing. The sensation of physical oneness is inherent in its nature.

As we participate, we can't help but comprehend ourselves in the same way.

When the hologram ends, stunned silence fills the theater.

I remember my first exposure, the recognition of my own bloodstream as part of the cycle of water, the visceral knowing of the intricately woven bonds among all forms of life, across and around the whole planet. What has been conveyed takes time to absorb. There are no adequate words to describe the awe. No one utters a sound for the full five minutes of the break.

I rise and return to the center of the open circle. As I turn slowly, gratified by the vague smiles and faraway looks, I bide my time until I feel the return of a communal focus.

"I want to thank you all for your responses to each of these holograms. In every instance, they matched my own. As I mentioned earlier, the last one we are sharing with you this evening requires some explanation. My sister, having been out-of-body so frequently, knew what we have all come to know — that it is possible for us to choose when to leave for the last time. What still remains in the realm of possibility for most of us was an easy option for her. Julie Jameson made that choice about five years ago. Her eagerness to move on to new adventures was hampered only by her concern for the brother she'd be leaving behind. Me." I feel a wave of empathy from the people surrounding me. "As you've just witnessed, Julie's abilities to merge her consciousness with other life forms in other places was extraordinary. She was, in fact, able to do even more. Among the talents she developed was the ability to move her consciousness around in time." I pause to let that information sink in. "What you are about to experience is a recording that my sister produced by taking herself forward to her own departure from this life — before it happened. She wanted to leave me a peek into the new territory she would be entering. Her gift in doing so has been of immeasurable value to me. The word death now means the same to me as the word birth." My audience is so fully attentive,

I probably don't need to offer them this option: "If anyone here would prefer not to participate in one individual's entrance into the next realm of subtler dimensions, please feel free to leave." No one moves, other than to look around and notice that they've all made the same decision to stay. I nod. "I'm sure most of you are aware, from the plethora of near-death-experience accounts available online — some of you may even have had your own — that no one's encounter with what lies ahead is like anyone else's. As in life, so in the afterlife — despite comparable similarities, each individual is a unique creation, a singular combination of attitudes, expectations, reactions, interactions. Each individual's life is unlike any other. The same is true of each individual's transition into the next realm.

"But of course, we humans want and need to share our life experiences. The more we include what others have gone through, with acceptance, without judgement, the closer we come to the original nature of ourselves. It is in this spirit of sharing, in order to remind us of our common denominator, our original oneness, that I offer you my sister's final gift."

The hush that has descended over everyone in the theater is weighted with compassion and yet lightened by anticipation. I turn back toward my seat, where Louisa is standing with so much pride and love in her eyes that I feel an upsurge in the fabric of time, a cresting moment of outward rippling changes. I take her into my arms, rest my cheek against her temple, close my eyes, and feel my way through how difficult it was to do what I just did, feel through it into how amazingly wonderful it is to be doing this, to be on the threshold of sharing with the world Julie's legacy, to be doing it with this woman who loves me.

When we turn to sit down, we both notice that everyone in the theater has their hands raised, this time not palms purposely forward in blessing, but hands relaxed in an open gesture of holding the space in stillness and in grace. Louisa's hands go to her heart and tears spring to her eyes as she sends silent gratitude around the room. This cohesive, generous attention from everyone present is so much more than either of us expected. Before we sit down, Carlos and Addie give each of us a hug, long and centering, in the patient, understanding atmosphere of the theater.

The last hologram begins.

*

I'm calm. I'm excited! This is probably the strangest thing I've done… and it feels like the perfect culmination to my life: looking at a preview of the culmination! Another twist for Great Mystery to smile about. I'm dancing with time. We're waltzing to a backstep beat.

Okay, so here we go. Up and out. Forward in time. There's my body, resting on my bed. There is the me of two days hence, already having said all my good-byes and settled all my accounts and made peace with all the elements of my life.

Isn't this the ultimate rush! Being out-of-body, watching myself lift out-of-body! I merge my two into one, and I/we are in a tunnel of streaking starlight, movement without motion, bursting outward into light that is more than light, so indescribably beautiful, filled with such incredible love, like nothing I've ever known, infinite and eternal love that dissolves me and caresses me and billows me into fluid musical colors of delicious comfort and electric awareness and profound joy and pure, clear truth.

I am luxuriating in this love, being held in this love as if I am precious beyond belief, for what feels like hours, or eons… or no time at all…

…knowing that I can release myself into it instantly… or I can return to it at any moment… I can bask in it forever, this love that overflows within me and around me… I can become it… or I can respond to the desire to greet these beings beginning to show themselves to me, emerging from the love as if they are — because indeed they are — the perceivable ways in which Great Mystery lets me know how much I am loved. Here you are, you aspects of Great Mystery who have left the density of four-dimensional reality before me.

Mama! Aren't you radiant! This love that flows between us is the sweetest, most colorful music! Look at our heart songs, feel all these colors! I love you so much.

Papa! You have stripped yourself of the role you played. Your essence is like that of a handsome actor who has removed his scary costume and frightening mask, welcoming me with an open heart. No trace of our earthly past remains. I overflow with gratitude.

Maudie and Mary Etta! Twin aspects of one ancient and wise goddess. You went in to add your magic touch to the play we were all performing in the midst of chaos, igniting the remembrance of <u>this</u> so we wouldn't get lost in the density. What a happy reunion!

And who is this? I know you. Samantha! Your early departure from the play changed its course into a story worth living for so many. Had you stayed, Jeely and I would never have met Louisa. How wonderful to find you here!

And I remember you, Clay! From the hospital. And Rim! Didn't you each do a magnificent job. You were so convincing! What's that? You were convinced yourselves! Weren't we all. We were completely immersed. We felt the suffering that so many feel when they forget. And we all persevered, to help alleviate that suffering and to herald in and ride the wave of the shift. Every one of us was an essential element in the masterful work of art we created by being our individual selves and making our individual choices.

Thank you all for greeting me, for condensing yourselves into your former forms so I could recognize you. I love you all so much!

They beam their loving light at me, they dissolve into it, and I am greeted by a young angel who has taken the shape of my own twelve-year-old self. What a hoot! This is so much fun! What am I laughing with?! How can this light body tingle with so much pleasure at these mirrors within mirrors?

Sweet little girl that I was, how I love her! She takes me by the hand, and as she does, my entire life is revealed in review, every moment of it, those choices that inadvertently caused pain in others, those choices that caused me a moment of sorrow, and it's all as beautiful and heart-warming as if I'm watching children finger-painting a large mural and accidentally — or not — smearing one another with random colors as they try to portray what they want to contribute. They get in each other's way, they paint over someone else's work, they argue and laugh and cry and try again, and they are learning, and becoming encouraging and cooperative. Whatever it looks like in the end, they can see what they've created, and that's the whole point. Every detail of my life is so perfectly vivid, every sound, every scent and flavor and touch is surprising in its clarity. How is it possible that I am in a form without solidity, without actual brain and nerves to trigger these sensations, yet able to be sensing these moments in time all at once? Ah, it's possible in the same way that it was possible for me to convey the same, and more, in the holograms. It's possible because within Great Mystery nothing is impossible. Absolutely nothing is impossible.

My little angel self moves me — forward? sideways? — these have no meaning here — and we are in a field of light that rearranges itself to give me reference points, so that I can recognize within one Being many versions of itself. The forms this Being has taken in order to walk among and interact with humans shimmer and overlap within this single creative force. I see the Buddha, Jesus, Quan Yin, Rama, the Rainbow Serpent, Quetzlcoatl, Isis, Artemis, and many more. I am receiving the understanding that these are all manifestations of the focus of Great Mystery that we call the solar system. I am inundated with the love of creation that emanates from this god/goddess Being, even as I expand into understanding that while this Being is several dimensions outward from humanity, at the same time it is another focus inward from the galaxy, which is another focus inward from the universe, which is another focus inward from the multiverse, which is another focus inward from Great Mystery.

The immensity of peace beyond the beyond becomes the void, the nothingness that is nothing more than infinite potential.

All space and time disappear...

Within the void, which is neither light nor dark, a spark of an idea ignites itself, a tiny point of desire, a question that wants to answer itself. The first note in the orchestration of all that follows. The first note that is also the last and the middle and within and without, as there is no first or last, no beginning, no end.

And the question is who-what-how-when-where-why-and-why-not?

Suddenly I've returned to my personal light body, and I'm laughing with insight and delight. Love consists of curiosity and play, discovery and invention, creation and recreation, breathing in and out of existence, becoming and dissolving, expanding and contracting in order to experience and to be experienced.

My little angel self holds my hand, and what I have been perceiving transitions again, this time into an array of possibilities, as far away as the stars and as close as my little guide. I see so many possibilities I would not be able to count them all in a trillion lifetimes. There are inter-dimensional realities inhabited by masters of space and time. There are planets with life forms that stupefy the imagination. There are universes within droplets of water and timelines that branch out from each event like a tree on steroids! There are trillions of ways to learn and to love on planet Earth alone. There is the peaceful retreat into nothingness and the basking in the love light until you're fulfilled. Great Mystery, you have outdone yourself! No wonder you need so many of us to tell you who you are and what you are capable of!

The love that you elicit from me is you loving yourself. The love you radiate into me is you loving yourself. The love that I feel for you and from you is me loving myself!

I am on the brink of a playing field so vast I will never finish exploring it. My excitement is uncontainable. I am in full-blown ecstatic bliss!

But before I preview some possibilities, I turn around to wherever I am being viewed from. I pull my girl self into me so that we contain and radiate all of our ages at once... so that Jeely remembers what he already knows: how much I have loved and admired him throughout our wonderful sibling time together.

I still do and always will, Jeely. Love you!

I blow him a kiss, and I wave, and the light envelops me.

Addie

Neither Carlos nor I had previously viewed the hologram that Jeely and Louisa chose as the last feature of our presentation to the audience in New Zealand, so both of us were in the same emotional state as everyone else in the theater. Stunned. In awe. Grateful beyond belief. Turned inside out. No more fear. So much love.

So much love for Jeely!

And for one another, and for ourselves, and for all of creation.

The silence lasted for several seconds, and then suddenly everyone was on their feet applauding, and then hugging one another, spilling out of their seats and cascading like a waterfall from the outer ring of seats down into the circle. Strangers were embracing with tears in their eyes. All around the room, people were seeing themselves in one another, and loving what they saw, and being loved by what they saw. Each person was receiving dozens of warm hugs. The people who came to hug us, respectfully waiting a turn, found the only words speakable to be ***Thank you***.

Jeely's face was wet with tears. He received each embrace as if he'd been found by a long-lost relative. Which, it seemed, was the emotion rising into the theater from all the hugs among everyone. Carlos' face, too, was wet, when he took my face in his hands and kissed it all over, making me laugh through my own tears. Louisa was meeting each embrace with the same softly swaying, comforting love that my once somewhat of a lonely grandmother used to share with me whenever I visited her.

The four of us received with open arms the same reaction from audiences all over the world.

But after that first three-month tour, Carlos and I decided to stay home, as my pregnancy was beginning to slow me down.

Isn't it lovely that human gestation suggests, as does one fragment of a holograph, the greater picture. The single cell, a complete universe of potential unto itself, when joined by one tiny identity, becomes an entity that multiplies itself by dividing, that grows into innumerable communities of cells that make up a multi-trillion-cell being that becomes so cramped in the space that once protected it that it has to burst into a greater space so it can become that which creates the actual from the potential in a greater set of dimensions... until it becomes so limited that it must burst again, from the confines of that once-useful physical vehicle into whatever even more expanded realm awaits to be explored. On a personal level, on a social level, on a cultural level, on a human level, growth makes its quantum leaps. Life is a fractal, a spiral, a masterpiece of symmetry.

Jeely and Louisa did one more tour. Then they handed the whole distribution project over to a young couple who'd stayed to talk after the presentation in New Zealand. We're all back home now, awaiting the arrival of our new family member, keeping up with an added load of correspondence, going to gift-and-trade gatherings to look for baby clothes, enjoying quiet moments on the pier as the sun disappears behind the eastward roll of this beautiful being we call Earth.

With so much life to look forward to, the memory of Julie's final gift has drifted into the background, along with the knowledge that when we feel our lives to be completed, we can choose to leave them. At the same time, if we want to.

I've been working at odd hours to finish writing down their stories, Julie's, Jeely's, and Louisa's, enjoying every minute of it, because I know, when I peek into the future, that this book wanted to be read by you. This book wanted to be read by You.

You and I are emerging from this now limiting space of one book. It's time to put it down and step into that larger set of dimensions we call life. Before we part, though, let us perceive one another's essence and recognize for a moment, in a wash of light filled with stars that cascade through the atoms of our inner spaces, zooming us out beyond the beyond while encompassing all of creation, let us receive, reflected in an other that is self, this infinitely multifaceted, wildly divine adventure we call

Love.

Mary Etta, do you see that? They love Jeely!
Some people just can't get enough attention!
Mary Etta! Don't you love what Louisa is doing with her life?
I do. I love them all. And I'd love some ice cream right now, but do they serve it here? No.
Are you saying you want to go back in?
Maudie, isn't Addie about to have twins?
Ooh, you think?
Let's!

Author's Note

I wrote the first five sections of this book about 12 years ago. And then life happened, and it got tucked into a documents folder on my laptop, not to be discovered again until after I had moved from Pennsylvania to Maui and was suddenly freed up time wise. When I read that early introduction to a few of the characters, I felt an insistent urge to get to know them better, and they were so cooperative in spilling out their story to me that I finished the book in 5 weeks, an unprecedented experience for me! I was awakened at all hours of the night listening to a conversation already in full tilt in my mind. I was aware of their presence the way you know that a friend might call at any time to catch you up on the latest. And what surprised me even more was that while I'd started out under the impression that I was writing this book, I was to learn that I had no idea where it was going to take me. I'd wait and listen for a chapter to crystalize its first sentence from a vague concept, and from the moment I wrote it down, I was led around unforeseen corners and into unimagined territory. But what surprised me the most was that things that happened in earlier chapters were set-ups for what was to come, as if there'd been a plan all along, while my personal experience of the process was to go with the flow and see where it led me. Is this a common experience among writers? I don't know.

    I have to admit that I fell in love with these characters. You know how when you fall in love you can't eat, can't sleep, can't wait to be together again? I lost five pounds and countless hours of beauty rest, I was at the beck and call of the one I loved, whoever he or she was in the moment, and all I wanted was to know more.

And then there were the assists and confirmations from other sources. I was halfway through *Why Not* when I picked up, at the local used book store, a book entitled *Awakening into Oneness,* by Arjuna Ardagh. Before reading about Sri Bhagavan and his wife Sri Amma — their Oneness Blessing movement has healed and enlightened millions of people — I had no idea that it was possible to move someone into a transcendent state with nothing more than a simple touch or a clear intention, and that it could then be passed on to others. That people can be miraculously healed in that way, yes — that transcendence can be achieved through meditation, yes — that the kind of enlightenment that accompanies a near-death experience is transferable in minutes? Maudie had taught me something new!

In one of my meanderings through what's available on the internet, I came across this tidbit of information: the U.S. military has already invented a device that transfers mental images from remote viewers to computer screens. If that's the case — I don't know if the truth of it can be verified — then at the rate of our present technological advancement, we could well have access to what Jeely and Julie showed me would be in the realm of possibility in a few decades.

Before I started writing, I had already been listening to the healing meditation music videos on Youtube published by Elke Neher. She offers intentionally designed messages and music that help to heal the pain body, leave the old paradigm behind, reconnect with one's higher self, reclaim one's energy, reactivate one's ascension DNA, and many more. It wasn't until after I'd started witnessing the encounter between Jeely and Louisa as adults that I came across Elke's videos about balancing the divine masculine and the divine feminine within. Those videos became my theme song, because they resonated so deeply with one of the themes that had just started showing up in *Why Not*. So many men are fatherless — whether because of war, work, or emotional distance — and so many women are motherless — whether because of suppression, lack of equality, self-abnegation — that both men and women are needing to resolve the imbalance within themselves, to redefine themselves, as parents and as people, to reinvent themselves altogether.

Along with my sense of being coached by my characters, I felt a personal urgency to get this message out there: we have an amazing future to look forward to. The world portrayed to us by the very real events covered by the media doesn't feel at all promising, nor does the level of unconsciousness in those that have assumed domination throughout history suggest that we have a future at all. But the more of us who see that bright future, the greater becomes the potential for us to open a timeline for ourselves to experience it. I hope I've given you a glimpse into the possibilities that lie ahead, so that you can move forward not in fear or doubt, but with enthusiasm and confidence. Can we dream it beautiful?

Why not?

Lesta Bertoia
Sept.2017